ROBERT COLBURN

The Sultan's Helmsman

The Sultan's Helmsman is a work of fiction. Names, characters, places, and incidents are products of the author's imagination or are used fictitiously. Any resemblance to actual events, locales, or persons, living or dead, is entirely coincidental.

ISBN :1-4392-4953-9
ISBN-13: 9781439249536
Library of Congress Control Number: 2009907035

To order additional copies, please contact us.
BookSurge
www.booksurge.com
1-866-308-6235
orders@booksurge.com

DEDICATION

Dedicated to my Turkish rowing teammates,

And to everyone who is willing to cross cultural boundaries

Cover illustration by Bruce Colburn

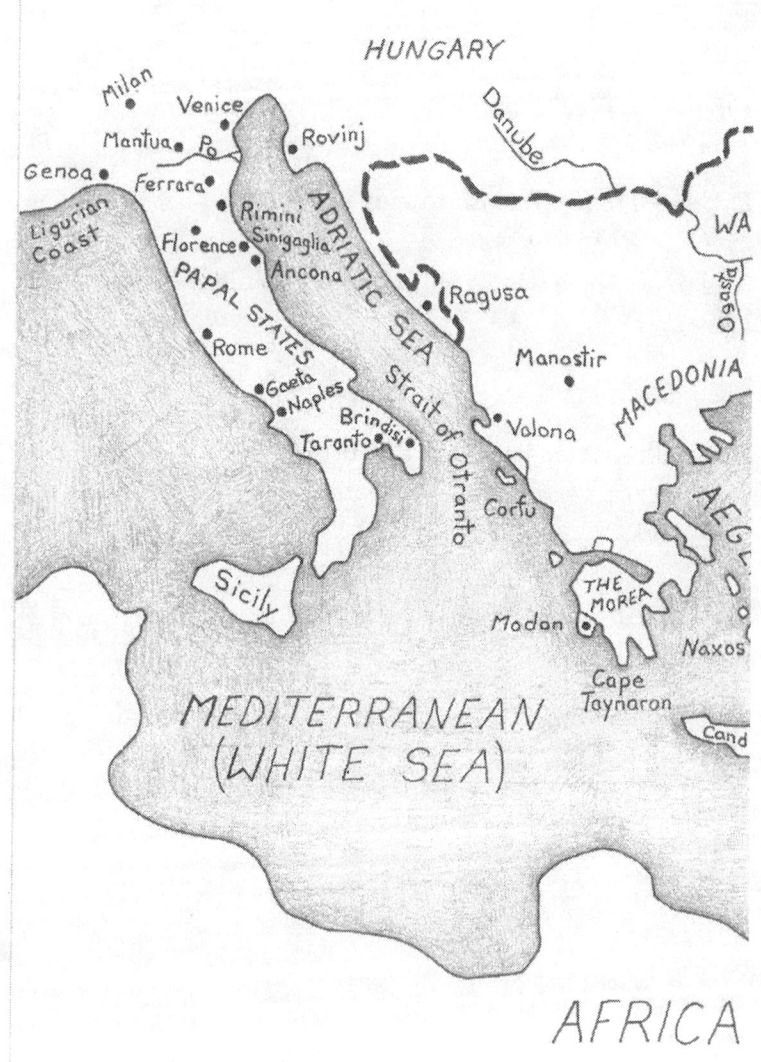

---- 1492 Boundries of the Ottoman Empire.

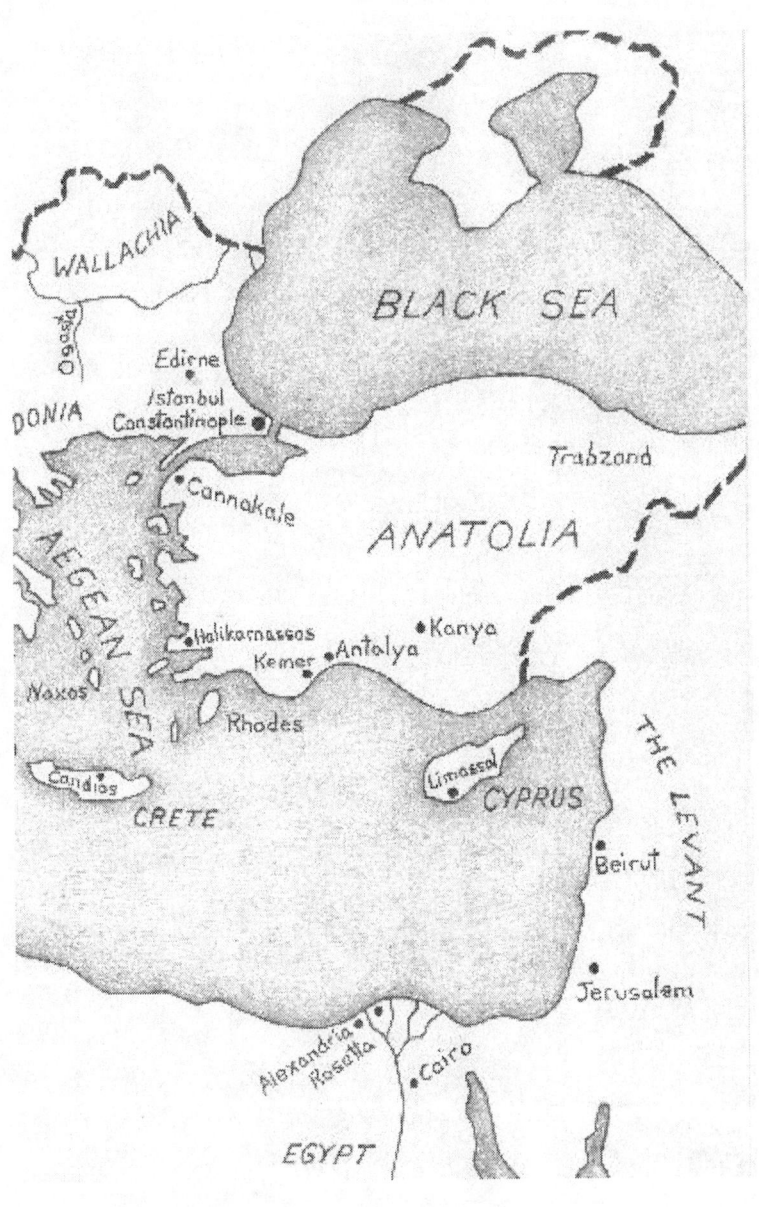

MEDITERRANEAN SEA (WHITE SEA)

Chapter I
The colors of the threads

Four Turkish galleys spread out in a line abreast, sailing easily with the wind on their beam, their hulls sharp and fast. *Yildirim* (Lightningbolt), the squadron leader, was easily recognizeable by her size and by the three brass lanterns on her stern. *Hilal* (Crescent) kept station on *Yildirim*'s port side, while the *Bayezidiye* (Bayezid's Gift)—which in size came midway between a galley and a smaller class of galleot—kept to *Yildirim*'s starboard. *Akdogan* (White Falcon), the fastest ship in the squadron, had been given the picket post on the port side of *Hilal*. Like all fast galleys, *Akdogan* had a tendency to try to stand on her nose when under sail. Her "playfulness" Captain Hasan called it, and I—her helmsman—had to keep a firm but light touch on her tiller to bring her back down off the backcrest of a wave whenever she tried it. *Akdogan,* with her two masts, was very fast indeed. In the Mediterranean's hierarchy of speed, it was common knowledge that Venetian galleys were faster than Spanish, Genoese or Florentine galleys, and that Turkish galleys, with their shallower and lower-cut hulls, were faster even than a Venetian.

Yildirim hardened up her foresail, a sign that she was preparing to come about, and we prepared to do the same. At a nod from Captain Hasan, Berk and Ozkan—the chiefs of the starboard and portside oars—went forward onto *Akdogan*'s beak to prepare the foresail. I watched them sitting out over the water ahead of the bow, their feet dangling on either side of the beak as they hauled the foresail brace tight against the wind ready to haul it across to the other side. When the ship is under way, the beak is the most dangerous place to be. One slip, and the ship will run down anyone who falls; there is no time to stop or turn, and little hope for anyone suddenly in the water to get out of the way.

Akdogan's bow rose to a wave, tossing sheets of spray over her gun deck, the drops spattering against the taut foresail like drumbeats. Three sailors were standing at the foot of each mast, ready to release the foresail and mainsail sheets. The secret to executing this maneuver smoothly was to keep the aft part of the sails from getting too loose and flapping around madly, flinging their blocks and ropes in all directions and becoming generally dangerous to anyone within their reach. Berk and Ozkan glanced sternwards at me, then at the captain, who looked back to them, then to me. Four pairs of eyes, all ready.

Yildirim's mainsail shivered once at the leech as she began her tack. "Rudder hard on starboard," I called out, putting the helm down to bring *Akdogan* across the eye of the wind, noting out of the corner of my eye that *Hilal* and *Bayezidiye* were tacking exactly alongside us. The windward braces ran in through their blocks with the purposeful "sheee" that I always liked because it signaled a maneuver well-carried out. The foresail barely slapped once as Berk and Ozkan hauled the massive boom behind the mast and let it pay out on the other side. The crew at the mainsail did the same, in unison, and I added the little momentary reverse on the rudder as we crossed the exact center of the wind, easing *Akdogan*'s bow gently over a wave and onto her new course as the sheets were hauled in. Our ambition is one day to do it so smoothly that the sails stay full, even across the very eye of the wind, without even a single flap.

Do I sound proud of my ship and the crew I am part of? I, who have not a drop of Turkish blood in me, but yet have risen to be the helmsman of one of the Padishah Sultan's galleys? I do; of course I am. The dark greenish-blue penant with the star and crescent flying from the aft end of *Yildirim*'s main yardarm was a gift to Admiral Bahadir and the squadron from the Sultan's own hand.

I have my "capture story" well-prepared in case I am ever a prisoner of the Europeans again. All of us non-Turks in Ottoman service—and there are many of us—have rehearsed our stories against the day of need that we hope will never come. We will say we were captured as youths in the *devshirme*, or that we were taken as hostages in the siege of Kefalonia or a hundred other similar places. Whether the Inquisition truly believes those stories or not, they were what they wanted to hear. It's true in enough cases that they will believe it when they hear it from the rest of us. The penance assigned in such cases is usually light, the Inquisition's public position being that the apostasy took place at the point of a sword. The Offices of the Inquisition dare not—for policy sake—admit the possibility that so many persons might willingly have turned their backs on strife-torn, illiterate Europe wracked by its interminable religious wars, and had found a refuge of tolerance, culture, and ideas in Constantinople. (We were only beginning to refer to it as Istanbul, and most of us still used both names). For anyone with a skill, there was a welcome.

"Every time the Europeans chase a heretic out of his home, or confiscate a Hussite's goods, they send us a talented gunner or shipwright," our Sultan had written in the preamble of a fatwa ordering his soldiers on the borders to give refuge to anyone wishing to cross. "Every time they close a synagogue or force a Jew to convert, they send us a physician. Every time they burn a scholar's books, they send us a mathematician."

It was this blend of nationalities which gave the Sultan's armies and navies the best of everything. The Turks rejoiced greatly when they found exceptional persons, and spared no efforts in cultivating their talents. Our guns were stronger, lighter, and safer than those of the Europeans, with longer and thinner barrels and wider bores. We could afford to cast our guns in bronze; the Europeans, with the exception of Venice, relied on iron. More brittle and not as safe. Ottoman guns could load a more powerful charge of powder, and the barrels cooled more quickly for reloading. We knew this. Every Ottoman sailor went to sea in full confidence that the guns aboard his ship were more accurate, possessed a longer range, and could be fired more often than those aboard any ship he was likely to meet. This same mix of talents applied to the designs of our ships. The shipwrights at the Tersane arsenal were encouraged to blend the knowledge that they brought with them, giving full scope to the best designs. *Akdogan* and her sister ships were the fruit of that mix of nationalities; there was nothing afloat in Europe to compare with them.

I glanced over at *Hilal*'s sterndeck. Her helmsman and I "know each other's handwriting" so well that we can steer our galleys oar blade to blade with barely the span of a man's arms distance between them. We've done it often enough too, especially when coming into harbor where there are plenty of people watching from shore, dropping the sails at the same moment, with the oars on one side holding water to turn the ships in a tight half-circle, then gently backing our galleys stern-first into the arsenal quay side by side in unison.

"Showoff," Ozkan had whispered to me with a smile as he padded barefoot aft along the center walkway to heave the springline ashore the first time we had done it as a crew. It's something the whole fleet can take pleasure in when it is done right.

Hilal's helmsman, I should note, has not a drop of Turkish blood in him either. In aspect and intensity, "Little Eagle"—no one ever calls him anything but that—is more Turkish than the Turks. His nickname suits the sharpness of his features and alertness of his eye. Hasan once observed that Little Eagle handles a ship as if it were a musical instrument; every maneuver precise and economical, and beautiful to watch. I've learnt much of my trade by watching him practice his. Of few words, he and I can carry on entire conversations with barely more than scraps of sentences.

Five miles to leeward of us, there was a pair of Florentine galleys on their way to the Levant. Their cargo weighed them down, and we had to keep tacking and spilling wind to stay well upwind of them. Florence had been granted trading concessions with the Ottoman empire; they were our allies. On this particular afternoon they were also our bait. We hoped that their presence would lure out the *corsos*, the corsairs who hide in the bays and coves of the islands of Khalki and Alimnia along the southern corner of Turkey's coast where the 'chin' of Anatolia meets the Mediterannean. The nearby Karpathas Strait was the bottleneck through which all of Istanbul's grain supply from Egypt had to pass. The corsairs lurking there, preying on ships of all faiths and flags, could choke it off. The long, low shape of a galley or galleot lurking against the shore virtually disappears against the land behind it, and it takes a sharp lookout indeed to spot one.

Three of our ships on their way from Alexandria to Istanbul were taken in the Karpathas Strait last month—July 1493 in the European calendar. There were pilgrims aboard, who were now being held for ransom by the Knights of Rhodes. The mother and father of *Bayezidiye*'s helmsman were among them. The reaction as soon as the news had reached Istanbul, via one of the ships which had gotten away, had been swift and angry. No sooner had the *Phoenix* limped into the Golden Horn with her damaged mizzenmast lashed to her gunwale, than the word of what had happened had gone around the docks of Istanbul in a furious buzz. Even before our squadron had received any orders, Captain Hasan sent us to the Tersane on the double with wagons for rice, gunpowder, and all the supplies for sea in case we were sent out. "If they send another squadron instead of us, you can always take this stuff back. I want to be ready to sail tomorrow morning."

Thirty miles off our starboard bow lay the island of Karpathas itself, surmounted by the mountainous peak of Pigadhia, which was where the corsairs were accustomed to light their beacon fires to alert them to any ships approaching the strait. If our plan worked, their watchers would see the Florentines, but would not see us farther out to sea behind them. When they lit the beacons to alert their comrades, they would flush them out for us.

"And if they do see us, and do not light the beacons," Captain Hasan said, "then Bayulken and Bahadir have another plan. And it's just as good."

By late afternoon, the crest of Pighadia was visible over the horizon, and the Florentine galleys ahead of us should have been well visible to any watchers on the ridge. We trusted to the setting sun behind us to hide us from their notice. *Hilal*, *Bayezidiye*, and *Akdogan* were painted the Ottoman navy's time-honored colors, colors carefully chosen to take on the quality of the light surrounding them, and which blended especially well—no matter what the time of day—with the color of the sea and the pale Mediterranean horizon. At the waterline, the ships carried a thin white stripe, so like the white caps on a line of waves; above it, the bottom half of the hull was a light blue-green. "Turkish blue" or "tourquoise" the Europeans called it, topped with a pale yellowish-buff band along the gunwales. From even a moderate distance, an Ottoman galley painted those colors virtually disappeared against the light reflected off the water. Especially at dusk and dawn, an Ottoman galley was all-but-invisible unless very close. *Yildirim*'s hull was painted the other favored color of the Ottoman navy, dark slate blue with a hint of green it—another color which was extremely difficult to pick out against the water, and particularly suited for night action.

How different, I thought, from the drawings of European galleys we had studied in the Hall of the Expeditionary Forces at the palace. The galley captains of Europe, it seemed, couldn't bear to put to sea without dressing their ships up with as much red paint as their rank would let them get away with. Red was supposedly reserved for the flagships, to make it easier for the rest of the ships in the fleet to keep formation with them. Thus, the more vermillion paint a western captain could pour on his hull, the closer to a flagship it became, to the enlargement of the captain's pride and the enduring gratification of Ottoman gunners everywhere.

Yildirim did not light her lanterns that evening. We approached Karpathas Island in the dark, still under sail. We watched for the beacon fires, but nothing showed. Had they seen us despite our precautions and chosen not to light them? We ate our supper at sea that evening. Whenever possible, galleys put ashore for the night, or tied up in a raft alongside their supply ship, if they were travelling with one. On this occasion, we were not. For reasons of speed, and because our supply carracks—with their higher masts and large sails— would have been too visible against the horizon, our squadron had left its carrack at a place called Vathi, on a peninsula about thirty miles to the north, to wait for our return.

Akdogan, like most galleys, had a small cooking stove on the port side near the stern. The stove occupied a space which would otherwise have been used for two sets of rowing benches. This small sacrifice of speed allowed a galley to stay at sea if the shore was too rocky to land, or if other necessity demanded it. The fishing lines strung over the stern had been active all day. Whenever possible, a galley fed herself as she went. I'm no longer distracted, even on those occasions when—for instance—Berk suddenly darts to the stern rail, hauls in one of the lines, and beats something large and wet and grey to death on the deck behind me. Tonight there was fresh fish and barley stew, with bread and cheese. I took my bowl and plunked myself down cross-legged on the stern deck next to Berk, and Ozkan, leaning my back against the gunwale to eat while Semih, my underhelmsman, took over. Atakan, the chief gunner, came over to join us.

"Howcome I always seem to get the piece with the most bones in it?"

"I guess God must be angrier at you than he is at me."

"Not possible. Your soul is a pit of malice as yet unplumbed—"

"—hidden from the world by a face serene," I finished the quote, and handed him the clay jar of olives in garlic that we had been sharing. Perhaps because garlic had been strictly forbidden to us oglans during our schooling and service at the palace, I had developed quite a taste for the stuff while at sea. As sailors know well, it keeps away sickness, cleans the blood, and increases its flow. Perhaps for this reason, it is said to make you dream clearly and vividly.

Ozkan's nickname was "Shark" because he eats everything. Atakan was originally from Trabzond, last holdout of the Byzantines. "He's crazy," Berk had told me once, "everyone from there is."

"No crazier than you," Atakan had responded brightly. "I just happen to like things that belch flame and make a lot of noise. Just ask any Hapsburg ship captain you meet." And he began to tell a very funny story about a camel, an uphill road, and a raven.

By midnight, we were off the coast of Karpathas, and *Akdogan* launched its jali boat with ten of her janissaries aboard. Their task was to go ashore, climb to the windy ridgetop of Pigadhia, and light the beacon just before dawn. *Akdogan* and *Hilal* were to wait at anchor for them in the lee of a cliff, while *Yildirim* and *Bayezidiye* sailed on ahead to be in position for the next morning when, we hoped, our signal would lure the corsairs to sea.

An Ottoman soldier or sailor learns to sleep whenever nothing else is happening. An hour is defined by the task allotted to it—there is no "early" or "late" for us, just the "now." It was something I had learned early in my training. I curled up on the stern deck, under the tiller, while the rest of the crew, bar a handful of lookouts, slept too. Captain Hasan wanted the rowers fresh for tomorrow. There are many sailors who are so attuned to their ship that they can wake out of deep sleep at the slightest change of motion or shift of the wind. I'm afraid I'm not a very good sailor that way. I can—and have—slept through a storm. To compensate, I can also stay awake at sea for three days running. Perhaps for that reason, I did not wake when our lookouts shortened up the anchor upon sighting the glow on top of Prigadhia, the glow which meant that the janissaries had succeeded in their task and we now had only to wait for them to make the long climb down and rejoin us. Ozkan nudged me awake sometime after that. "They've done it," he said.

I sat up.

He pointed to the glow on Pighadia's crest. "About an hour ago. The boat'll be back soon, and we'll need to be ready to sail. We don't want to be near *this* shore when dawn comes."

Berk came up beside me, a reassuring presence in the darkness. Wordlessly I took the cover off the compass and opened the chart lantern's front so that the merest glow spread over it, enough to point out to him the direction Mecca lay. He pressed his head to the deck soundlessly, and a number of his rowers followed his lead.

Not long afterwards, Janissary Captain Yigit's cap appeared over the gunwale, with Yigit—and Yigit's wide grin—under it. They had brought the jali boat alongside the hull without even the slightest bump. They had brought the beacon guards down the mountain with them, tied up and gagged as prisoners. "What is, what isn't," he explained in a whisper with a shrug. "No sense leaving them there to put the beacon out, and it's more prisoners to exchange."

With the anchors already shortened up, it required only a few turns on the capstan to haul them to the surface. Hasan gave an almost imperceptible nod to Berk and Ozkan, and they began to row.

Good rowing is silent rowing. When all the oars are in time, when all the pressure is even, a ship can move nearly as silently under oars as sail. The even slapping of the wavelets against our hull changed its rhythm, and there was the slightest hiss of a bow wave from *Akdogan*'s prow as she began to gather way. I took a deep breath. To be out on the water at night was a special feeling, suspended between the stars in the sky and the reflected stars in the water. It was how I imagine journeying through the sky might feel.

Two hours later as the sun rose, we were east of Karpathas in the strait between the island and the shoals of Saria. What little morning breeze there was, was against us, so we lowered the sails, furling them with dried grass gaskets which could be quickly broken if the sail needed to be hoisted in a hurry, and moved the ship by oars alone. Semih smeared half a barrel of butter on the foredeck and the center walkway. It smelled terrible after an hour or so in the sun, but if the Europeans in their heavy boots did attempt to board us (we Turks usually went barefoot while at sea in all but the coldest weather), they would find the decks very slippery beneath them. A light morning mist on the surface of the water, common at that time of year, hid us for an extra hour, an advantage we made good use of.

When it cleared, we could see the Florentine galleys, about three gun ranges ahead of us with no fewer than six corsair galleots in pursuit of them. "Now that is a glorious sight," Hasan said. "One fifth for the Sultan, the rest for us. The trap is sprung."

If *Yildirim* and *Hilal* were in position somewhere ahead of us as planned, the trap was indeed sprung.

Three of the corsair galleots broke off the chase and turned to meet *Akdogan* and *Bayezidiye*, thinking no doubt to outnumber us and add us their spoils while their comrades took care of the Florentines. Puffs of gunsmoke showed at the bow of one of them, first the demiculverin on the starboard side, then the outboard one on the port, but raggedly, not in disciplined sequence. These were hesitant ranging shots, which splashed into the water well short of us.

"That's what I wanted to know," Captain Hasan said. "They aim their guns, not their ship."

I could hear Atakan's snort of derision all the way from the gun platform as he sighted along the *Akdogan*'s beak. He turned and said something to Inanc, his gun captain, who grinned widely before stooping over the breech of the starboard falconetti. No Ottoman ship would have done that. The extra gun crews needed to aim the guns would have crowded each other on the gun platform and gotten in the way of the soldiers, an invitation to chaos. And what would be the point anyway, as the aim changed every time the ship rose to a wave? Much easier, and many times more accurate, to triangulate the guns ever so slightly towards each other so that their aim converged on a point at a fixed distance ahead of the ship. *Akdogan* carried five beautifully-cast bronze guns in a row across her bow platform. In the center, because it was the heaviest, was the enormous basilisk—its muzzle more than a hand span wide—with a pair of smaller culverins on either side. Outboard of the culverins at the edges of the bow platform, *Akdogan* carried a pair of slightly smaller falconctti, which were still pretty good size. Above the guns, there was a raised fighting platform for the janissaries in front of her foremast. Two small cannons called demisakers were mounted up on the sides of this fighting platform for close-range work.

Akdogan's guns were aimed to converge at a distance of twelve hundred *arshin*—about nine hundred European yards—ahead of her bow. Although that might have seemed an overly ambitious range, Atakan's gunners had proven over and again in training that they could make good on it. The range meant that Atakan could almost certainly get off a salvo while closing on an enemy ship, well before the enemy ship considered the distance close enough to fire.

Not only was the Method of the Triangle more accurate, but it saved us time by not having to re-aim the guns each time they were fired. An Ottoman galley could usually bring her guns to bear first, and could almost always fire a second time before the enemy could aim and fire again. Having already wasted a salvo, it would take the corsair galleot several minutes to cool her guns down enough to reload them. The first meaningful shots would be ours.

Several of the janissaries on the fighting platform gave a cheer. They had seen the flash of sunlight glinting off of moving oars ahead of us. *Yildirim*'s dark hull detached itself from the grey rocky shore against which she had been lurking all but invisible, with *Hilal* beside her.

The corsair ships saw them too and hauled their wind in confusion, attempting to get into some sort of formation to face us.

"Pick one," Hasan said.

"The red-hulled one," I suggested. "After we deal with her, we can go after whichever one *Bayezidiye* hasn't taken." Which left the three southernmost ones to *Yildirim* and *Hilal*, who in any case would reach them first.

Atakan signalled to the sterndeck by raising his hand, that his guns were loaded and ready. My task as helmsman now was to sight along *Akdogan*'s two masts to keep her bow perfectly pointed at the enemy ship. A gunner on each of the side guns would raise his hand when the ship got to the exact distance where his gun's point converged on the target. When both their hands were raised along with Atakan's, it meant that all five guns had converged and the aiming point had been reached.

The port gun chief's hand went up briefly, then down again, now the starboard. Almost there. I steadied the tiller, compensating for a wave which had lifted *Akdogan*'s stern slightly, and brought her back on course.

All three hands were up. "Shoot!" Captain Hasan commanded, almost softly.

"Shoot," Atakan repeated. The gunners touched their linstocks to the touchholes and *Akdogan*'s foredeck guns fired in a ripple of red and orange moving inboard from the lighter outer guns to the heavier ones in the center—deliberately not precisely in unison because of the enormous stress the simultaneous shock would have placed on the hull—but in very close sequence. The enormous bronze basilisk on the centerline fired last and alone because its strong recoil inevitably halted the galley's momentum temporarily. The deck jolted under our feet.

The bow of the enemy galleot disintegrated into a chaos of flying wood. I saw one of her falconetti upend and go rearing over the side. Our cannonballs, converging on a point with pounding accuracy, shattered the forepart of her hull. One of our shots threw a column of water close to her portside, but that was the only splash I saw; the four others must have all been hits. What was left of her bow immediately began to subside into the water, the galleot's remaining movement forward still pushing an enormous white wave in front of it.

"Full pressure on the oars," Hasan commanded Ozkan and Berk, "there will be Turk prisoners chained to her benches. We must get to them before she sinks."

The corsair galleot's remaining forward motion had pushed her bow wave up over her crushed bow, and the foredeck was now entirely awash. *Yildirim* and *Hilal's* guns were speaking too. Another of the galleots staggered under a salvo and heeled halfway over, as—a moment later—*Bayezidiye* found her range.

"Ask them in Greek if they surrender," Hasan ordered, and Atakan bellowed it out in the precise Byzantine-influenced Greek of his Trabzond homeland.

"Fuck yes, we surrender," came the reply in Frankish. "We're fucking sinking."

"Frankish? Well, well." I heard Hasan comment.

"If they can get the guns off her, she'll probably stay afloat," I said. Indeed, it looked as if they were doing just that, levering the culverin forward to push it over the bow. I shot Atakan a look of sympathy at the thought of all that valuable metal going into the sea, which he returned with a resigned shrug. It was probably only iron anyway. With luck, we'd still get the ones off the other ships.

"Unchain your rowers," Captain Hasan ordered Atakan to shout across the water between the two ships. "The more of them who live, the more of you I'll spare." Shrewd, very shrewd. Corsairs in general could not hope for mercy, and usually fought to the last man. By allowing quarter, the example might induce the others to surrender quickly.

"And tell them not to throw their chart chests into the water either," Hasan said, but it was too late. A figure had already run aft and tipped a box, no doubt containing the charts and ship's papers over the sternrail. A not surprising precaution when they were about to be boarded.

We approached the side of the stricken galleot carefully from behind her stern. "Starboard oars, run in," Hasan ordered just before we came close. Yigit's janissaries up on the fighting platform kept the two demisakers ready to sweep her decks in case of any last-minute resistance. Those janissaries not serving the demisakers had arrows ready in their bows. At close range, arrows were just as effective as arquebuses, and skilled archers could get off twenty times as many shots. There was not a janissary up on the platform who could not have put an arrow through a two-finger's thickness of plank at a hundred arshin. They could cover the corsair galleot's deck in a withering curtain of fire, and the corsair galleot's crew knew it. Atakan meanwhile was waiting for the bow guns to cool enough to reload, timing them with a small sandglass measured for the purpose, while Inanc timed the enemy guns with a similar hourglass to warn us when they might be ready to fire again.

The galleot's rowers were a collection of Turks, Mamluk Egyptians, some Genoese sentenced to the galleys for debt, even a few free adventurers (these were distinguished by not

having their heads shaved in the same manner as the others).
The Turks and the Mamluks we freed, the others we chained
to our own masts with their officers. Prisoners to exchange
for Turks held on Crete.

Two of the galleots, the ones which had had the good
fortune not to suffer our initial salvoes, showed some signs of
attempting to make a run for it and leave their fellows to their
fate. Two yellow and red flags shot to the end of *Yildirim*'s main
yard, together with *Hilal*'s and *Akdogan*'s indicator flags, which
we interpreted as meaning that the admiral wanted *Hilal* and
us to give chase to the remaining two galleots while *Bayezidiye*
accompanied *Yildirim* in rounding up the four galleots which
already surrendered. If we had read the signal wrong, *Yildirim*
would merely fire one of her smaller guns to get our attention,
and send up a longer, more detailed string of flags. The chase
did not last long. With Kapathas to one side, the Astakidha
Shoals to the other, and us behind them, there really wasn't
anywhere for them to go except upwind in a bid for the open
sea. For that, they would have to risk not only the wrath of the
Florentine galleys, so lately their prey, but also our guns rak-
ing their undefended sterns. Against a headwind under oars,
as we were now, a heavier ship has an advantage in speed over
the lighter one.

Akdogan and *Hilal* closed the distance steadily. We had
willing rowers at our benches, eager for spoil. Not for the first
time, I gave thanks for our admirals' long-standing insistence
that there should be no slaves or prisoners of war aboard expeditionary ships to pose the threat of an uprising during a
battle, or reluctance in a chase.

"We want no enemies aboard," Gedik Pasha is supposed to have told the Imperial Divan to their faces, and our admirals since then have held them to it. Paid rowers of our own blood is a luxury that our navy shares with the Venetians. Spain, France, and Naples cannot afford it. It is a small part of the reason our ships are faster than theirs.

The galleots, despairing of escape, broke for the land. This was the one risk we couldn't do much about, that they would dart back to one of their coves where, either we be unable to pry them out, or—beached with their sterns to the land—present us with an unsinkable, and very dangerous, combined gun battery if we tried to enter a bay after them.

Our crew were pulling madly at the oars, frantic not to let these prizes get away.

"After them, sirs!" I yelled in encouragement, "We're catching them, like we're stuck to their rudders."

Atakan darted aft along the walkway to ask Hasan for permission to try a long range shot. I watched as they discussed it. It would mean altering our course to aim at the galleots, instead of steering at an angle between them and the shore in a last attempt to close the triangle and cut them off. Either choice was a calculated risk.

Hasan assented. "See what you can do."

Atakan sprinted forward, "Pull the quoins all the way out" he yelled to Inanc before he even reached the gun platform, "Full charge." Pulling the quoins entirely out from under the breeches of the guns would elevate the muzzles and increase their range. It would also drive the recoil down into the hull and, for all we knew, spring the frames under the bow. The shipwrights at Tersane would no doubt have plenty to say about that, if we floated long enough to give them the opportunity.

I altered course and aligned the masts with our quarry. This time the shocks from the guns on the deck under my feet were so prodigious that I almost staggered as the *Akdogan* pitched her bow down and came nearly to a stop. All of us on the sterndeck held our breaths as we watched to see where the shots would fall.

Five sharp splashes, on the other side of the galleot. Overs! They were in range after all. Running from us, they could not bring their guns to bear. *Hilal*'s gunners had seen the fall of our shot, and opened fire themselves. Two of her shots hit, and one of the galleots raised her oars out of the water as a sign of surrender. The other tried to run herself ashore, but grounded on some shoals. Her officers leaped into the jali boat and fled for the bay behind her, leaving her rowers chained to their benches. Under cover of our guns, we sent a small boat of our own to put a towline aboard and, all oars straining, pulled her off and took her under tow.

In their haste, the galleot's officers had not jettisoned their chart box, and Yigit brought it back on board and broke it open with a spear butt. This was a prize indeed, and it turned out to contain something far more important than charts. Folded among the lists of cargoes taken and sold and the shares due the crew, was a letter bearing the magisterial HHM, which were the Latin initials of the Knights of Rhodes, and the seal of the grand master himself. The letter was in four languages, Latin, Greek, Italian, and Frankish. With Hasan and our other officers peering over my shoulder, I began to piece my way through the Italian, and looked up startled half-way through. "This is a letter of *marque*," I said in real surprise. "It authorizes the bearer '...*to prey at will on all shipping in the waters between Cyprus and Zante...*' and it asks the governors of '*any ports belonging to Ferrara, Naples, Spain or the Papacy to permit them shelter, provision, and repair.*" In return, the *corsos* agree to give the Knights of Rhodes one tenth of the spoils."

"We have a treaty with them, dammit. When is it dated?"

I scanned down to the bottom and the signature. "February...three years ago!"

The Knights of Rhodes were playing a deep game indeed, and now we had the proof. I wondered who among the Divan or at the Admiralty back in Istanbul had guessed this plot, and how long ago. Someone had been clever enough to send us here to get the proof. Now too we could guess the reason the latest batch of prisoners were being kept on Crete instead of on Rhodes itself—to avoid provoking Turkish retaliation.

"I'll take these on board the *Yildirim*," Hasan said. "We need to get these back to Constantinople as fast as we can."

With the slight breeze now behind us, we set our sails, and in company with *Hilal*, who had taken the other galleot in tow, we sailed back to join *Yildirim* and *Bayezidiye* and the prizes. The Florentine galleys continued on their way, unmolested and unperturbed, but not—we hoped—ungrateful.

Hasan sent Semih down into the hold to see whether our long-range shots had sprung any timbers. He took a bucket and disappeared through the hatch like a rabbit, poking his head up a few minutes later with the bucket half full. "There's about a hand's breadth of water in the hold, seeping slowly."

"Take five men with buckets below; five more on deck. Make a bailing chain," Hasan ordered. "We'll tar an old sail and put it over the bow to help seal it."

Hasan and the other captains were summoned by the admiral on board the *Yildirim* to plan what to do next, which was to find a good sandy bay to beach *Akdogan* and the damaged galleots and repair them enough to sail or tow back to Istanbul, before heading for Crete to exchange our prisoners for theirs. Other corsairs would no doubt take up their predatory trade along this shore in time, but we had given them a setback for the moment at least. This year's sailing season would be that much safer, and that much more grain would get through to Istanbul this autumn.

We slung ropes under the trunions of the four smaller cannon and swung them into *Akdogan*'s jali boats to lighten the bow. The basilisk was too heavy for this; it would have taken the foremast right out of the ship if we had tried it. The basilisk's carriage could be run aft along the center walkway to take the weight out of the bow, and this we did. While the gun crews were hauling away, I found a bay on the chart which the ship's navigation book described as having a gently-shelving sandy beach. We ran *Akdogan*'s chin up on it, stripped to our shorts, and waded into the shallows with caulking mallets over our shoulders to repair the leaks. The frames in the bow had been sprung, but not cracked, by the force of the guns, so it was a relatively straightforward matter to tamp more caulking into the seams and seal them with tar heated over a fire that Atakan's gunners built in the sand. It took us a good part of the afternoon, and the patching of the galleots took even longer. Atakan and his gun crews came in for a lot of good-natured ribbing over the very effective mess their accuracy had made of the galleot's bow. It took a lot of tarred sail, and we stuffed every empty biscuit barrel we could find into the galleot's forehold to make her float. "She'll need constant bailing, but as long as you don't punch into too many northerly winds, she'll get you home," was Hasan's assessment to the prize crew who would be taking her to Istanbul.

It being already evening and too late to put to sea, we spent the night more comfortably ashore, and took the opportunity—always valued—of refilling our water casks. The following morning, the patched up galleots—the less seriously-damaged ones towing the more damaged ones (stern-first if need be) set off with all possible speed to Istanbul carrying the damming letters to show to the Divan, whose fury we could predict, while the galleys sailed for Crete. According to Hasan, there had been some discussion of sending *Akdogan* straight back to Istanbul with them for speed's sake, but if we were going into possibly hostile waters to negotiate, Admiral Bahadir wanted to keep all four galleys together for a show of strength.

It took us but two days to sail to Crete, but the Venetian *podesta* in charge of the island kept us waiting another two days offshore, hoping to wear us down so that we would reduce the numbers of Turks we were asking them to release. He was reluctant to deprive his colony of so much free agricultural labor, offering at first to let only three Turks go in return for every four Europeans we released, but Bahadir stayed firm, and insisted on one-to-one. I was one of the ones he took with him in the boat that went ashore to negotiate.

"Keep your eyes down, but notice everything, guns, walls, defenses," Bahadir told me, "so that you can write it down when you get back to the Hall of the Expeditionary Forces. It may be of use someday."

It took a further morning of arguing, but in the end, the *podesta*—under pressure from the abbot of a local monastery who urged the freeing of Christians as a holy duty—agreed to a one-for-one exchange. The customs records which showed which landowners had been given Turkish prisoners were brought in and copied, and we were sent with an escort of soldiers to gather them in from the outlying farms while our own boats ferried our prisoners ashore.

And so, rejoicing, we brought our countrymen to freedom.

"But this one here is not a Turk," the blade of the Cretan captain's dirk was leveled at my chest. With one foot already in the boat, Hasan looked up from the boarding ramp, surprised. "Come, lad, this is your chance to get away," the captain hissed to me in Italian.

"You are mistaken, sir. I am Turkish," I said, uncoiling the rope quickly from the post on the quay, and praying that Little Eagle kept his head down so that they wouldn't notice him too. Like me, he was wearing only his sea cap, not a turban. Turbans were reserved for Turkish-born, or—as an exceptional honor—for very high-ranking non-Turks. Two of the Cretan troop were armed with arquebuses, their matchlocks lit. They propped them on their forked aiming sticks, pointing them variously at Bahadir, Hassan, and the others in the boat.

"I say you are not. I was a prisoner of the Turks too, once. I can tell the difference." The fool was grinning in a self-satisfied way. I couldn't tell whether the idiot really thought that he was rescuing me. Or was he taking a last-minute retribution to counter our success? One of his soldiers grabbed me by the arms. "You're coming with us. We've freed you."

"He'll do no such thing," Hasan snapped, stepping back out of the boat. The soldiers were already pulling me away, and more were running down onto the quay from the street behind us. I saw them push Hasan roughly back into the boat with the flat of a sword. I had to distract them for my comrades' sake. "Fly, fly!" I yelled in Turkish, then twisted around and down, attempting to throw the Cretan who had my arms. It half worked. I wrenched an arm free and hit back as hard as I could, but punching someone who is wearing a helmet and breastplate of Milanese steel is not very effective, especially for someone my size. I was grabbed from behind and found myself on the ground on my back under a lot of people wearing the wrong color uniform. Someone's arquebus went off nearby, by accident, I think. Then the soldiers closed around me and were dragging me up the street from the port. Over one of their shoulders, I had a glimpse of the boat making for the open sea, and of Bahadir staring fixedly back at the land as though to engrave every detail in his mind.

They took me in front of the *podesta* himself, attended by the abbot and a Dominican monk sitting at a small table acting as secretary. Unlike the other nations of Europe, the Venetians had kept the Church's Offices of Inquiry relatively powerless and firmly subordinated to the civil authorities. This explained the presence of the *podesta,* and his controlling of the proceedings. The Dominican's eyes had a dark and empty look, as if something had crawled up behind them and died there. I knew what they wanted me to tell them: some variation on the not uncommon story of being taken prisoner by the Turks, forced to live among them, and now—having been captured (freed)—that I welcomed this heaven-sent chance to return to the arms of Holy Mother Church. There would be a token penance, as was customary in the case of those whose sin was assumed to have been forced on them. Whether truth or fiction, the Church was glad enough to believe it and to hear it said publicly. The alternative: that some might have "turned Turk" willingly, was too threatening an idea to allow.

I could say what they want and satisfy them; walk out of this windowless room with its damp stone walls a free man to a new beginning in Italy or wherever I choose. Would it bother me so very much to lie to these small-minded men? After all, I had my capture story ready and rehearsed for just such an occasion.

I would much rather tell the *podesta* what he does *not* want to hear: that our charts are better than theirs, that there are schools and libraries everywhere in Constantinople, that our training is more rigorous, that our galleys stay at sea well into November while Europeans return to port by mid-October, that an Ottoman believes himself the equal of three of any other nationality.

The three men at the table stared at me with growing annoyance. Prisoners of the Inquisition were supposed to do the talking, to unburden themselves. Sinners know their sin and are supposed to confess, unprompted, because it is tearing at them from inside. The secretary slid a paper across the table, perhaps to prompt me.

It is not solely my "confession" they want to hear, nor is it only under the spurious pretense of saving my soul that they wish to hear my story. Curiosity is eating at them. They are dying to know just how a European such as me had risen to become the helmsman of a Turkish galley.

I let the silence linger.

"Perhaps you wish to see your home again? To hear your native language?"

Did he not know that my homeland no longer existed? My village was burned to the ground in one of the baronial feuds forever tearing Europe apart. What was left of the region was later hacked into fiefs by other nobles taking advantage of the chaos to add to their estates and fighting among themselves. Small wonder that, in so many places in eastern Europe, the peasants, the small tradesmen, and even many of the wealthier merchants had preferred Ottoman stability and law to the factionalism and arbitrary extractions of the feudal nobility.

"Show him the instruments."

The monk rose from his chair and walked to the side of the room. Abruptly, he pulled a canvass covering away from a rack, its ropes incongruously neatly laid out. There were some sharp metal instruments laid out alongside, though for exactly what use was not clear to me. The mere sight of the instruments of "persuasion" was supposed to put the prisoner in the mind of confessing freely. Perhaps they would most people, but I had come of age in the rigorous mental and physical discipline of the elite palace school in Istanbul. I won't claim that I am impervious to pain—no human being is—but if you have swum in the Merich River morning after morning, winter and summer, and trained in the rough and dangerous game of throwing wooden darts at your fellow oglans on horseback, (and been hit by a few yourself), pain does not immediately daunt you. "They treat their bodies as though they belonged to someone else, as far as pain and danger are concerned," the present Sultan's father once remarked of his Turkish soldiers. That example had been read out to us frequently in our training at Edirne and Istanbul as an example always to be followed.

"No need for those," the *podesta* smiled ingratiatingly. "You are our guest. We have rescued you. No doubt your mind is unsettled by the suddenness of what has happened." He stood up and walked around the table to stand next to me, and his smile grew wider still. In a voice as smooth as honey, he continued, "Or perhaps you cannot believe your good fortune at being free, and are afraid to speak lest it is all a dream and your former masters are waiting outside the door to take you back. Tomorrow, perhaps, you will be more yourself."

After another long silence, the *podesta* drew an exasperated breath and ordered the guard at the back of the room to take me back to my cell to ponder the state of my soul.

Renegadoes they called people like me. By an odd twist, it was similar in meaning to the name the Turks called me among friends—Kachak—which means "fugitive" or "runaway," because they said they missed me whenever I was away from Istanbul at sea for too long. It was also a sideways pun on the Turkish word for "little," a reference to my height. I am small and light, the falcon's quickness has always been of more service to me than the ox's power.

It was the falcon I thought of now. No doubt my interrogators would have been disappointed if they knew that I was not spending the time they had given me on ruminations on the state of my soul—but on thoughts of escape.

Imagine, reader, how it feels to know that the place you sprang from no longer exists. How much that loss diminishes you, and removes part of the self which formed you. When your village goes into the flames, part of you goes into the flames with it, and that part does not come back. After the raid, I spent the next two nights hiding between two ridges of rock in the hills above our valley, in a crevice which I desperately roofed with branches, unable to escape the smell of smoke which seemed to follow me into the rocks. The second night, I dreamed of the spirit of the nearby stream, who I had imagined all through my childhood had looked after me.

"Are you willing to wander?" she asked. "To live like a shadow in the woods, always running? Until you learn enough that you're stronger than they? What they cannot see, they cannot touch, and what they cannot touch, they cannot kill."

No. I was not willing to live like a shadow. And for the first time in two days, I was actually hungry.

It was while I was out looking for berries in the hedges that I saw the pataran in the dirt of the road. Eyes untrained to the ways of our people would not have noticed it—a longer stick lying across a shorter one as if fallen there by chance, the longer stick pointing the direction of, say a previous hunting parting, or the way to water. Some others must have escaped the raid also. This pataran pointed south. A good direction; with summer ending soon and the cold weather coming on, it would be easier to live off the land to the south than if I stayed where I was.

Thus, I wasn't actually a product of the *devshirme* levy, although people later—not unreasonably—often assumed I was. Nor was I captured at sea; or been sent to the Ottomans as a treaty hostage, or any of the other more interesting ways so many Europeans found themselves serving under the crescent and the star. For every *renegado* with one of those dramatic tales, there were ten ordinary ones like me. Sultan Bayezid's scouts were slipping in and out of the disputed lands west of the Ogosta River, and his gold was freely on offer to all those with talent and energy to earn it. Genoese shipwrights, Venetian painters, Jewish book printers, soldiers, gunners, sailors, masons, craftsmen, in short anyone with energy. There was much work to be done and few enough to do it. We left a Europe of sword and fire, a Europe where you could be burnt at the stake for reading a forbidden book, to a place they would not dare to follow, to the place where many of those forbidden books came from. Books that European scholars were now paying fortunes for.

We came across the Turkish scouts somewhere south of the River Kojma, roasting their supper in a field. In return for our tending their horses, and doing odd jobs around the camp, they fed us. The Sultan's armies were always in need of recruits; they asked if we would be willing to go with them—that was assuming they could get their captain's permission. It was as simple as that. It didn't take much thinking to say yes.

To my surprise, the captain's accents carried the distinctive shortened vowels of a region which was only a few mountain ridges removed from my home. "Varensi?" I asked.

"Very close," he said, barely surprised. "And you're from somewhere not far from there either, by my ear."

"But how," I pointed to his uniform, "how is that you've become…?"

"A Turk?" he finished with a laugh. "Oh, that's not so unusual. There's lots of us. The Turks take talent wherever they find it, and they reward it too. Our former Grand Vezier—Mahmud Pasha Angelovic, peace be upon him—began his court service as a prisoner of war. Our present Grand Vezier is Albanian. It is like that."

I must have looked surprised.

"Truly. Such is the rise that is possible," he half chuckled. "That's my tune too, may I rise half so far. So, if I'm ever captured by the Christians, I'll say I was taken against my will. They'll feel sorry for me; give me a light penance, and I'll thank them for my freedom and then sneak back across the

Ogosta the moment I get the chance." He pointed to the scar which ran across his forehead.

"The Turks did that?"

"Oh no. A Firenkish overseer gave me this. Before I ran away." 'Firenk,' I was to learn in the coming days, was a flexible term encompassing—according to context—Europeans, Christians, Latins, Franks, assorted western non-Turks, or any disagreeable persons in general. His pronunciation of the term—longer or shorter vowels—varied depending on degree of antipathy felt towards whomever it was being applied to at the moment. The fact that he was 'Firenk' himself impinged not at all on his use of the term.

"You were taken in the *devshirme*?"

"I was part of the intake, yes. Oh, it's not the group kidnapping the Europeans in their lurid tales of Turkish bloodthirstiness make it out to be. They—that is, we—are very selective. To me and the three other lads selected that day, it was the doorway to a wider world."

Over the next few days, he told me his story in bits and pieces.

"My village, which you won't find on any maps—even if it were still there, which it isn't—offered me the same life that a thousand similar villages offered. Reasonably productive farming on lands owned by some petty noble—who took most of the fruit of our labors. Had I stayed, the most adventure I could have looked forward to was perhaps an occasional journey across some mountains to a fair in a larger town. Or perhaps if I was restless enough, a pilgrimage later in life to an important city in Greece or the Balkans."

He paused to consider. "Not a bad life by any means. But one year, a man returned to our village. He had been one of the lads selected in our village *devshirme* some years before. He had been taken into the palace school, and eventually rose to become an important commander in the Sultan's service in Constantinople. We heard of others from nearby villages who became officers in the elite janissary troops, or in the administration. The money they sent home to their families was proof enough of their success.

"There were a few who tried to avoid the *devshirme*, and there always plenty of ways to get out of it if one wanted. The officers' journey from village to village was arranged months in advance, probably for just that reason. They only wanted the eager ones. They never took more than one boy from every forty households, and some *devshirme*s they took only two from each village.

"A colonel—himself a European and likely himself a product of a *devshirme*—and his *sürücü* had arrived the night before and had lodged in the village headman's house. They made sort of enclosure in the square, fenced off with waist-high curtain of beautifully embroidered cloth, and there was a sort of gate in it, as if it was part of a tent. Behind that, there was the colonel sitting on a dais covered with Turkish carpets—it was all very stately, designed to make us feel as if we were being called to something grand. The *sürücü* stood at the entranceway and examined each one of us as we came forward, our height, the shape of our skulls. If he nodded to us, we could enter and speak to the colonel. The village priest with his baptismal rolls, stood beside the colonel, making sure no one was taken who was an only child, or the son of a widow.

"In the end, there were five of us standing in a group beside the colonel's dais. The priest wrote out our names on duplicate lists, one for the colonel and one for the *sürücü*, and each handed the copies to the other to compare them. They gave us red jackets, which our parents paid a small tax to cover the cost of, and we marched off in a column to join the rest of the troop, making our way from village to village until they had collected enough recruits. One of my friends decided after a few days that he didn't want to go after all, and ran away during the night. They caught him, beat him on the soles of his feet, and then sent him back to the village anyway. Two others tried to join us on the march. That's what the guards are for mostly—if you want to know the truth—not to keep us from escaping, but to keep the unchosen from joining. After a while, the colonel and the *sürücü* whispered together, and added their names to the list, although they're not supposed to do that."

I held up my hand to stop him and pointed over towards our left. "Someone over there," I mouthed. "About a mile distant."

Without speaking, he ran his forefinger over his right eyebrow to mean, "Are you sure?"

I nodded. To my surprise, he accepted what I said, and swiftly took the bow from his shoulder and notched an arrow. At a jerk of his head, two of his scouts, bows drawn, circled around to our left and disappeared without a sound into the undergrowth.

"He's right," they reported when they returned. "Hungarian cavalry. At least a hundred."

We kept well south of them, and as far as we knew, they never suspected we were there.

"That was clever work today," the captain said at supper. "You're a sharp one. How did you know?"

"It's the way the forest changes sound," I answered, "certain birds call out louder; others go silent. The palette changes. You learn to sense it." It sounded a little foolish.

"Can you swim?"

"Fairly well."

"How many nights between the new moon and full?"

"Fifteen, but every second fifteen, it's fourteen."

"What has five branches but only one leaf?"

"My hand."

"How do the trees tell us that a storm is coming?"

"By turning their hands—I mean their leaves, to show us the white beneath."

Faster and faster questions, designed to test my quickness in thinking and how alertly I observed the world around me. There was a pattern to the questions too; they were looking, not only for original answers, but also the reasons behind the reasons.

"What is the carpet all stand on, but no one can roll up?"

I looked around me in confusion, trying to make sense of it. The expectant silence grew. Then in a flash I saw the meadow, bright with wildflowers. "The Earth?"

"Bravo. The Earth indeed."

One night we were camped somewhere in southern Wallachia. I had gone to gather firewood. As I returned to the circle of light, the conversation ceased in that sudden way which told me that the subject of the conversation had been myself.

"Kachak," one of them began, very solemnly, "we have a question to ask you. You told us you have nothing to go back to?"

I nodded. "That's true."

"You can be of great service to us. And probably to yourself too."

I waited for what he had to say.

"Let me tell you how it works. The Sultan gets one fifth of all spoils; it's the law. But in our case, the stuff we're bringing back doesn't divide very easily. We'd have to sell some of it to pay our share, and in the wake of the campaign season, the markets will be full of the same stuff, all trying to sell for the same reason, and we'd get a terrible price for it."

I nodded. I understood that principle from the country fairs when everything was in season.

"But," he held up all five fingers, "if you're our fifth, we can keep the goods we have, and you will have a roof over your head, food in your belly, and coin in your purse in the service of a general or admiral—"

"He's too small for a janissary," one of them remarked.

"Hmm. Well, if not a janissary, then some other discipline. Istanbul is full of *kolejler* to train quick-witted people for service to the empire—scouts, translators, mapmakers, cannon founders. Would you like to be something like that?"

I nodded again.

"And within all those, there is a *kolej* more special than the rest. They call it the inner school, the Enderun Kolej. It trains the best and brightest *oglans* for the navy, the army, and for the highest levels of the government."

"We'll get him into the Inner School then. He's quick-witted enough."

"But first, if we are to present you to the Sultan's steward, Mehmet here will teach you to read and write."

"You can read?"

"All of us can. It's part of the training. Can't run an army without people who can read, whether it's maps, orders, messages, or even just lists of supplies."

Mehmet traced some beautifully curved signs in the dirt with a stick, gracefully. "Each one of these has a sound. These here make the sounds of your name."

"My name looks like that?" I was entranced. I had never thought that my name might be a thing I could see.

He handed me the stick. "Now you try."

I carefully copied the same signs in the dirt. They were straggly next to the ones he had made, so I rubbed them out and made them again.

"Good. Don't worry, it takes practice." He made more signs. "This is my name. This is the captain's name—"

The captain rubbed it out in mock anger. "Oh no it's not." He made a new sign. "Like that. A lion." The others laughed. Clearly there was some joke here. Mehmet wrote all their names, and I looked from one to another and to the signs in the dirt. I could picture the signs as I looked at each of them.

The writing came easily to me. It seemed both magic and yet the clearest thing in the world that each sound should have its own mark. In a few days, I could write everyone's name in the troop, and very soon after that, I could write simple words as Mehmet spoke them to me. Mehmet went looking for some paper in a village we came to, and with a stick whose end I charcoaled in the cook fire, I worked at them whenever I got the chance.

In October, at the end of the campaign season of the western year 1484, which coincided that year with the end of Ramazan, the Turkish armies returned to the empire by way of the road to Edirne. After a week of rest, we continued onwards to Constantinople. At Edirne, which the Europeans still call by its Roman name, Adrianople, or often just "Andi" for short, we were examined again, physically and mentally, and given new Muslim names. They had called me Kachak on the road, and it had stuck. The captain took me to Vezier Daud Pasha's tent, where a group of soldiers mounted guard over a growing pile of campaign spoils.

"This one is for the Sultan. He's our detachment's fifth."

"Name and unit?" one of *pencikis* responsible for collecting the Sultan's share asked.

The captain gave it. It was written into a notebook, and I was left standing among the piles of saddles, cloth, weapons, and other property. There were other 'captives' like myself, given as fifths by the detachments of scouts, probably according to the same mathematics as I had been. A steward came out of the tent and asked us the same sorts of questions the captain had tested me with, only harder ones, asked more rapidly. To prove we could read and write, we each had to write something then hand it to another to read aloud. After two weeks of rest in Edirne, the army and the court officials continued on the Istanbul road.

Topkapi palace was not at all like the stony, gloomy fortresses of Europe I had heard of in stories. (I had never, given my life in my village, seen one myself). Its many buildings, its gracious columned arcades, and its pavilions were designed for harmony and the enjoyment of life. Many opened to the outdoors and had been sited by their architects in such a way as to present spectacular views. Some over the Sea of Marmara, some of the Bosphoros, the hills of Istanbul, or of the Golden Horn. Topkapi was full of gardens, and the memory which will forever bring my mind's eye back to the place of the shaping of my new life was the wonderful smell of baking bread which every hour of the day or night wafted from the enormous kitchen wing and pervaded the entire palace.

Once inside the gate to the third court, we turned to the right, along a long white arcaded building of pleasant proportions and many windows. This was the Newcomers' Hall, one of the four halls of the elite Inner College. Family name and rank counted for nothing here, and to erase any distinctions, everyone here was given a new name anyway. Turk, non-Turk, did not matter either. We were new people, relying on ourselves alone, for our talents to lead us wherever they might.

Inside, the building was airy and light, with a high curved ceiling, and three-sided alcoves along the walls. There was a balcony around the second storey.

Our instructors, *lalas*, were there to greet us, and—lined up formally behind them—the oglans who had already been there a season or more. These oglans would be our leaders and guides in the way of the Kolej, our older 'cousins.' At a nod from the *lalas*, they stepped forward and—as each of us newcomers walked through the door and humbly selammed—took each one of us by the arm, and paired us off one by one down the line so that each one of us was given a cousin to settle us in and teach us the ropes.

If most Europeans carried a picture in their minds of the quintessential fierce Turk, I now found myself standing in front of one. The *oglan* paired with me had the intense face and sharply articulated features that one would have expected, while the quickness of his eyes immediately spoke of intelligence. His hair was cut short along the sides of his head and longer on the top, increasing the determined aspect of his bearing. The fierceness, however, was not directed at me, being reserved only for the Sultan's enemies, and the smile assured me I was not one of those.

"I'm Bilgetai, from Üsküdar," he said in my own language, barely accented, "Welcome."

I attempted to return the greeting in what little I had learned so far of his. My attempt pleased him.

Each alcove contained beds for ten students. In the day, the beds would be folded away and the alcoves used for study.

Bilgetai—the name meant 'wise colt'—led me down the hall
to the alcove which I would share.

"This will be yours," he said. "And this is the chest for
your things, and to use as your writing desk."

I must have hesitated, for of course I had no things. He
nodded again. "Yes, open it."

I lifted the lid of the fine rosewood chest. Neatly folded
in it were clothes such as I had never worn before; two jackets of blue, a pair of soft boots, shirts of blazing red, and the
loose, comfortable pants that the Turks wore, one for every
day of the week, a woolen coverlet for my bed, and a cloak,
which doubled as a second covering for my bed, as well as to
wear on festival days. "Are these really for me?"

"Everything belongs to the Sultan, but they are for you
to wear in his name."

The *lala* made a speech welcoming us, and exhorting us
always to do our best. "Each of you holds your future—and
your real fortune—in his own head and in his hand. The Inner College cares not whether you are the sons of lords, or of
fishermen, or of shepherds."

Our days began a half hour before dawn, to bathe in the
separate hamam attached to our hall, after which we folded
away our bedrolls, and heaven help any one of us whose things
were not put away by the time the trumpets sounded the dawn
salute. If we were not out of bed in time on our own, one of
the older oglans would cheerfully tip us out of it and pull it
away from us. Once bathed and dressed, one of us would read
aloud a passage from the book designated to be read for that
day of the year, then we had our breakfast of bread, yogurt,

honey and figs. During the morning, we studied philosophy, mathematics, history, and languages—Turkish for everyday use, Persian for literature and court ceremonial, Arabic for law. We were encouraged to add to that a language beyond the empire, if we chose. Midday meals were hearty soups usually made from lentil, cheeses, and more bread. On Thursdays, we got a special pilaf and whichever vegetables were in season. We ate meat sparingly. Sultan Bayezid was himself a vegetarian, eating nothing that had had blood or life in it. He did not impose his tastes on others, but the rest of the court tended to follow his lead. Afternoons were taken up by musical and physical training—swimming, archery, medicine, swordsmanship, and horsemanship. A janissary colonel taught us wrestling, not the brute force tussling and grunting Europeans think of, but the precise, swift moves and holds of the Turkish style. In the study of the bow, I began to see the deep discipline in the Turkish character that underlies the supposed wildness. We spent months just practicing the movements without actually drawing the string, holding it in our outstretched hand and pulling back the other hand—empty—to our ear, faster and faster.

"The bowstring will take the end of your thumb off if you release it even the slightest bit wrong, and then you'll be spoiled forever as an archer. That is why you must spend months getting the motion perfect before we allow you to touch the string. Then you will spend months just drawing the bow before you put an arrow to the string. And then, only then, will you begin to learn archery."

To show us what he meant by archery, we were taken many times to see the sipahi calvalry practicing—shooting from their horses at a brass ball, arrow after arrow in rapid and accurate succession. The sword came easier to me than the bow; my size may have had something to do with that. Under the skilled eye of my alcovemates Cihan and Inanc, I made rapid progress. Cihan's family was from Macedonia, and he practiced relentlessly and always with a cheerful humor. Inanc was blessed with a quick aptitude for everything he did. The first afternoon he picked up a sword, it was as if—after an hour of practice—he had been born with one in his hand.

Evenings were taken up by study in a subject of the student's choice. Bilgetai had noticed my interest in the history of the sea (coming from a landlocked region, I had never seen the sea until I arrived in Constantinople, and was entranced by it, its moods, its changes, its boundlessness). He suggested that I study charts and navigation. He himself had chosen calligraphy, and already was developing a very fine hand, though his teachers—in their quest for perfection—were stinting with their praise, admitting only that perhaps after forty years of practice his work might not be entirely unreadable. Calligraphy, as I soon learned, was a subject valued by the government on a level above all the others. No fewer than twelve different styles were taught.

In the spring, we were sent to across the Bosphoros to work on the rich farms in Anatolia, to strengthen our muscles, and to improve our Turkish. We were sent to Anatolia again in the autumn to help gather the harvest. Apart from the language, it was not so very different from home for me, and we returned to Istanbul wiry and fit. It was the philosophy of the Enderun Kolej that useful manual trades were as important as book learning, and that one could not be complete without the other. Frequently we were sent out into the city to lay water pipes, unload ships in the port, or to repair ruined buildings. Bilgetai's drawings and designs were much valued by the masons for this work. He could look at a ruined building, whether storehouse or mosque and see it in his mind's eye, perfect and whole again, then sketch it wonderfully clearly in his planbook.

At the Tophane, I spent more than a week helping with and learning the rudiments of the casting of bronze cannon, work which I particularly enjoyed, though I would be lying if I said I understood even a tenth of the details of alloys, rates of cooling, the mathematics of bore lengths, and the other secrets of the foundry.

We took turns standing guard along the high wall, though against what I was never sure. I enjoyed that, having the roofs of Istanbul spread out at my feet in the dark, feeling the night breeze in my hair, and having time to think in the quiet. I loved to stare across the Sea of Marmara, which takes its name from the marble the Greeks quarried on its islands, and which we now called, along with the rest of the Mediterranean, the White Sea. Beneath the palace there was an enormous labyrinth of stone storerooms. We helped unload the wagon loads of grain, raw hemp for making rope, flax, and the precious copper ingots from Anatolia which were kept within the safety of the palace to be doled out, under guard and only as needed, to the cannon foundries.

Whenever someone of high rank was coming into a room or courtyard, a special small trumpet signaled the approach in order to give us junior oglans—whose standing did not permit us to stay behind and selam—time to run and hide ourselves. There wasn't always time or a convenient exit to make a clean getaway, and this led to a number of comical incidents when we were forced to obscure ourselves behind whatever piece of furniture or tapestry was near at hand. Sometimes we were privy to discussions we no doubt should not have heard, such as the time Erhan, Inanc, Cihan, and I had been in the conservatory putting away manuscripts when we were caught by surprise by the trumpet. Unfortunately for us, there was only the one doorway, which left us no opportunity to leave in time. Even to try was to invite the far worse possibility of blundering directly into whatever grand personage was about to enter. Erhan shot a desperate glance at a low table piled with books and fortunately draped with an expensive brocade, and we dove behind this rather inadequate cover.

Trapped, and in fear of a beating, we overheard Grand Vezier Daud Pasha and the second and third veziers—Ishak Pasha and Mesih Pasha—worriedly discussing the conspiracies of Cem, the Sultan's rebellious younger brother. Cem, after a series of unsuccessful revolts in the eastern provinces, had ill-advisedly fled to the Knights of Rhodes for sanctuary. He now found himself a virtual prisoner and hostage in one of their castles in France. The Europeans knew a useful pawn when they saw one, and they were keeping him as a threat to lead a crusade against us. Cem himself was doubling on his hosts, secretly corresponding with the Mamluks of Egypt in hopes they would give him an army to lead against us from the east and take the throne. A Venetian ship captain, it seemed, had intercepted Cem's courier and some of the letters aboard a ship which had put in at Modon on its way to Rosetta. Wary of the growing intrigues and power of Charles VIII of France, the Signoria had forwarded copies of the letters secretly to Istanbul.

Whether our hiding place had really been sufficient to conceal us, or whether Daud Pasha knew we were there all along but had considered it sufficiently polite that we had attempted to hide, none of us ever learned. Perhaps the Grand Vezier saw the chance to educate us by sharing an impromptu lesson in diplomacy. In any case, we were grateful to him, and privately swore eternal loyalty to his commands, believing that he, by sharing with us his secrets and burdens, had in some unspoken way sealed us into the band of those he trusted most closely.

As my training progressed, the *lala*s set me to copying maritime charts in the palace treasury. There were ten of us altogether, at a long table with our pens and inks. Beautiful charts, refined by hard-won experience on the seas. Squadron Admiral Bahadir would unroll the originals, which were kept in locked chests in a guarded room in the inner treasury, valued as highly as jewels, and we would copy them, feature by feature. First the coastlines, then the wind roses and rhumb lines, and finally Bilgetai, with his fine calligraphy, would add the place names in red or black ink depending on the importance of each. European sailors have dismissed Turkish charts as inexact and crude. Instead of the detailed bays and promontories drawn to scale, and exact depictions of shoals and reefs as shown on European charts (the palace possessed copies of captured western charts for Ottoman captains to study) Ottoman charts showed each bay simply as a semicircle. The promontories of land along the coast were designated by the points where the arcs of the bays intersected. It made it easier for the helmsman in the course of a voyage simply to keep a count of points of land as the ship passed them, and to know which were the bays to avoid and which were safe to turn into. A red dot at the mouth of a bay meant there were shoals and sandbanks; black dots marked reefs where one could see the waves breaking on them, and a black 'x' indicated submerged rocks or reefs or some other especial danger which lurked unseen. If there were no marks at the mouth of the bay, it was a safe harbor.

Simple to use, unambiguous. No unnecessary details or clutter. If a part of the coastline has reefs, then it is enough to know that they are there, and steer well away. The exact depth and outline are irrelevant, since you're not going into that particular bay anyway. No captain in his right mind will be bringing a ship into known danger. And just try reading all those little marks and shadings on European charts by deck lantern at evening on a pitching galley trying to make shore for the night with darkness coming on and the wind rising. Not to mention all the coats-of-arms, embellished compass roses, drawings of kings and half-imaginary animals that the Europeans obscure their charts with.

"They're made as if for hanging on a wall," Bilgetai murmured half to me and half to himself as we studied a Catalan chart captured from a caravelle off the coast of the Morea, "Very beautiful, but not at all what you want on the deck of a ship. You see, our method of making charts has been honed over many years. What we need to know, the sea has taught us."

Apart from the charts, the really detailed information about a coastline is stored in the notebooks which every captain carries on board and in which he—or his amanuensis—records every detail: prevailing winds, quality of the anchorages, availability of fresh water, siting of cities, fortresses, even the likelihood of earthquakes. Upon returning from a journey, the captain sends a copy to the Treasury so that the knowledge collected in it can in turn be copied into notebooks for other captains to take with them on their voyages. Thus the knowledge of our fleet is constantly being increased and shared.

Our charts have another advantage, which the Europeans in their scorn are apparently not aware of; they can be rapidly copied—with much less opportunity for error—by any decently-trained naval clerk. With more than one hundred and twenty galleys in our war fleet—not to mention the countless merchantmen at sea all over the Levant—what use were charts which took years to copy and wouldn't be ready in sufficient quantities when the galleys sailed?

One evening, after the news of Admiral Hersekoglu's capture of several papal galleys loaded with treasure off the Ligurian coast had been cheered throughout Istanbul, Bilgetai mischievously labeled the entire Mediterranean as *Osmanlin Gölu* (Lake of the Ottomans) in charcoal on the chart he was copying. Admiral Bahadir laughed at the joke before making him rub it out.

The afternoon the earthquake struck Constantinople, Cihan, Inanc, and I were practicing swordsmanship in the meadow adjoining the palace grounds which sloped down to the Bosphoros. It was late autumn; the last of the wildflowers were still in bloom. Cihan was teaching me a difficult counterparry, with a feint and advance, when I stumbled clumsily on my left foot, the point of my yatagan going wide. I whirled it back, expecting a jab, and it was then that I noticed that he had staggered as well and dropped his guard. The ground seemed to shift slightly under my feet, the way it feels when you are ill, then shifted again, more sharply, seeming to thump against our feet. The other oglans had stopped their practice and were looking around in surprise. Inanc and Cihan, being from that part of the world, recognized instantly what was happening. "Zelzele," Inanc said sharply, "Earthquake." I had read the word, but had never heard it spoken, nor imagined that the solid earth itself could so betray one's trust as to move. After the initial moments of surprise, discipline reasserted itself. "Form up," one of the older 'cousins' shouted, and we did. People were flooding out of every doorway in the palace, the halberdiers in the inner courtyard forming ranks around the Padishah and the women of the court. "Make sure everyone is out," the kapubashi ordered. We oglans instinctively checked around us for our alcovemates to make sure they were accounted for. Then five of us from each hall were sent to the doors to make sure there was no one still inside.

The earthquake went on intermittently for several hours, but the buildings of the palace weathered it unscathed. That night, although the ground had stilled by evening, we slept outside in the courtyard in the chill autumn air for caution's sake. In the morning, we were told that the dome of the Conqueror's mosque had burst and collapsed. Of all of Constantinople's stone buildings, that was the only one which had suffered major damage. As most of the city was built of wood, it flexed and withstood the shocks. Bilgetai was sent to the palace library where the original plans of the mosque were kept, and ordered to bring them to the imperial architect whose was returning hurriedly to the capital from Edirne where he had been overseeing the building of a bridge. For a week, we oglans joined the squads of janissaries who had been detailed to the special duty of clearing the rubble away and to stack as much of the tile and stones as were able to be reused. There was no question in anyone's mind that the dome would be rebuilt exactly as it had been.

Some six weeks later, I came awake to a similar shaking. My first thought was that I must have overslept and that one of the older cousins was about to shake me out of my bed and turn it over. The faint grey light in the windows showed me it was still not yet dawn, however. "Out, out, get out!" someone was shouting. I sat up and swung my feet to the stone floor. It was moving too. I scrambled with my alcovemates and the other oglans in the hall to pull on some clothes and rush out of the building into the predawn cold of the courtyard. "Another one?" I asked Erhan. He nodded grimly.

A number of minarets collapsed in various parts of the city. As far as I know, no one was hurt, there being no one around when they did. The wooden houses, where most people were still asleep, withstood the earthquake well. It being too early in the morning for most cooking stoves to have been lit, Istanbul was spared the catastrophic fires which I was told often did the worst damage. I began to understand how frail a thing even a great city surrounded by thick walls could be.

As palace oglans, we took part in the many festivals which filled the year. The celebrations accompanying the wedding of Princess Hadirga, the Sultan's daughter, to Prince Ahmed Mirza of Kharaman were especially costly and brilliant. Ambassadors and noble visitors were invited from every state and province of the empire, and from every country on our borders. Processions of janissaries and cavalry marched through the streets and into the hippodrome past the reviewing stand where the Sultan, the Sultana and the princess—both veiled—the veziers, and Mirza himself watched and applauded. The cavalry played their mounted and very dangerous game of *jerid*, charging and throwing their blunted wooden javelins at each other from their saddles. They had new brightly-colored uniforms for the festival, and they made a brilliant show. The captain of the Thracian team had something of an arm, and showed it, launching shot after shot. An opposing midfielder, charging unsupported up the field, managed to duck one, but the second or two of hesitation that the movement cost him allowed the entire defense to surround him. They pummeled him, nearly knocking him off his horse.

Prince Mirza was the grandson of the same Uzun Hasan who had revolted so often against the present Sultan's father, and the display of military prowess was partly intended to remind the groom's family of Ottoman power at the same time that everyone hoped that the wedding would ally the eastern provinces with the capital and pacify our borders. Mustafa, Daud Pasha's eldest son, was married to the sultan's second daughter, Princess Fatimah, at the same time.

Each of the guilds of the city prepared elaborate displays of their crafts on wagons, which were pulled along in the procession. The bakers' guild set their wagon up with a real brick oven in which they baked bread as it was wheeled along, throwing small loaves into the crowd. The sweetmakers came next, stirring their boiled candies and tossing handfuls of them to the crowd as well. Acrobats, jugglers and tightrope walkers performed, and puppet shows were given on the street corners. Some of them made ribald fun of local officials; one puppeteer in particular had the accent of the Agha of the janissaries off pat.

The Enderun Kolej's contribution to the celebrations was a large paper-mache castle, thirty feet high, which we built at one end of the hippodrome. It took weeks to construct, each level having to dry before the next one could be built on top of it. Curious crowds came to watch the progress in the days leading up to the festival, and public interest was kept high by the speculation about what part it was to play. On the last day of the celebrations, we staged a mock siege and battle in front of it. We had been issued real shediks, the old-fashioned conical pointed helmets of the janissaries, and wooden swords (which could still hurt) from the palace armory for the occasion. Some of the shediks were more than a hundred years old and bore nicks and dents which we knew had come from real battles. Cihan's came down low over his eyes, giving him a slightly quizzical look. We thought ourselves quite fierce-looking in them, and enjoyed wearing them around in the hall as often as we could before the big day. I wondered about the soldiers who had worn it before me, what had been their names, where had they come from, what were their thoughts and fears, and whether any of them had been killed wearing it.

Our mock battle was noisy, energetic, and fierce with a few accidental bloody noses on both sides. When it was over, we staggered sweating, laughing, and exhausted to one side while a three-quarters life-sized catapult shot a flaming ball of tar into the paper-mache tower. We had coated the paper beforehand with copper salts and linseed oil so that it would burn in different colors, and placed squibs of gunpowder in strategic nooks. It burned and exploded spectacularly with periodic bangs and sprays of blue and green sparks, drawing appreciative oohs and aahs from the crowd, and the princess threw coins to us from the reviewing stand in appreciation.

I followed Erhan, Inanc, and Cihan to the shade of a plane tree at the edge of the parade ground where we collapsed happily on the grass together, eating the sweetbreads we had bought with some of the princess' coins, and enjoying the people pointing at us and talking about us behind their hands. "*That* was enormously fun," Erhan observed. "I suppose they won't let us keep our shediks?" he added hopefully.

"They'll probably make us turn them in to the armory tonight, or at latest tomorrow."

"Let's walk around in them some more. We don't have to be back at the palace until this evening." At festival times, the customary restrictions of life were relaxed by common accord. We wandered the city in the soft evening, returning to the Gulhane gate much later than we ought to have. At any other time, this would have earned us a beating, but we got off with a scolding and a warning.

One morning of my fifth year, as our *lala* was taking us through the history of the wars against the Kharaminids, he suddenly stopped, mid-sentence, his eyes up and on the door behind us. Then he bowed, something none of us had ever seen him do, then motioned for us all to stand.

A man of average height, perhaps forty years old, brown bearded, wearing a golden kaftan and an enormous turban with an aigrette of heron plumes, walked slowly up the aisle between our seats. I heard a quick intake of breath from Erhan, who sat behind me, and the quiet rustle as the oglans in the back rows touched their hearts and foreheads and bowed as he passed. Padishah Sultan II Bayezid, Refuge of the World, Ruler of the Black Sea and of the White, Lord of the Horizons, walked past me so close that his sleeve almost brushed my shoulder. There had been no trumpet. The implication was that he meant for us to stay in his presence.

The *lala* murmured a polished greeting, switching effortlessly to Persian, "Long life and prosperity, my Padishah."

"And to you my good *lala*. Please continue. The course of knowledge must ever flow. I am here to steal a few moments rest from my work and to enjoy a few moments of the mind. You were discussing the end of the Seljuks. Which of your students can recite the *Lay of the Sons of the Night Wind*?

The *lala* nodded to Bilgetai, who had copied parts of it in his fine hand, and whose memory for history was faultless. He stood and recited,

> And they brought the humbled Pir Ahmed
> before the victorious Sultan, who asked,
> "Why have you broken your treaties,
> wasted both our lands, and deprived your people of peace?
> My own enemies speak better of me
> than your friends do of you."

The Sultan said nothing for a moment, then nodded his approval. "Those lines were well chosen and well spoken. The making and keeping of treaties is one of the foundations of the justice of a ruler. 'My treasure in this world is justice'," Bayezid quoted in Persian from the *Shahnameh*. "The Karaminid state was far more powerful than we. Yet, they are nothing now."

We considered this in silence. We knew that he was thinking of our current war in the east with the Mamluks and of the broken treaties which had led to it.

"And why was that?"

I looked at the *lala* for permission to stand. He nodded. "Because they broke their treaties?" I said hesitantly, and added, "Like the Hungarians did with us at Varna?"

Bayezid smiled. "You have touched on something very important. To keep our treaties is the Ottoman way. To keep those treaties we make to ourselves, to our friends, to our comrades, is even more so. Who of you can say why?"

A number of hands, Erhan, who was the best of us for history, being the first. "Because our treaties to our enemies are written on silk; our treaties to our friends are written deep in our blood, and our treaties to ourselves are written on our souls."

And so it went for some time. Bayezid pronounced himself pleased with us, and when he stood up to leave, he leaned over and whispered something in the *lala*'s ear that must have been a compliment, because the lala seemed to grow several inches taller on the spot. Nor was this the only time Bayezid came, for he truly valued learning, and it was said he could read and speak at least five languages fluently.

Indeed, the padishah was present at the only examination I ever failed during my time at the Enderun Kolej, my oral recitation on the alliances of Europe. I had spent months studying to get it down—Venice was at war with Genoa; Florence was at war with Milan; Milan and Ferrara were at war with Venice; France was at war with the part of Naples that France claimed, while the people of that part of Naples who did not want to be French fought back. The other part of Naples was at war with Venice and the papal states, who were meantime at war with each other despite sharing enemies-in-common. Naples and Genoa were allies, but distrusted each other; France was at war with Spain, and Spain was at war with itself. Hungary was about the only stable constant, only because they never stopped raiding us whether we were at peace or at war with them. I would have had the whole thing off fine, if a ship had not arrived in Istanbul two days before my examination with the news that the Papal States had made peace with Venice, turned on Naples, and reconciled a number of the other warring states to an uneasy league (aimed, not surprisingly, against us).

I tried to redo it at the last minute, but there wasn't time. "Venice" and "Florence" do not rhyme in Turkish, for one thing, and now they had to go at the ends of different lines. When the time came, I got it hopelessly muddled. As I stammered to an embarrassed stop, the three examining lalas were staring, shamed, at the ground. I wanted to sink into the loam of the garden.

The padishah eased the painful silence with a small laugh and turned to look at Vezier Daud Pasha. "Now he knows what we have to deal with every day."

One of the *lala*s looked up.

"I think you have learned more than you have learned," Daud said. "Describing the world as it isn't, you have told it as it is. Forget the colors of the threads, but remember the pattern."

I nodded, thankful to be let off so easily. Years later, I was to remember what he said, and to realize that I had indeed learned more than I had known.

That day happened to be a Thursday of the year 895, or April 1490 in western reckoning, Thursday was the day of the week we got our special pilaf for the evening meal. When Bilgetai and I entered the treasury room after dinner for our chart copying, the other oglans were not there. Admiral Bahadir sat alone at the head of the table.

"Bolt the door," he said formally.

I did.

Bahadir slowly unrolled a chart. It was of a coastline neither of us had ever copied before. "This was captured a week ago. I want you two—and only you two—to copy it. Quickly, but with absolutely no mistakes. The galley *Yildirim* sails in two days, and she must have a copy of this chart on board when she does."

I heard Bilgetai draw in his breath.

It was the coast of Spain.

"These are the notebooks pertaining to that coast. You must copy them also."

"*...sheltered from sight from the land by an overhanging cliff, and the shallow bay makes the waves steep and breaking. All four of a galley's anchors must be set to keep her from dragging against a lee shore,*" I read as one of them fell open to the page. I looked closely. Interlaced with the Turkish were many Spanish and Portuguese words, which—thanks to the many words of Latin left over from when my native country had been a province of the Romans—I found I could understand surprisingly easily. The entries were signed "Onur."

I looked up as if with the pleasure of coming across the trace of an old friend. "Is that *our* Onur?" Onur had been one of the older 'cousins' my first year.

"The same," Bahadir answered. "He goes ahead of his fellows into danger, and puts his learning to good use."

When the chart was finished the following afternoon, the Admiral allowed us to accompany him to the port. "It is time you saw the importance of what you do."

There were almost fifty galleys and smaller galleots berthed side by side against the shore, their square sterns to the quay and their sharp bows pointed outwards. Long, low, and dark in the water, their hulls looked as sharp and purposeful as knife blades. And this was not even the whole of our fleet; more galleys were stationed at Gelibolu and Cannakele on the Dardanelles. To my eye, the ships were graceful and alive, the curve of their hulls whispering of speed and the desire to be on their way to distant places. There was a captured Milanese galley tied up alongside several of ours, having its guns taken off to be melted down and recast with longer barrels and larger bores to make them lighter and add to their range. A shipwright and his assistant were standing on the quay, studying her lines.

"Cut her gun platforms down, do you think? Make her a little bit trimmer and more seaworthy?"

The shipwright was shaking his head. "Hardly worth it. That hull will never be fast. Make more sense to take her apart completely and resteam the wood to build a new one."

We climbed up the short ladder from the quay to *Yildirim*'s stern deck. Flag Captain Bayulken and his officers selammed, then stood along either rail of the stern deck while the rowers stood at their benches, and the sail handlers lined up along the center walkway in front of the mast, and the gun crews on the fighting platform.

Bahadir nodded to Bayulken to have the crew stand at ease while he conferred with the officers and inspected the ship. We made our way gradually forward along the walkway. My presence did not seem to be needed at that particular moment, and I knew that the admiral intended for Bilgetai and me to see as much as we could, so I took the bold and probably impertinent step of asking Captain Bayulken, "May I go out on the beak?"

"On such a day as this," Bayülken said, looking pleased at what was an indirect compliment to his ship, "You may do anything."

In truth, I did not know whether I would actually have the nerve for it or not. The beak narrowed as it arched up from the bow. It was not for ramming, being too high off the water and delicate for that; it served as a boarding bridge in battle. I had never been out on a ship's beak before, but it was something new, and I wanted to try. I walked along the walkway between the rowers' benches, where loops of rope were fastened over the oar handles to hold them down so that the blade ends stayed up and out of the water when under sail or in port. Beyond the rowers' benches were the guns.

Two of the crew were perched far out on the beak, flaking out the braces of the foresail yard, their feet dangling over.

"The Captain said I could come out," I called out to them.

One of them waved me along, and I began feel my way cautiously. The beak had a little spring to it under my feet, which was a trifle disconcerting, and I placed my feet tentatively for the first few steps, trying not to look down at the water on either side. It was wonderful to be suspended between air and water out ahead of the ship. Even if my steps were slow and uncertain, I imagined what a thrill it would be to do this when the ship was at sea and under way.

"When you reach the end, swing your legs forward and over."

"Thanks, my name's Kachak," I said when I was sitting astride the beak.

The one who had waved to me held out his hand. "From the palace?" he asked looking at my clothes. "I'm Mete, crew chief for the starboard oars, and,"—pointing his crewmate—"he's Canni, chief of the portside oars."

Canni gave me a wide grin. "Welcome and Peace."

The view from the beak was glorious. To be projected out into the harbor, with the mass of the ship behind me—businesslike and purposeful—was to have a privileged view of the goings-on of a new world.

"Tell me about your ship. Where have you sailed to? What adventures have you had?"

"Lefkada."

"You were at *Lefkada* ?" I asked, delighted. We had all heard the story of how our ships, brilliantly handled, had worked their way in close to the shore at night and threaded their way undetected through the difficult passages between the myriad small islands that ringed the coast. They had surprised the enemy galleys on shore, burning scores of them. They began to tell me of it, how they had avoided the sandbars, oars muffled with strips of cloth, inching through the darkness.

"Come, the admiral is about to address the ship," Canni broke off his story, motioning me forward.

Bahadir made a short speech to the officers and crew. "You do not yet know where you are going, or what you will be doing. Your captain will tell you those things only when you are well away at sea, away from the eyes and ears of the land. What you do know—what you do not need to be told—is that your voyage is important. If you succeed, you will bring back something far more precious than gold."

Then he gave them the spur that no Ottoman crew worth its salt could resist. "What you are about to do is not possible. That is why the Sultan has every confidence that you will accomplish it."

The crew gave a cheer, and, with the admiral going in front, we turned and climbed down the stern ladder to the quay. *Yildirim*'s stern lines were cast off; her oars splashed down into the water as if part of one enormous wing, blades squared smartly. They paused for a beat, then the water turned to white as the blades surged through the water in a single motion. The wash of the puddles lapped against the stone quay, and *Yildirim* began to move out into the harbor like a thing alive. I felt my heart beat with the beauty of it.

"Because we are sailors and superstitious," Bahadir Reis said, "We do not watch our ships out of sight. We let them go upon their business, and turn instead to our own."

When *Yildirim* did return two months later, it was with a long scrape down her port side—which her helmsman swore up and down through all the quaysides of Fener was not his fault—and with tales well worth the hearing. She had made a lightning dash clear across the length of the Mediterranean, out of sight of land, slipping silently at night into dangerous bays along the Andalusian coast to bring off families of Mooriscos and Jews fleeing the growing terror of the Inquisition in Spain. She had evaded Aragonese galleys among the islands, then dashed across to the north African coast to land her refugees where they could embark in safer and more comfortable merchant convoys to Ottoman lands, only to sail back to Andalusia to rescue more. Among the stories circulating—though officially denied—was that once, in order to evade capture, *Yildirim* had sailed west through the strait of Jebel Al-Tariq, which the Europeans call Gibraltar, into the very Karanlikin Denizi itself, the Atlantic, the Sea of Darkness. She brought with her the best Andalusian sailmakers, the best swordsmiths, the most widely-travelled merchants, the best gunpowder mixers, and the best chartmakers of that now unhappy land.

"How can you call this king a wise man," our Sultan later asked an ambassador, "when he is expelling from his kingdom the very people who will enrich mine?"

Indeed, their talents were needed now more than ever before. A July evening storm had struck Istanbul, and a lightning bolt had caused the gunpowder works at the Gongormez Kilisesi to explode with horrific casualties among the workers. Once alight, the fire spread rapidly through the surrounding neighborhoods of wooden houses. From the palace walls, it looked as if much of the old part of the city was engulfed. We were sent to help the troops who were fighting the fires all through the night and into the following day. We tore down houses to make firebreaks and hauled buckets from the cisterns until the muscles of our shoulders and backs burned.

Those oglans and janissaries with medical skills treated the injured in the temporary hospital which had been set up in the Atmeydan janissary school. It was said that more than five thousand people died. By the second evening, we were beginning to hold it. It was burning itself out in the neighborhoods where it had already done its worst. Bilgetai and Erhan's faces were streaked with soot, making their eyes seem unnaturally large in the glow cast by the islands of flame which still danced. We were staring silently down the hill towards Kuchuk Aya Sofya street at the blackened scars that the fire had left. I was so weary I had not even realized that my shoulders were heaving with silent sobs, until I saw Bilgetai and Erhan look away quickly to give me space, pretending not to notice.

"Sorry," I wiped my face. Smears of soot and tears. "It's the second time a town that I call home has burned."

Bilgetai and Erhan swung their gazes back to my face and held it. Erhan nodded, more with his eyes than with his head, in that way he had, and did not look away again. I thanked him silently inside for that. Friends do not need to spare your feelings.

As the summer wore on, we chartcopiers gradually made the transition from oglan to something more like assistants to the admiral. Bahadir entrusted us with more and more sensitive work, teaching us as he went. We learned the complexities of supplies for an enormous fleet, and the meticulous planning that must be done before even one ship can sail. "Sea battles are won on land," he was fond of saying. He began to tell us of events in the wider world. King Korvinus of Hungary, sometime open enemy and always scheming, had died that April, removing for a time part of the longstanding threat to our western border. But by no means the only one.

"There was a congress of Christian rulers in Rome this spring," Bahadir told us, "trying to stir up a crusade of all Europe against us. As usual, they want to use our Sultan's rebellious brother as the spearhead. Our reports say even the Mamluks sent an envoy."

Bilgetai looked up from his work, surprised.

"Yes, truly. They are even going so far as to cast us as being involved in the death of Christ now. One of our agents writes that there is a painter named Luca Signorelli in Orvietto, not far from Rome, who has a commission to paint a crucifixion scene. In addition to the usual Roman soldiers, the painter has included a Turkish cavalryman, no less. Just to make sure there's no question, there's a pennon with the crescent and star fluttering from the lance."

"Well that's one event we had nothing to do with."

"Truly not. Our fathers' fathers' fathers' were still in eastern Asia when it took place." He turned solemn. "Kachak, how would you like to go to sea on a galley next summer instead of hauling wheat in Anatolia? Small size may not be much help on land, but it is valued aboard a galley. You already know how to read a chart; you have a feel for ships. It is the logical next step in your training."

"I would be pleased and honored, my admiral."

"Good. I will ask Grand Admiral Hersekoglu Ahmed. He will grant it, I am sure."

My first ship was the *Emniyet* (Confidence), a trim little galleot which had begun her life as the *Trinitas* under the flag of Naples before being captured and towed back to Istanbul. Repainted and renamed, she now patiently suffered the awkwardness of trainee maneuvers as—season after season—she produced each new crop of Ottoman sailors. Poor *Emniyet*. She had had a hard life even before she came to us, having been capsized twice and almost sunk. If there was a waterlogged tree trunk floating just under the surface anywhere within miles, *Emniyet* was sure to hit it, giving her cadets plenty of practice in patching hull strakes. She had survived a waterspout at sea off the coast of Egypt, and been struck by lightning while in port at Gelibolu. Throughout the fleet, many of us carried slivers of her lightning-struck mast with us as protective talismans. It is the most powerful amulet a sailor knows.

Much repetitive training in harbor at first, learning to handle the sails and oars, learning to row in time with the oars a precise distance above the water so that not a single blade ticked the water on the backstroke. The Europeans say that we Ottomans feather our oars upside-down (to their eyes anyway), but there is a reason for this. Your wrists roll up over the handle rather than down under it, and thus are ready in hook position to pull the handle towards you strongly as soon as the blade dips into the water for the next stroke. When we had begun to learn the feel of the ship, we made short voyages out into the Marmara and back. Drills and more drills to hone what we learned, each maneuver done faster and more surely than it had been the day before. In a month's time we were pretty proud of our quickness, until the officers took the ship down to Gelibolu "to show you how real ships are handled," (and no doubt to nip the beginnings of our pride in the bud).

"So that's how it's done," Cihan said as we watched two galleys sweep past us under oars almost as if we had been standing still, banners flying, their banks of oars in perfect time, everything sharp and precise. Humbled, but also determined, we returned to Istanbul for two days of leave, before going on a longer cruise, destination a surprise.

"This morning, we will put the *Emniyet* to sea more sharply, more skillfully, more soundlessly, than we have ever done," the first lieutenant said, addressing us from the stern deck, both hands behind his back, "and you will do it—" here he brought his hands out from behind his back, and there were strips of cloth in them "—blindfolded."

"And I hope every Hapsburg, Vatican, and Firenk spy in the city is watching," he said more quietly, but just loudly enough for us to hear. For that, of course, was part of the point. "Victories are won before we sail," our training officers repeated constantly. Among the Europeans, the Ottoman fleet's reputation for uncompromising training was one of its weapons.

It was an exhilarating challenge. We did it, and we did it well. The feel of the ship was in each of our limbs by now; touch and hearing supplied what we needed to know. We ran through the entire gun drill blindfolded for good measure, swabbing, loading and unloading, everything except the firing itself. That we would do down at Cannakale, out of sight of western eyes.

We learned the skill of navigating at night and telling time and direction precisely by the phases of the moon. For each day of the year, and for each phase of the moon, there were charts with concentric half-circles drawn up to tell us exactly how much later every evening the moon rose and set and which point of the compass it was in, and against which stars. From the angle of the moon above the horizon measured with a cross staff (astrolabes were too expensive for most galley captains, and a cross staff was easier to use at sea anyway), one could calibrate against the chart—in the circle of light cast by the lantern at the stern—which direction the ship was heading and exactly how long until dawn. It was not a matter of having to match it to a particular hour; the moon was its own time. We learned from the janissaries the skill of sleeping only when we needed to and being awake when duty called for it.

I returned to the Hall of the Expeditionary Forces that autumn confident and happy. My fellow oglans, Bilgetai, Erhan, Ahmethamid, all had stories to tell too. I returned to my chart copying with a new appreciation for the task. The Mamluks had sent envoys to Istanbul, and the peace talks which had dragged on all summer finally resulted in a treaty which was signed in the middle of September. Bahadir gave us all five days of holiday, and we went down to the shore of the Bosphoros each night to watch the fireworks which celebrated the end of the dreadful war in the east.

The following summer, I was assigned to a "real ship" not a training vessel—the *Akdogan*,—as her underhelmsman. Bilgetai was aboard a ship in the Black Sea squadron as the navigator and captain's amanuensis. We spent the summer patrolling the islands of the Aegean, sometimes in company with the main fleet under Admiral Kemalladdin, sometimes as part of a detached squadron. In July, we sailed to the dangerous coast of Spain to spirit away Mooriscos and Jews from the Inquisition. We undertook wild landings by small boats in dangerous bays, climbing the cliffs with lanterns in our teeth to make the secret signals while *Hilal* and the rest of the squadron "made themselves obvious" off of Majocar to draw away the attention of any Spanish troops or ships which might have been in the area and who might have hindered our evacuees. *Akdogan* was forced to show her speed several times, her sharp prow driving through the waves with the north wind at our stern and Spanish galleys in angry pursuit. Officially, the Spanish had already confiscated all the belongings of the exiles before they left, but this had been a cumbersome and bureaucratic process, and many—having seen this persecution coming— had had time to transfer their valuables to bankers in Florence or Antwerp or Galata, or to secrete them in outbound cargoes. Many a crate of oranges on its way to the Golden Horn destined for the kitchens of the Padishah carried rubies in false bottoms. The Spanish, having belatedly tumbled to this, hoped their galleys would have a last chance at squeezing our passengers' wealth before we left their waters. We made twenty-three journeys back and forth to Tangiers before autumn's worsening weather, and the attentions of the resentful Spanish galleys, made the western waters too turbulent for us. On the long sail back to our home waters and Istanbul, we had aboard one Andalusian Moor in particular who spent a large part of each day staring mournfully over the stern at the waters receding in the direction of his former home. His town, he told me, had been burnt by Ferdinand's soldiers. He was by trade a book printer.

"Mine was burnt too."

"So we are both without a place to be from."

It was on this voyage that I first heard the haunting and lilting music of Andalusia that the Mooriscos and Jews brought with them, rhythms which they sang softly on the stern deck to pass the evenings when the weather allowed, songs which would soon be heard in taverns all along the dockyards of the Horn. Istanbul would blend them with its own melodies and form an emotional continuation of a Granada and a Cordoba which no longer existed. I have never seen Al-hambra, nor walked the streets of Granada in the flesh, but when I close my eyes, I tread every corridor and corner of them in that place within my mind where music draws its pictures.

We caught a papal galley and her escorting brigantina southwest of Sicily; she was on her way west to Spain, and she clearly did not expect Turkish ships so far west in the Mediterranean. Assuming we were friendly, her officers neglected even the rudimentary precaution of altering course when they first sighted us. The galley hauled down her flag as soon as we opened fire. The brigantine, being too fast for us to catch, backed her sails smartly when she saw what was going on, and got away. From the galley's officers we learned—though doubtless the news had already reached Istanbul before us—that the corrupt Roderic Borgia had been elected Pope Alexander VI. The news brought a certain gloom to our passengers, for it had been Borgia's diplomatic efforts while a cardinal that had helped fuse the Aragonese and Castillian alliance, an alliance which had then become strong enough to break the centuries of peace with the Moorish cities, and to attack and drive their citizens out of Spain. Our passengers held Borgia at least partly responsible for their present exile, and his accession to the papacy confirmed their wisdom in leaving Spain to make a new life elsewhere. The news that the new pope was pursuing a policy of tolerance towards the Moors and Jews who had settled in Rome only partly mitigated their distrust.

We learned more gratifying news from the captive Turks we liberated from the galley's oars. Our increased ship construction of the previous spring had triggered waves of panic in the west. The Knights of Rhodes—certain the build-up had been directed against them—had sent a flurry of letters to Rome announcing the threat. The Neapolitans, equally convinced that Sicily or Naples was the intended target, had spent fortunes they didn't have repairing their neglected fleet. The Hungarians meanwhile assumed that the hammer had been about to fall on their coast. When the Ottoman fleet passed the Dardanelles and vanished, without reappearing in any of the expected places, it had caught all of Europe entirely by surprise. No one had imagined that our fleet would sail to the far end of the western Mediterranean, nor that evacuation, and not conquest, would be our purpose.

The papal ship was loaded down with the tribute that the Vatican was squeezing out of its domains in Europe to cover the increasing expenses of the pope's mistresses and the gifts he wished to lavish on his relatives. She did not even attempt to jettison her chart box, and when we hauled it over and broke it open, we found out why not. In addition to the charts and papers one would expect to find, there was also a packet of documents transferring the titles to numerous Church estates and benefices in Valencia and in the Papal States to Borgia's relatives and to his two illegitimate sons and daughter.

Each of us received a share of the captured galley's worth as prize money at the end of the summer when she was towed into the dockyards of the Horn and added to our fleet, while her cargo was put up for sale. Captain Hasan was invited to a meeting of the Divan and given a robe of honor. The dockyards of the Horn were busier than ever; sixty new ships were being built—agile as sea snakes, to use the Padishah's own phrase—and the Venetians were already becoming thoroughly nervous about the size of our new navy. Their *bailo,* Hironimo Marcello, wrote secret reports back to Venice. Several of these were intercepted by some clever lads employed by the vezier's office, who waylaid the unlucky courier in the backstreets of Pera on his way to the harbor to board his ship. The Divan ordered Marcello's expulsion from Istanbul, and sent word to his masters back in Venice not to bother to send any replacement for the time being. As the Divan no doubt intended, the secondary effect of this diplomatic tit-for-tat was that those of Marcello's reports which had already gotten back to Europe were then given even more weight. "They'll take our fleet seriously now," Bahadir commented with satisfaction.

It was a nervous autumn. No one was supposed to know about the event, and I have no doubt that whippings had been promised—and no doubt meted out—to any who told, but the news went through Istanbul like flames through dried grass that there had been an assassination attempt on the sultan while he was campaigning in Macedonia. At Manastir, a dervish of the anarchical Kalenderi sect had called out to the sultan from the crowd lining the route of his march. Bayezid had heard him, bent down from his saddle, and invited him to accompany the army for the rest of the day's march. Conversing—as our Sultan loved to do—on philosophical matters in the Sultan's campaign tent that evening, the kalenderi had suddenly jumped up, yelling blasphemously "I am the Mehdi," and waving a saber he had concealed under his robes. The guards had not wished to search a holy man closely, and their carelessness nearly cost the Padishah his life. The kalenderi wounded Bayezid in the shoulder before Second Vezier Iskender, who was present at the discussion, grabbed the imperial mace and caved in the left side of the fanatic's skull with it.

The Sultan's wound was not serious, Iskender's prompt reactions had seen to that. The campaign continued. In the interests of order and public safety, the Kalenderi were expelled from the western territories of the empire, and many of their lodges were ordered closed. Handwritten sheets were plastered to the walls of Istanbul's buildings at night, the first wave of a whispering campaign claiming that the expulsions and the closing of the Kalenderi lodges indicated that Bayezid was turning into a religious bigot. This was unfair. Bayezid was curious about many religions, and loved discussing them. He had almost paid with his life for that curiosity. The palace library—as we oglans had seen for ourselves because we sometimes shelved the books there—contained bibles as well as Korans. The library contained texts some might have considered heretical. His mother was a Christian. Bayezid understood better than most people the distinction between religion, and those who merely drape religion over their own excesses like a cloak.

Akdogan's helmsman was promoted out of the ship to become the captured galley's new helmsman, leaving a vacancy. It was thus that, the following March,—one cold, rainy, miserable, *glorious* morning—I became the helmsman of the *Akdogan*, and that was something no one else in the world was. We winged our yardarms and sailed down the Bosphoros, hurried on our way by a northerly breeze sweeping down from the Black Sea, with our mainsail and foresails sheeted in at the bottom. From the land, this may look like the easiest point of sailing, but this is a galley's or galleot's most unstable rig. The hull tends to skip off the waves rising under the stern, especially as the rudder rises part way out of the water and has less to work against, and the helmsman must have a deft touch to keep the ship exactly before the wind. Even a slight change in course, or a surprise gust, can cause one of the sails to gybe over hard to the other side, heeling the galley dangerously or—in a really strong wind—take the mast with it. The helmsman must read the catspaws on the water for the slightest wind shift, and gently ease the galley's rudder to meet it, easing back when the gust has passed. Fortunately for me, that morning's breeze was steady and gentle and gave me several days of good running to regain the feel of the ship.

We ran down the Sea of Marmara, past the Prince's Islands, and came to Gelibolu in the Dardanelles at evening. There we took on additional supplies, and sighted in the guns using marks painted on the cliffs. One week later, the squadron sailed for Macedonia to escort a convoy of round-hulled sailing ships carrying barrels of saltpeter back to Istanbul. We were back in the Horn when the battered *Phoenix* limped into harbor.

The rest of my tale you already know, or the important parts anyway. These then, were the circumstances which had brought me to this cell in Crete, where people who knew nothing about me disputed what nation I belonged to, and attempted to claim me as one of their own.

Chapter II
Dressed to suit their image

My reverie was interrupted by a parade of faces—male and female—peering in at the grated opening in the cell door. The guards were making themselves some pocket money by selling admission to the curious of Crete who wished to see the terrible Turk *renegado* for themselves. After some time of this, which I did my best to ignore, the cell door grated open against the stone floor, and the Dominican monk from the interrogation entered. I braced myself for this unwelcome intrusion into my thoughts. Keeping his back to the door, he asked in a low voice which would not carry, "Why do you not say what they want you to say?"

Ah, a new tack. "'They'? Not 'we'?"

"It would be the easiest way to get you out of here. One less captive your friends would have to exchange for you. A captive they could use to exchange for another Turk."

I was startled at this, for the pragmatic reasoning echoed one of the lines of thought I had been testing out myself.

"Why do 'they' need my confession so badly?"

He knelt beside me, back to the door, in order to be able to converse even more quietly. To those looking in it would seem as if he were contending for my soul. "Because it raises their credit in the eyes of those they would convince. To be able to parade you around the town as someone they have rescued makes their stories true."

"I do not wish to lend credence to their stories."

"Nor do I. I know, even better than you, how they use those stories as an excuse for piracy, killing, and theft. They raid your ships for profit with one hand, and write treaties with you with the other."

In four languages, I thought to myself. I locked my thoughts against what I assumed was an attempt to gain my trust.

"I'll tell you something. The *podesta* cannot be sure what to do with you. He dares not offend the order of Rhodes, but Venice also has a treaty with the Turks. Venice's Levant trade is the basis of her wealth, so he is under strict orders not to provoke the Sultan either." He thought for a moment. "Imagine I am the Grand Master of the Knights of Rhodes, Pierre d'Aubusson, who is also Cardinal of Sant Andrien—"

Without meaning to, I looked up in surprise.

"It's not a title he uses often. After all, being a cardinal is very little compared to the power of the Grand Master of the Order. A cardinal, moreover, who can snap his fingers at a pope and all the other cardinals combined."

As his description unfolded, I began to sense the awful power our squadron had challenged and perhaps provoked.

"The order," he continued, "the 'Religion' as it calls itself, is its own kingdom, and a very powerful one. It recognizes no law, except the will of its grand master. The order is accountable only to the Pope. It knows this is an empty restraint; the Vatican dares not enforce any instruction that the order doesn't choose to obey. The Order owns more land in France than the king of France does. It is wealthier than the whole of England. Only Spain is more wealthy, but Spain is at the other end of the Mediterranean and cares not what the order does as long as it calls itself the eastern bulwark of Christendom."

"And so the *podesta* agrees quietly to keep 'the Religion's' captives for it," I said.

"Exactly. But now," he let his shoulders droop almost comically, "I am the *podesta*.. Appointed to this island either as a stepping stone on my career upwards...or as a way station on my career down. I dare not offend the Religion. I dare not offend the sultan. I—" he let out an exaggerated sigh, "I dare not offend the Signoria of Venice which appointed me. Yet, in the seasons when the Ottoman galleys patrol, more cargoes get through, not fewer. The farmers have someone to sell their grain to; the merchants get their cargoes of pepper and silk from Aleppo. Profits are better; the colony prospers. And through it all, no one likes to admit the reason." He paused for a moment and recited some Latin in a louder voice for the benefit of those beyond the door. "You are the card in his hand, but he doesn't know how to play you for the most value."

He paused, then said in a grimmer tone, "If he did, you would be facing a much more terrifying side of the Offices of Inquiry than you presently are. They destroy people."

"I know. I have heard of what they do. But, why are you telling me this?"

"I'm Jewish."

I stared at his monk's habit.

"They forced my family to convert. Two years later, they decided our conversion wasn't sincere enough for them, so they confiscated half of what we owned. That wasn't enough, so they demand a payment—a very large one—every year. My parents couldn't afford to keep me and my two sisters on what was left, so my father pledged me to the Church. It was his way of getting revenge, 'I'll make the Church keep you, since I no longer can.' He also hoped it would guarantee a little protection for the rest of the family."

The story had its own internal plausibility, in the madness of such times.

"Promise me that, when you get back to sea, you will hurt the people who did this? Hurt them badly?"

"But Crete is an island. Even if you get me out of here, I still have to get off the island."

"You might have to become someone other than who you are. Don't worry about how. My people have long experience with that."

"So do I," I said wryly.

Under the pretext that he was making progress reconverting me, he was allowed to visit almost daily. We planned my escape so many different ways that it became a sort of pastime for us. In one version he would bring me food and wine, counting on the fact that Turks did not drink alcohol, he would put some drug into it, and when the guards confiscated it and were asleep, he would sneak me out and across the island to Sittia, from which—we imagined not very realistically—an

Ottoman galley could sweep close inshore at night according to some prearranged signal and spirit me away. In another, he would get me off the island by selling me to a ship captain as a rower with some story of unpaid debts. In another—even more impractical—I would disguise myself as a Jewish merchant and take a ship to Rosetta, and from there work my way back to Istanbul.

Each version was brought up short by the same obstacle. The sea. In the meantime, he used the time to teach me some Latin, which I knew would be useful anywhere in the Mediterranean.

"If you reconvert, and they let you out, they may still put you to work in the fields or the galleys. The Christians have no law, as the Turks do, against enslaving their own kind."

"It's a risk," I agreed. "But then so is any other method. And it would raise your standing, to have converted a renegado. That could be useful."

"You and I keep our oaths by breaking them," he observed.

"A strange and strong form of loyalty, perhaps."

Time was growing short and the sailing season would end soon. I took the easiest way out. I reconverted. The *podesta* was much pleased, and gave orders that my return to grace would be celebrated in a very public way with a special mass at the abbey church of St. Sebastian. They made quite a show of it. Handbills announcing the conversion were posted in the town. The morning of the service, my Dominican friend—I will not tell you his name even now, for in such discretion does his continued safety lie—came into my cell chanting the psalm "*Oh Lord my God thou hast set me up and not made my enemies to triumph over me*——" and stood with a turban (folded wrong), boots, and other deliberately Turkish clothes over his arm.

"What on earth are these for?"

"——*I cried unto the Lord and the Lord hast healed me*——um, well, they want you to dress the part of the repentant Turk, and ride you through the town."

"And this is their idea of one, is it? These are janissary boots; I'm not a janissary, don't they know the difference? What are they expecting, scimitars and turbans?"

"*Thou hast brought my soul out of hell*——yes, as a matter of fact they are."

I thought of Berk and Ozkan and how they would split their sides laughing if they knew. "If any real Turks see me like this, I'll never hear the end of it back in Istanbul."

"Ah, but you're not a real Turk, actually," he reminded me.

"True enough, but realer than this," I grumbled. "No, it's worn like this; you've got it inside out. And no, I will *not* wear a *taj*."

Last, he held out an archer's thumb ring, magnificently carved from amber to protect from the release of the string, and he——not understanding what it was——tried to put it on my middle finger, for which, naturally, it was too large.

"I have not earned the right to wear this," I said, explaining its correct purpose. "I will not, no matter what they ask."

"I do not understand. You make no conditions converting from one religion to another, yet you remain loyal to your *training?*"

I remain loyal to what I am and to what I am not."

"But who would even know?"

"I would."

Thus, dressed to suit their image, I rode across the town with soldiers and monks escorting me through streets lined with the curious, some of them sympathetic, some not. At the door of the church, the *podesta* himself removed the turban, which partially unwrapped as he lifted it so that one end of it flapped comically in my face as the breeze caught it. The captain who had 'freed' me removed the kaftan, a merchant prominent in the city took off my boots; one by one they stripped me symbolically of my Turkishness until, in my white penitents' smock, I prostrated myself in front of the altar. The abbot himself said the mass. When I rose to my feet and approached the altar, I looked into his eyes for any sign that he suspected. I didn't feel a very good dissembler. Surely my face must be blaring the truth to anyone who looked. Could they not see through my mask? Surely they must all suspect? The abbot smiled as I knelt for his blessing, and his expression told me this was his day, not mine. I looked around the half-circle of the leading townsfolk—who had no doubt purchased their place in the ceremony by means of a substantial donation—standing by me as my spiritual helpers. There was not a skeptical glance in the whole place. No, they believed it because they wanted to believe it; they needed to believe it. It occurred to me that even if I shook myself and shouted loudly up to the dome, "So sorry, everyone, this is just a pretence I am carrying out in order to get home, in order to get back to being myself," the abbot would simply have shushed me and continued with the service.

After the *Veni creator spiritus* had been chanted over my head, there was a feast. They served pork and wine to test me, of course, and I ate and drank it without a qualm. In this, they erred in their assumption. Not all who served the sultan were Muslim, and many were not. Talent was what concerned the Ottomans. As long as you showed respect and paid the poll tax, your individual beliefs were your affair. For a few days after the feast, I was allowed the freedom of the town. Everyone's curiosity was soon filled and I—having served their purpose—was sent to semi-arrest in the abbey.

I was in its library one afternoon, poring over one of the many printed books that the busy print shops of Venice—where so many books were printed which were banned in other parts of Europe—had sent to the island, when the street outside the gates erupted into a loud discussion that reached even into the grounds. I caught a word here and there as a group of people gathered. Then one of the monks went out to see what the fuss was about. A ship had arrived from Venice with staggering news. The corsairs of the Knights of Rhodes, not content to prey solely on Muslim shipping, had now arrogated to themselves the right to board and search any ship carrying either cargo or passengers to, or from, any Muslim port, or carrying any cargo owned by Muslim or Jewish merchants. This for all practical purposes meant that any ship in the Mediterranean, no matter what flag it flew, would be meat for their appetite. An entire Venetian convoy returning from the Levant had been detained because—among its other cargoes, five of the ships were carrying taffeta from Aleppo. Five ships and their entire cargoes had been impounded on the pretext of a few bolts of cloth. Venice's Signoria was furious and had sent letters of complaint to the pope and to Rhodes. Pope Alexander had written back saying that the matter was out of his hands. This only added fire to Venetian resentment because the pope himself collected customs duties on Muslim cargoes shipped through Ancona, nominally a free port in the Papal States.

The Religion in its turn had written to say that—if the Venetians wanted their ships, crews, and cargoes back—they could appeal their case like everyone else to the *charge d'affairs* at Rhodes, who of course was a member of the order and unlikely to give a fair hearing to outsiders, or decide anything that would cost the order financially.

I was summoned to an evening meeting at the residence of the *podesta*, who summarized the details of the dilemma Venice and—by extension—Candios found itself in. At the end of the meeting, I was handed two secret letters addressed to the Grand Vezier and the Grand Admiral in Istanbul containing suggestions for cooperation.

"This is Captain Andreas," the *podesta* said, introducing me to a short, bearded Venetian, "of the galleot *Lion*. His orders are to take you and these letters to Istanbul." He turned to the captain, "You're to sail only at night, at least until you are clear of any waters where any of the Religion's ships might sight you. While in Istanbul, you are to have no contact whatsoever with any Venetian officials. Not the *bailo*, not any of his staff, none of the merchants there, nobody. The word must never get back to Rhodes or to Europe that the Serene Republic is even talking to the Ottomans. That is why the letters are being sent from Candios and not directly from Venice."

He turned back to me. "Here is your license to sail, and sixty gold ducats to compensate you for any, er, inconvenience you have experienced in your time with us. My valet will give you clothes appropriate for your audience as an envoy."

We sailed within the hour, and after five nights darting from one hidden island cove to the next, we found ourselves north of Mykonos and safely in Ottoman waters. I was pleased to see that our lads were up to scratch; no sooner were we exactly ten miles north of Mykonos when two galleys flying the star and crescent swept over to inspect us.

Captain Andreas swore at them. "The devil must be whispering in their ears! How else could they know we were here so quickly?"

So I told him about the special mirror that each Ottoman sea captain keeps in his cabin which, when he looks into it, shows him where hostile ships are, through fog or night. Andreas crossed himself and glared at me, while also making the sign against the evil eye for good measure. All made up on the spot, of course, with liberal borrowings from the *Lay of the Sons of the Night Wind*—did I not mention, reader, that I am a good storyteller? Good, let him take that tale back to Europe then, with as many embellishments as he chooses. The more Hapsburg sea captains who believe they can't evade our ships in mist nor darkness, the more intimidating our navy will be.

Captain Andreas reluctantly ordered the sail lowered and our oars raised out of the water as a sign of our peaceful intentions, and I could see that it fretted his pride to do so. We bobbed in the water waiting for the galleys to come alongside.

"Time to earn your money," Andreas said gruffly to me as a small boat with an officer and several janissaries from one of the galleys rowed across to us and boarded. I translated as Andreas explained the purpose of our journey. The Turkish officer explained graciously—but using that subtle verb tense which indicated it was not a request, even if the polite formalness of the language made it sound like one—that one of the galleys would escort us as far as Cannakale, and that, once we had passed through the Dardanelles, another galley from Cannakale would escort us the rest of the way across the Marmara to Istanbul.

Eight days later, after a slow upwind slog mostly under oars, we put into Istanbul. We were flying a crescent flag by that point, and we docked not at the foreigners' wharf at Galata, but at the better-guarded imperial docks at Yenikapi on the south side of the city peninsula, a district where the average foreigner was not permitted to wander. The city walls run close along the Marmara shore there, and there is an opening and a breakwater for small ships to dock behind. With our masts and yards lowered, the galleot would be all but invisible from either the water, or from on land, unless someone were to get inside within the walls. There was a guard of janissaries to make sure that did not happen. The chances of any European becoming aware of our mission was thus sizably reduced.

With an escort of a dozen Venetians from the ship, I made my way up the hill to the palace to deliver the letters. Instantly the sounds and smells of Istanbul warmed my heart. I had not known how much I missed even the faintest strains of music drifting across the water from a dockside tavern. My Venetian escort stared eagerly at everything they were seeing for the first time, and chatted eagerly about how they might even see the sultan himself, until I told them that the Padishah and the grand vezier were in any case away with the army, and the grand admiral was almost certainly away at sea as well. By virtue of my status as an envoy, I entered the first courtyard of the palace by way of the Imperial gate, which I had never entered in all my time as an oglan; we always used the Gulhane gate instead. I asked merely to see whoever the most senior naval commander who was not away on sea duty.

Ahmethamid was one of the sentries on duty at the gate to the Divan court, and his face jumped in momentary surprise as he grounded the butt of his halberd with his best military precision, questions darting from his eyes. Hemmed in by my escort as I was, I managed to give him only the barest blink of my eyes in recognition, as I stooped to remove my boots and replace them with a pair of indoor slippers, silk of course, lined up for the use of visitors. Discipline reasserted itself and he made his face blank, saluting as formally and correctly as if he had never seen me before. I left my Venetian escort to cool their heels under guard in the portico outside, sitting among the waiting professional letter-writers who could be hired to pen petitions (and who also handled bribes), and was taken in to present my letters.

Court protocol demands that, whenever a foreign ambassador has an audience with anyone important, his arms are held, presumably to prevent him from leaping forward and assaulting the sultan or whatever official is giving the audience. With an expression on his face which I interpreted to mean that he intended to play the scene for my full benefit as well as for his own, Ahmethamid and another halberdier duly held my arms as they accompanied me to the office of the most senior naval commander present, which happened to be Bahadir, who thought this was hilarious.

He was very glad to see me, but showed no real surprise, as if it were the most natural thing in the world for his lost sailors to turn up at the palace as accredited Venetian envoys. Indeed, I was to learn, this was far from being the strangest thing that had happened in his long career.

"It's alright, Ahmethamid, you can let this one go, I think," he said with just the hint of a smile. "No doubt he has a reasonable, believable, and thoroughly entertaining explanation. One which enlightens the hearer while not departing—overly far—from the truth?"

I touched my chest and forehead. "Selamlar," I said, and held out the letters. Ahmethamid and the other halberdier glanced at the admiral, unsure whether their duty was to stand guard as protocol dictated, or whether this was now a confidential meeting. Bahadir indicated for them to stay. "By all means let us be formal; besides it will save him having to tell his story twice."

"The letters first, then your tale, perhaps over a meal? It's not every day I get to entertain a fully-accredited Venetian diplomat." He motioned to a page to set the midday meal for two in his office.

"Oh, I'm not fully-accredited," I said, "I'm only a temporary courier, if that."

He opened and read the letter addressed to the grand admiral, putting the one for the grand vezier aside unopened. "I assume the contents are similar?"

"I do not know; they were sealed before I read them, but from what the *podesta* said, I believe so."

The letter was in Greek, the usual diplomatic language between Venice and Constantinople. Bahadir translated the letter himself, nodding occasionally at certain points, frowning at others. "These are interesting suggestions. The Venetians are very practical; they know where their interests lie, even if it sometimes takes them a while. The Genoese, by the way, are likewise furious, their *bailo* has been making similar suggestions."

"Venetians and Genoese agreeing on something?"

Bahadir chuckled. "Quite a picture for the world, isn't it. But we shouldn't joke too soon. How would you like to find yourself facing a joint Venetian-Genoese fleet someday?"

"A lot better than I would like to try commanding one in a joint operation, I would think," I answered, quite seriously. We both knew how the mutual jealousies between the two maritime cities had torn their previous attempts at cooperation apart in a matter of weeks. "Throw in a galley or two from Naples or Milan, and watch the pot break into a hundred pieces."

"With Ottoman ships keeping the peace between them?"

I suddenly saw what he was getting at. There was a beautiful symmetry to it. "Why, it's what we've been doing all along, isn't it?"

He smiled the way one of our lalas might have at a pupil who has just figured out an algebra problem. "In our subtle way, yes. And each time our Padishah plays one off against the other, it buys us time.

"Is it as precarious as all that then? Surely our army..?"

Bahadir nodded heavily. "It is every bit as precarious as that. If the Europeans ever put aside their own quarrels and united against us—as they keep saying one day they will do— they could sweep through the Ottoman lands like a broom. Against one, or even two at a time, our armies are formidable, but against all of Europe? Against France, Spain, Naples, Milan, Hungary, Rhodes, the Papal States?" Bahadir let the sentence hang. The pope still has Cem to use as a puppet to lend legitimacy to such an army. If Cem were to lead it, then it is always possible that some of our eastern provinces, where Cem was the governor as a young man, might revolt in his name. We would find ourselves between two fires. I don't think we could fight both, and neither do Daud Pasha or Beyazid."

"Surely an Ottoman prince would never lead an army against his own country, not even to take the Sultanate?"

"I do not think there is anything that man would not do to be Sultan. Years ago—before you came to us—when his father was still alive, he even tried to usurp the throne."

"While the Conqueror was still *alive*?" I was stunned. The idea of anyone attempting the throne while Sultan Fatih Mehmet, the Conqueror of Constantinople, was ruling was so rash as to be absolute madness.

"Yes, incredible as that may seem. Mehmet II was on campaign with the army, and he had left Cem in Edirne as regent. Cem, prompted by some unscrupulous advisors who were out to feather their own nests, took advantage of his father's absence, and put about rumours that Mehmet was dead. Cem had himself proclaimed Sultan."

"What happened?"

"Oh, the janissaries put a very quick stop to it. Mehmet returned; Cem pleaded for forgiveness, claiming he meant no treason. It was only the absence of news from the front, he said, that made him think his father was dead. Mehmet publicly forgave him and packed him off to govern Konya, but he kept Cem's wife and son at Topkapi, no doubt as hostages to make sure Cem behaved himself in future."

I shook my head.

"That is just one of the many spear points leveled against us. We have almost always been outnumbered. Even fighting against one enemy at a time."

"And won each time." I was thinking again of Varna, and the admiral could see that I was.

"At Varna, the enemy marched themselves into a trap between the swampy edges of a lake, and some thickly-forested hills, before they even knew our army was nearby. Their troops were fighting for plunder, ours for their homes. Even so, it was a very, very close thing. They let their greed lure them into an ambush, and our troops fell on them from the ravines and wiped them out. Their failure to use their scouts cost them dearly."

And our discipline and training cost them too, I thought.

"But that was forty years ago. The Europeans—if united—could put three quarters of a million men or more into the field. We? At most, a hundred twenty thousand."

I gasped at the number. My imagination could not even contain such an image.

"Of course, they would lose half of them to starvation or sickness, but still…"

That much at least was true. The Europeans' inattention to the details of securing adequate provisions for their campaigns was a constant source of wonderment to Ottoman soldiers. 'A hungry bear won't dance,' the saying went. Starvation and the accompanying diseases had ravaged the Europeans' attempted invasion of 1481. That campaign—very fortunately—had collapsed before it could even embark from Italy.

"It is only in our navy which—thanks to Bayezid's foresight—we continue to outnumber them, even all of them together. Venice is the only one with a truly sizeable fleet of her own, and they would much rather trade with us than take orders from the pope." He changed tack. "So, you see, Kachak, that the sea is our only sure defense. It is the silver breastplate which keeps us safe."

I nodded.

"That is why," he continued in a low and serious voice, "we must never, ever let the navy weaken, nor relax our vigilance. The key to it all is the papacy. Alone, the Papal States are no threat. They have barely four thousand troops in the field, most of them hired mercenaries whom the pope can't always pay anyway. At sea, the papacy has six galleys and two galleots. Not even enough to carry the Vatican's mail half the time. But the papacy is the center point around which any large attack against us would have to coalesce. Without the pope to stir them, the others will never come together of their own accord. Not for any length of time, anyway."

There was a silence, then he brightened his mood, "And it is why we must always keep our ears to the wind for any divisions and squabbling to the west. Their discords are our best troops. Now, these Venetians of yours, whom you seem to have so nicely on your leash, do they instruct you to return to them to Candios with an answer?"

"They expect it, but I have no intention. That is, I would prefer to shrug off my Firenk habit, having finally made my way home—unless you have some reason in mind whereby it would serve. They expect me to report on our—that is, the Turkish—response." I told him then the story of my 're-conversion' and the pretense I had gone through in order to return. I also told him everything I had observed about the harbor and shipping in Candios while I was there.

"Ah, now that you are back, you will enter those facts in the notebooks in the treasury. They will be helpful. But I would have you wear your Venetian clothes a little longer." He chuckled. "They don't look at all comfortable."

"They're not very practical," I pulled at the ridiculous doublet, and the annoying lace collar. "Of course I will do as you wish. The squadron is back at sea?"

"*Yildirim, Halil, Bayezidne*, and *Akdogan* and a few other galleys are escorting a convoy to Rosetta. Routine, which is why I am better used here on land. I could use Captains Bayulken and Hasan's brains here too, of course, but their initiative is needed at sea. They are expected back at the end of September."

The page came in with a tray of food, and my mouth watered at the sight and smell of the warm brown bread. The page piled a plate of it for me with olives and cheeses, and handed me a goblet, cooled with snow from the mountains outside of Bursa, filled with that wonderful and—later—justly famous Ottoman drink we make from boiled morello cherries.

The admiral smiled at my unconcealed enjoyment. "Home again. You're now a man of some means, by the way. Your share from the captured galleots came to almost seven thousand *akce*. You may collect it, as well as your back pay, from the Treasury tomorrow. If I were you, I would seek out some of those Andalusian merchants you helped convey here, and invest some of it with them. Some of them have set up in business in Galata and are doing quite well."

Seven thousand akce was almost four years' regular pay. I was, if not entirely a wealthy man, at least very well provided for.

"And Bilgetai?"

"With the Black Sea squadron. You're itching to be at sea again?"

"Yes. I want to be useful."

"Oh, you will be. And I promise the time will not be empty while you wait for the squadron to return. Meanwhile, keep your Venetian escort away from the Terhane, and especially from the Tophane gun foundry. I want them to see only what we choose for them to see." He took an appreciative drink from his goblet. "I think it would be good for us if they spread the word in Europe of the marksmanship of our janissaries. There's a competition the day after tomorrow in the Hippodrome. Why don't you invite them? They'll have to dress as Turks, of course, but that will make them think they're learning secrets. And the more secret they think it is, the more people they will tell."

"And getting a little of my own back for making me dress like them?"

Bahadir gave me an innocent look. "Such petty vindictiveness would absolutely never cross my mind. More bread?"

"Oh, I almost forgot, can we have someone make me a small mirror? Something with just enough ornamentation on it to be mysterious, but not so much as to make it impractical for everyday use? Say, aboard a ship?" I told him the story I had told the Europeans. "I thought I might 'steal' one and send it back with them to make the story stick."

This time he really did laugh, long and full, almost doubling over. "They'll stare themselves blind looking into it for a ship. Kachak, your soul really is a pit of malice as yet unplumbed. Erhan always said you must have djinns whispering in your ears; he must be right."

'My' Venetians had also been fed while they waited outside in the courtyard, though not with the same enjoyably home-found associations as I had been. They were sweating in their western clothes, and cross as two sticks at me because of it. "Well, what was the response?" they wanted to know as soon as we had left the palace and were—they assumed—safe from listening ears. In this they were quite wrong. I knew that at any given time at least a dozen people on the street seeming to amble past us or around us at random belonged to the Office of the Vezier, and that they would watch us constantly for as long as we were in Turkey.

"It hasn't been three hours yet, let alone three days," I answered.

"Three days?"

"It's the Ottoman way. One day to think about it; one day to discuss the possible responses, and one day to think about the discussion and choose the best response. Albeit, I can at least tell you that the letters were received graciously."

So I spent the following days showing them what we wanted them to see; dropped obscure hints, even pretended to sneak them along the quayside of the Horn (dressed not very convincingly as Turks) where I made sure they had an opportunity to count the berths and the drying sails, and see the ships under repair. We laid on a little performance to increase their appreciation of our naval might, moving the same batches of sails into several successive warehouses so they could surreptitiously count them three times. From one of those warehouses, I 'stole' the ship-finding mirror and slipped it quickly down the front of one of their jackets. "Give this to Andreas," I whispered. "He'll know what it is. And whatever you do, don't get caught with it."

One of the Venetians stopped short with an excited cry of recognition. "That's the *Acireale*; I'd know the rake of that mast anywhere." He was pointing at the captured galleot that Atakan's gunners had so thoroughly pounded and which was entering the final stage of repairs. Shipwrights were swarming over her, repairing her bows and repainting her hull in proper Ottoman colors.

"She used to belong to Naples," he continued angrily.

"Aren't we at war with Naples now?" one of the others asked.

"Yes. No. We're at peace, I think. Never mind. She boarded one of my father's ships off Brindisi; took a whole cargo of cinnamon from us." He walked over to her berth and for a moment I thought he was actually going to kick the hull.

"Well she's been punished for her deeds, and she certainly wasn't flying the flag of Naples when we caught her," I said, giving them a carefully edited account of how she had been captured. I took special pains to point out that all that damage to her bows they were looking at had been done with one salvo at extreme range.

"Karpathas? What on earth she was doing there?"

As it happened, I was wondering that myself. Whose orders had she been under, and why had she had a Frankish crew aboard?

Severing my tenuous contact with the Venetians and from the west was not difficult. One of my escort picked a fight with some Genoese sailors—or perhaps the Genoese picked it with them. As the fracas erupted into a rather satisfying brawl, gathering intensity and participants as they punched and kicked their way along Jankaturan Street, I slipped quietly away and left them to it. Two figures detached themselves soundlessly from the shadows thrown by a store wall, and took their places on either side of me. "Good evening, efendim." It was the first time anyone had addressed me by that title.

"Oh, I'm not efendim yet," I said, "Sorry, did you want to join in?" The one on my left was looking wistfully down the street. He shrugged. "Not this evening, I think. In any case, our orders are to get you back to the palace quickly and safely."

Which they did. I entered modestly and Turkishly at the accustomed Gulhane gate. Bahadir sent his letters of reply down to the ship by some other hand than mine, and bid them be off back to Candios. Captain Andreas made some noise about refusing to sail without me on board, but the guns along the walls at Yenikapi convinced him that perhaps getting the letters quickly back to Crete was a more pertinent concern. I never learned exactly what Bahadir had replied to their suggestions. In the end it didn't matter anyway because we subsequently learned that, at the same time all this had been going on, the Venetians had also sent an envoy to the pope attempting to stir up a crusade (against us, naturally) in hopes that the pope—in return for the support—would command the Knights of Rhodes to give them their ships and cargoes back.

I spent the rest of the sailing season adding notes to the captains' notebooks about Candios, updating charts, and once I was invited to lecture to this year's crop of oglans in the Enderun on topics of navigation and life at sea. My rank entitled me to a room at the naval barracks at the Tersane, across the Horn from the main part of the city, which was where the galley crews lived while in port if they did not have homes of their own, or if their homes were inconveniently far. It was an old building, inherited from the Byzantines, full of arches and pillars and long dark corridors, intermittently lit by lamps in sconces, which was how Erhan was able to surprise me one evening, poking his head out of the shadows and announcing that he was back from Ragusa.

"Squirrel!" I exclaimed in delight; it had been one of his nicknames at the Enderun Kolej, and he still allowed those of us who had known him from those days to call him that. There was a new captain's alinlik in his sea cap, and a ship's dispatch bag hanging from his left, non-sword arm, shoulder. For a moment I was tempted to pretend that I did not notice them in the dim light, just to see how long I could string him along. I was too overjoyed to see him to hold back my congratulations for long though. "*Captain* Erhan! They've made you a captain! How long ago? Oh well done. You had some success off Ragusa, I see."

"We rooted out a nest of Catalan corsairs who had been bothering the convoys going in and out. The Venetians bottled up one strait; we the other. We took seven of their ships and shared them out between us. We needed some new crews and new captains to sail the captures home." He drew his shoulders up. "You have the honor to be addressing the new captain of the imperial…and only *slightly*-damaged…galleot *Bellagratia*. We're going to rename it, of course as soon as we repaint—"

"Well, I should hope so," I said laughing as I saluted formally. "What kind of name is *Bellagratia* for a pirate ship anyway? Let alone an Ottoman warship."

"Well, they were not very…fearsome…pirates."

"Mothermilks, you were going to say?"

"Yes. Plenty good against unarmed merchant ships; total pussies at the first flash of steel. Bullies, but nothing in a fight. The Ragusians are delighted to have their commerce restored to them; they kept feeding us and feeding us at one celebratory dinner after another."

"Well, then, my half-starved warrior, let's go get ourselves dinner. We both have tons of stories to exchange. Whoever tells the best one, gets his meal paid for by the other."

"Agreed! So, what's your latest tale?"

"Well, while you were off getting yourself promoted, I've been being a Venetian ambassador. Well, envoy anyway."

"Ending wars, or starting them?" he asked as we walked, laughing, down the stairs and out into the street that ran along the quay. "And where *did* you learn your verb tenses? Oh, and are Atakan and Inanc around?"

"Haven't seen them for several days. They've been down at the gun foundries, making loud bangs. Atakan says they have cast some new culverins that you can load with almost six pounds of powder without the barrels exploding."

"Good God, I hope he never tries that aboard *my* ship."

The proprietor of the 'Stork of Marmara's Kitchen' was delighted to see us. He seemed to know all the crews by sight, no matter what time of day or night one showed up at the Stork, or else he was extremely good at pretending to. Around the Istanbul waterfront, the word was that you weren't officially in the Ottoman navy until Tashlik said you were, and knew exactly how strong you liked your coffee. He could even tell apart the twin brothers who rowed aboard the *Katuhr*, something not all of their own officers could do.

"Welcome, Sirs, welcome. I have a table waiting. What can I get you on this chilly, misty evening?"

Erhan didn't hesitate, "A bowl of whatever I smelled as I came through the door," he grinned.

Tashlik beamed at the compliment to his cooking. "Mushrooms and peppers in cream, with pilaf. Tonight there is also cheese from Trabzond with the bread. You will be happy with your choice."

We were. The mushrooms were excellent, and so was the cheese. "I can see why the Trabzonders don't let many of these out of their city," Erhan said appreciatively.

"Naples and the Papal States have patched up their differences and made peace," Erhan told me after we had taken the edge off our hunger and caught each other up on our respective news.

"That's trouble for us. If it lasts."

"It could be," he agreed. "It ends one of the major quarrels on the Italian peninsula. Suddenly the papacy has a military ally it didn't have before."

"One with an army *and* a navy."

He nodded. "There's no reason—at least on paper—why the agreement won't last. On its own, it's not enough to form an alliance against us, but it could be the spear point of one."

"Even if it isn't, the end of hostilities could free the Neapolitan navy for more energetic activities against us. And the Knights of Rhodes, once they are deprived of Neapolitan cargo ships to prey on, might well turn their attentions even more towards ours."

Erhan bent forward and leaned his elbows on the table, considering it. "Did you know that one of Alexander's duties—before he got himself elected pope—was Cardinal-Protector of the Order of the Knights of Rhodes?"

"Nooo, I didn't. How on earth did you find that out? And what does that mean?"

"A Venetian captain explained it to me. He wanted to be sure we understood. It means that the Knights of Rhodes have nothing whatsoever to restrain them now."

"*Whatsoever thou bindest in my name shall be bound...*" I murmured. Those words had been read over my head in Candios, and they had chilled me. They were too broad, too encompassing. I liked them even less now. "It means *any* ship, flying *any* flag. Supreme forgiveness for any act they commit."

I think," Erhan said thoughtfully, "next sailing season will be a busy one."

They say a helmsman and his ship grow so close that they can sense each other. Whether true or not, I can attest that a helmsman gets to know every aspect of his charge. Each ship has its own way of moving, as distinctive as a signature, that sets her apart from even her own sister ships who were built in the same shipyard. A sailor can pick his own ship instantly out of a line of similarly-painted vessels just by the way she rides. Even on land, that feeling of rocking ever so slightly to that particular rhythm, is a reminder of that bond. One morning, I came awake unaccustomedly early, and strolled to the window of the long hall. It looked out over the Bosphoros and, beyond it, across the Marble Sea. There was a line of ships coming in. The Rosetta convoy. On the starboard wing was a familiar silhouette. No mistaking, even at this distance, that distinctive pitch of the bow into an oncoming wave. It was the *Akdogan*; My squadron and my friends were returning.

Chapter III

The Most Dangerous Books in the World

I was down at the quay to meet them, and it seemed that half of Istanbul joined me as I watched with a professional's eye the long and complicated business of bringing a fleet into harbor. With the convoy safely home, the galleys broke away from the main body and headed for their docks along the Azapkapi district shore, while the merchant ships sorted themselves out along the civilian docks in Fener on the other side of the Horn. People were counting the ships, how many had come back, how many had been lost (next to none). I heard people speculating on the fortunes which would be made today when the cargoes of spices, indigo, linen, wheat, soap, and other fine things were landed. The city would eat this winter. My Andalusian factors were there. I had taken Bahadir's advice and invested some of my prize money with them in shares in some of the cargoes.

"You will do well out of this; the convoy has come back safe. Your shipmates protected it well from the corsairs."

Yildirim, leading the other ships, fired her leeward guns in salute to the palace as she passed the point, then rapidly brailed up her foresail and lowered the yard to the deck.

Rounding up smartly into the wind under just her mainsail, she lowered her jali boat to take Lantern Captain Bayulken, who would be carrying the convoy's dispatch bag, to be rowed across the Horn to the palace. She then downed her oars to row the rest of the way into port. Two lengths from the quay, she dragged her portside oars in the water to help her turn, then backed water on both sides with short, rapid, precise strokes to bring her stern into her berth, showing the world how an Ottoman ship ought to be handled. Her oars paused as she coasted in, then dug into the water with the blades squared, bringing her to a stop exactly two arshins from the stone edge of the quay. Landing lines were thrown, uncoiling gracefully in the air as they flew. I caught one and made it fast around an iron bollard just as if I had been any other dockhand. *Akdogan* followed *Yildirim* into the quay a moment later, and I did the same for her, keeping my head down until I had made the last coil of the rope fast so as to deliberately heighten the effect of the surprise when I looked up into Ozkan's and Berk's faces staring down from the gunwales at me.

"So! Look what the ravens brought!" I heard Ozkan shout, his face opening wide with a huge grin. They had to wait for the oars to be cleated down and for Hasan to order the stern ladder lowered and to go ashore himself before they could come down the ladder to the quay, which they did two steps at a time, with Berk leaping the last three and risking ending up in the water the way Little Eagle had done once at Gelibolu, going in butt-first with a yell of surprise that the water closing over his head had smothered, and with *Hilal*'s order bag still strapped over his shoulder.

They were dancing around me, slapping my shoulders and demanding to know the whole story—at once, before the day was any older. I handed Captain Hasan the order bag (I had prevailed on Bahadir to allow me the privilege of being the one to give it to him), and he looked me up and down, smiling and shaking his head as I gave him the outlines of my story.

He suddenly looked worried when I came to the bit about the Venetian galleot. "You haven't been assigned to any other ship in the meantime, have you?"

"No, efendim," I answered quickly, "I am still the *Akdogan*'s helmsman, if you will have me."

"I'll have none other," he said.

We kept the ship in readiness for two weeks, in case the squadron was ordered to sail again for a late-season assignment, but as the season wore into mid-November and more and more of the distant squadrons returned from their stations, no such orders had come through. The fleet was gathering for the winter. Bilgetai was back, medals around his neck. The Black Sea squadron had been busy making those waters safe for merchant shipping, and now that the cargoes of tallow, furs, honey, and fish could be shipped unmolested and profitably, the Russians had sent a delegation to Istanbul to negotiate trade agreements with us and with the Khanate of Crimea. Bilgetai was summoned to the palace and given the task of lettering the signing copies of the treaty.

Hasan passed the word that we were to begin the long process of laying the ships up for the winter. We lined up on deck and lowered the flags from the end of the yards and folded them. Two by two, we carried the long oars ashore on our shoulders, and lined them up in racks in the enormous, multi-floored kurekhane along with those from all the other ships' to be repainted over the winter. A year ago we had chosen dark blue for *Akdogan*'s blades, with a thin white band on the tips. When moving through the water, the colors matched particularly well with the whitecaps thrown by the blades. *Yildirim*'s oars, because she was the lantern galley, were white with red tips. We swung the yards down, and unbent the sails to be hung up in the sheds.

"Good lord, what on earth have you done to this sail?"

"Sorry. We had to patch a hull with it."

"Dammit, when are you wave-donkeys going to learn to treat the Padishah's property with more respect?"

"No sooner than we learn to stop troubling his enemies."

As we did every autumn, we tried to find some combination of folding or rolling our sails which would keep them from dry-rotting in storage. Despite decades of experimentation, the method has yet to be found which can preserve them for certain. The only sure way to protect them from dry rot is to hang them, and then they chafe each other if the building is the slightest bit plagued by drafts. Moreover, there isn't a shed whose roofline is high enough hang the mainsails of the bigger ships properly; the foot of the sail always trails along the floor.

We levered the masts out of their steps for sanding and varnishing later, and hauled the rudder off its pintles to be taken ashore (my job). We then spent a day and a half prying every last one of *Akdogan*'s thole pins out of her gunwales for revarnishing—an incredibly time-consuming process because you have to keep turning them and letting the varnish dry before adding the next bit—but necessary to prevent them from swelling and splitting, or worse, rotting in their holes over the winter.

Oarless and mastless, we towed *Akdogan* to the Tophane wharf where its enormous oxen-powered crane could swing her cannons ashore to be stored with the other guns lined up in the armory under oiled burlap.

I was down in the hold one afternoon with Atakan, Inanc, and the other gunners, unloading the last of the provisions, when Inanc suddenly glanced over at me with a look of dismay. At his feet, nestling against one of the ribs of the hull, was—unmistakably—a cannon ball. He leaned down quickly to pick it up and hide it behind a sack of rice, doing his best to look innocent, but Atakan saw the motion before Inanc could completely secrete it. For a moment, we all shot embarrassed glances at each other, because of course we all knew exactly how it had gotten there. Fate catches up with all of us. Atakan suddenly burst out laughing. "So that's what was thumping around all that time. I knew there had to be one missing."

It was funny now, only because it had not actually punched a hole in the hull while rolling around, and I suppose—on looking back—that probably it had been funny at the time too, although each of us who had been aware of the "incident" when it had happened had desperately hoped that Atakan hadn't noticed. Small chance. Not a grain of powder goes into his guns that he doesn't know about.

What had happened was this. During one of the gun drills the summer before—carried out, I should note in the gun crew's defense—at speed and in challengingly rough seas, the crew loading the port culverin had lost their footing in their haste, and the cannon ball had escaped along the deck and had thumped its way ignominiously down a hatchway ladder and vanished into the hold. With no time to retrieve it, nor even a replacement ball, Inanc had simply grabbed an extra handful of wadding to stuff into the barrel so that the ramrod would show the proper length out of the muzzle. Atakan either hadn't noticed, or had pretended not to. I had watched the whole scene develop from my station at the tiller. When the culverin was fired, the extra wadding did what too much wadding always does—which is to catch fire—and it exited the muzzle in a blazing spike of flame, hanging in the air for a moment at the top of its arc before plunging hissing into the sea. Nothing had been said at the time about the absence of a fifth splash, the face-saving assumption being that perhaps it had been invisible amongst the whitecaps. I knew that the gunners had searched the hold desperately afterwards, but apparently without success. And now the shiny, accusing sphere had reappeared among us to make sure "the incident" was not forgotten.

With everything out of her that could be moved, we towed *Akdogan* with small boats farther up the Horn to the sandflats of Kagithane Island where several other ships were also being scraped as part of the usual preparations for being laid up for the winter. That done, we anchored her in the shallow water. Then we climbed in stages outboard on her columbarium, which is the part of the hull along the sides which flares outwards over the water to give leverage to the oars. I have no idea why we still use the Roman navy's term for it—a holdover from Byzantium, I suppose, when that part of the ship actually used to look like a dovecote. The growing weight heeled the hull more and more. "Bir, iki, UECH!" we shouted together as, with each roll, the gunwales dipped farther under, letting the water pour over them to fill the hull with a growing roar. One thing about galleys, when they go under, they go quickly. It's not like a sailing ship which usually subsides gradually, with a somewhat stately grace. Once a galley passes that point of no return, the motion is quick and violent. *Akdogan* sank suddenly into the shallows, flinging us with shouts and splashes into the water with the violence of her last roll, leaving only her raised stern deck poking above the surface. Ozkan broke the surface with the bight of a halyard in his mouth, grinning and shaking the water out of his hair in a spray of droplets. We swam around the ship, making her lines fast to rafts of barrels on the surface. The water by that time of year was quite cold, but each us would be damned if we would let it show on us in front of any of the others. I took a deep breath and swam down to her, relishing the unusual perspective of hovering above her deck. There is something intriguing, and a little unsettling about swimming around a ship in the water, of things not being in their usual orientation.

We let her lie there for five days to let the currents clean the inside of her hull thoroughly, then, with pulleys and rafts of barrels, raised her slowly to the surface (huge cheer as her deck and beak broke the surface), and nudged her over to the sloping shingle beach of Kagithane, pumping and bailing her foot by foot until she could be drawn up far enough on the flats to careen her.

It is hard to describe why this annual ritual of sinking our ships, then seeing them rise to the surface again is so important to us sailors, but it is. Landsmen do not understand it; to them it appears merely as over-energetic and irreverent skylarking. It is much more than that, a promise, perhaps, that our ship will take care of us on the rough seas. It will plow through the waves and return to the crests, a symbolic unsinkability.

Now the real work began. Careened first on one side, then the other, we scraped her hull of the weeds that inevitably grew on any hull after an extended period in the water. That done, we recaulked every strake in her hull, then painted it, getting blue paint all over our arms, our faces, and in our hair. Anywhere in Istanbul, you could always spot crews from ships newly-returned from a long cruise by the paint streaking their arms and faces; it usually took a week or more until soap and time wore it off. In the meantime, we wore it as a badge of honor, recognizing and being recognized by our comrades in the streets and in the bazaars by virtue of our similar markings. Our daubs brought us smiles and well-wishes from the civilians on shore wherever we went.

Her hull now tight, we towed *Akdogan* back down the Horn from Kagithane and hauled her up onto the shore along the Tersane. There were not enough sheds for all the ships, so some would spend the winter outside under tarpaulins, but our squadron was senior enough to rate being kept under sturdier shelter. As helmsman, it was my job to give the commands to coordinate the delicate job of hauling the ship foot by foot up the ways while part of the crew pounded in the *takozes*—the wooden wedges used to prop a ship upright when out of water—as she went. Every few feet, another set of takozes was pounded in to keep her steady while the last set at the stern was removed and brought around to the bow to be used again, and so on. The rhythm and coordination had to be exactly right: too slow and the ship might fall over to one side, or slide off the ways, too fast and the takozes could jam, then we would have to stop, push the ship back down the ways a few feet, and restart the process. A helmsman who could keep the process going smoothly and safely earned huge thanks from the crew for making the job relatively painless, a helmsman who could not brought loud curses down on his head from the crew straining at the blistering ropes and banging away at the stubborn takozes.

Akdogan slid up the ways as docile as a Erzurum lamb, and as her bow nestled into its slot, the last of the takozes were malleted in, and the hull tied down, everyone gave a loud cheer for the Sultan, and we went off to the taverns of Pera for a monstrously good meal to celebrate.

Ozkan had used some of his prize money to buy himself some magnificent Arabian horses to breed, and he, Erhan, Berk, and I spent spent the days between our on-shore duties exercising them on exhilarating rides across the hills above of Tuzla. That was how he got that scar on his forehead; he came off his horse rather fast and headfirst one afternoon. Any enemy crew seeing him come climbing over their gunwale with a knife in his hand would draw another—more bellicose—conclusion about the origin of the scar, which suited him just fine.

Atakan disappeared for days on end into the depths of the cannon foundries of the Tophane, surfacing occasionally with a delighted grin, but saying little about the work that was going on there. Over at the Tersane, new ships were being built, shallow-hulled and fast like *Akdogan* , for close inshore work.

The weather was closing in. Each morning, the Marmara seemed greyer and its waves higher and angrier, crested with more whitecaps than the day before. It was the season when the flags on the walls of the palace stood out from their flagstaffs every day now in the wind. As sailors, we notice the way flags blow without even trying to. In the Tersane, we began to talk worriedly of Admiral Kemaleddin's Ligurian squadron, which had still not returned. It was the only one still out.

We had gone to the ropewalks one particularly gusty day to spin the hundred-arshin lengths of rope *Akdogan* would need the following spring. The ropewalks were among the driest and warmest places to be in the city, and the work was pleasant, albeit slow and methodical. We alternated walking the strands down the long floor, left over right, as Ozkan cranked the spinner at the most even speed he could manage, and Erhan walked the grooved wooden wedge—the nut—backwards to keep the rope tight as it was twisted together. We had made up five of the hundred-arshin lengths, complete with crown-and-back splices at each end to keep them from unravelling, when the door burst open late in the afternoon and Yigit darted in.

"The Ligurian squadron's coming!" he yelled.

We all instinctively looked in the direction of the door. "Don't you dare," Ozkan hissed, knowing that if we stepped away before the last stretch we were working on was finished, the whole length would unwind and we would never get it tight again. "Finish this one first. There will be time."

Berk gave him a sort of crushed look, as if the thought of bolting out had never crossed our minds, and we stayed at our work long enough to wind it up. As soon as the ends were spliced, we dashed outside to the pier. Far out to sea, on the wings of the late afternoon gale, a file of galleys was coming in under double-reefed foresails, bones of white water under their cutwaters and spray driving across their bows. Even from this distance, we could see they were having a wild ride of it.

"They sure left it late," someone said.

They entered the mouth of the Bosphoros, hell for leather, and shot for the Horn. The hills blocked some of the wind as they came closer, and they even shook out their reefs for the last stretch. No salute today, in this weather that would have been folly, and in any case, the wooden muzzle tompions were firmly in place to keep the spray out of the barrels of the guns.

"*Civa* is missing her foremast," Erhan noticed as she rounded up and dropped her oars preparatory to docking. "Must have rolled it right out of the step."

"Hm, *and* her anchors," I noticed. "And she's not the only one, either." The observation brought me up short. They must have cut the anchors away to lighten the ships in heavy weather, a desperate step that no ship captain would order lightly. An anchor might be a ship's only salvation in a heavy wind against a lee shore.

"Those boys sure didn't take the easy route home."

Grand Admiral Kemaleddin himself, larger than life and wearing an enormous turban, stood laughing and shouting on his quarterdeck, bellowing greetings to the shore as the squadron came in.

They had braved autumnal gales that no western galley, and few Ottoman ones for that matter, would have dared sail in, and they brought astounding news. Yigit, who was friendly with some of the janissaries on the *Anadolu*, managed to get it first, darting back to us along the quay to share it.

"The pope made his illegitimate teenage son a cardinal," Yigit shouted out when he got closer. "Cesare Borgia, yes, *that* Cesare, has been a cardinal since last September. All of Europe is scandalized."

"Ha! Hooray!" I shouted, "We'll have peace for another year at least!"

"No Crusade!" Erhan yelled across the water in the general direction of Europe, "No Crusade!" then slapped me on the back, laughing, "Guess you're going to have to rewrite your exposition on firenk alliances again."

"At least this time it's simpler," I said, "no one in Europe is going to form an alliance under the papal banner after this."

I thumped Yigit's shoulder. "Show me your hand. You're sure about this? His own illegitimate son?"

"Oh yes, and there's more," Yigit said. "That's what made it worth Admiral Kemaleddin's staying out in the November gales. The Borgia pope elevated no fewer than eleven other cardinals at the same consistory-"

"What's a consistory?"

"That's what Demircan called it. I don't know. Doesn't matter. The point is, he had promised the existing cardinals he wouldn't make any more. One of the new ones is only fourteen years old! Demircan says the Vatican is seething with revolt. The Prefect of Rome—who is also, by the way, the Captain of the Church's army, was so furious he snuck out of Rome and went to Sinigaglia to sulk on his estates."

"So the papal army is headless for the moment," Ozkan chuckled. "And the Prefect himself has a brother who is a cardinal."

"Yes he does. Cardinal della Rovere. One of the angriest ones. Has his own fortress at Ostia," Yigit added, "on the mouth of the Tiber itself. It's the gateway to Rome! And della Rovere is said to have his eyes on the papacy himself, some say he is eager to step into Alexander's purple buskins without waiting for him to die."

"Angry enough…angry enough at the pope that he would make common cause with us to spite him? Let our ships use the harbor at Ostia, do you think?"

"Kachak! You are—" Ozkan began, then broke off as he saw the others staring at me with the same wicked smiles growing on their faces which must have also been visible on mine. It was not an entirely impossible thought. The same year I had come to Constantinople, some Neapolitan nobles—then in revolt—had taken the previously unthinkable step of offering our expeditionary forces the use of Osimo—just a few miles south of Ancona—in return for help against the papal forces.

"I want *Akdogan* to be the first Turkish ship to sail up the Tiber River," I said solemnly, knowing how utterly ridiculous I must have sounded, "and I want to be at her helm when she does."

No one said anything for a moment, then Ozkan nodded seriously and the others with him. "It may never happen, but we swear that if it does, it shall be us."

"Oh, and the French are furious too," Yigit said, bringing us back to a more realistic topic."

"Well good."

"And the Venetians are saying, 'we told you so,' to anyone who will listen, and going ahead with their war against Milan."

"Even better."

"And the pope has married his daughter to Giovanni Sforza, it was done in the Vatican itself. At the marriage feast, the cardinals amused themselves by throwing candies into the bodices of the women guests. The leftover cakes were scattered out of the windows to the crowds waiting below."

"S-c-a-n-d-a-l-o-u-s!" Berk drew out slowly.

"An alliance between Milan and the papacy then?" That could make some trouble for us, because of Milan's coziness with the French.

Yigit shrugged. "Small worry there. The papal states are still at war with the other branch of the Sforza family, in Milan."

"Which pretty much leaves Rhodes," I said.

"With the sea lanes closed for the season, we won't know their reaction until next spring, no matter what it is."

"They're not likely to do much on their own with only five galleys."

"Five galleys and a carrack," I reminded them. The *Grand Nef du Tresor* was one of the largest warships in the world. None of us had ever seen her, but we had heard descriptions of her from merchant sailors who had seen her moored at Genoa and Marseille.

So we celebrated the news, and Istanbul breathed more easily for a season.

In that, we may have been premature. The consistory, scandalous as it may have been to Europe, at least had the effect of balancing Pope Alexander's allies. There were new cardinals made from Hungary, Germany, France, Milan, Naples, and Spain. At the palace, there were some who worried that this might signal the hidden preparations for a very dangerous alliance indeed.

One grey drizzly winter evening, I found myself being rowed across the Horn in a navy caique and walking up the steep streets of Pera. The Andalusian book printer, Olaya, who had been so forlorn at Akdogan's rail during the journey from his homeland two summers ago, had opened a printing shop, and was thriving at it. Printing was still relatively new in the Ottoman empire, and as people discovered the usefulness of the new art, there was a quickly-rising demand, not only for books, but also for the printing of legal papers, government decrees, commercial documents. The agents of the Medici bank were spending money like water for copies of Latin and Greek texts by the ancient philosophers, and they were not the only Europeans busy in the search.

Bahadir wanted to try an experiment, and had sent for me to carry it out.

"If you are looking for philosophy, you'll find plenty of it in Istanbul," I heard Olaya's voice coming out of the shop door as I drew near. He was drinking tea with a customer—or a potential customer—sitting opposite each other on low divans in the shop's front room. "Ah, Kachak, come in. What a delightful surprise!" He turned to his guest, "this is the helmsman of the ship which brought me here."

He introduced his guest to me as Niccolo del Guercino, a sub-director of the branch of the Medici bank branch in Pera. "In addition to his commercial work, Signor del Guercino is also engaged in buying books to send back to Giucciardini de Medici's libraries in Florence."

"Giucciardini values books as highly as profits, probably more."

"Constantinople is certainly the place to find both."

The shopboy brought me a glass of apple tea on a silver tray.

"But not just any books. Works that have not already made their way to Europe. He is looking for even more untranslated works by the ancient philosophers. Surely there

must still be undiscovered works of Aristotle, or even Laes-
tice, lying neglected on some library shelf?"

"Possibly," Olaya said, "but—as you know—you Florentines already have the pick of the crop. Your Giovanni Aurispa
and Filelfo spent a lot of time searching libraries and collections here. They made a pretty thorough haul. Anything they
didn't find, well, it's either no longer here, or it must be in a
very neglected place indeed."

"He will be very disappointed if I do not send back something soon. Branch employees get special bonuses for finding
something rare."

"But perhaps there are other writers whose work would
interest him. Other than the Greek and Roman authors."

del Guercino sat up, interested. "You know of some?"

Olaya nodded slowly. "Yes, I do. I've even printed a few.
But, I should warn you that the manuscripts I am thinking of
are some of the most dangerous books in the world."

"Ha. The more dangerous the better. Cosimo and Brac-
cioloni were searching out and copying Roman manuscripts
in the monasteries of Switzerland at a time when to possess
even one of them might have gotten them burned at the stake.
However, the monk they paid to catalog their dangerous library went on to get himself elected pope. So everything
turned out fine."

"That was three popes ago. Your present pope might not
be so...open-minded."

Something in Olaya's tone stopped him, and it stopped
me too. This was a man who had been forced to run from his

own country. He had known danger and suspicion in plenty. If he thought something was dangerous, then it was.

"I see. What—in particular—makes these manuscripts so dangerous?"

"These authors I am thinking of, well, some of them think very differently from those authors the West is used to. Their works would be a different flavor, some of them very different. Not so different from the Greek writers perhaps, but very different from the European authors who came after them. Many who have read them find their ways of thinking very...freeing. Would your Giucciardini be such a reader?"

"He would. His father owned a translation of Averroes, for goodness sake."

Olaya sat up. "Did he indeed? That is no small thing." He turned to me and said quietly, "Long after Averroes died, his translator, a Spanish Jew, ended up in the Inquisition's cells. Although that was probably for reasons other than the translation."

"So, tell me," del Guercino continued, "in what ways are these books different?"

Olaya looked around the shop, shot a glance at me as if to ask, "should I tell him?" then plunged right in. "Westerners tend to see truth as a monolith. They look for a single deduction by which to explain every large concept. Aristotle and Augustinian tried to create vast systems—systems which they thought could answer every question in the world—using just a few first principles."

"Universals from specifics," del Guercino nodded, "and Aristotle's specifics were not always...correct."

"Exactly. And since that time—in the west—everything has had to be either one thing or another. Fitted into categories. Usually only one correct answer. Here, we admit of the possibility that there might be more.

"And thank goodness for it," del Guercino said, "There's more scope for initiative here. Tell me something, you two have been here longer than I have. Do you feel it too?"

"Feel what?" I asked.

"Well, it's hard to put into words. I feel as if I have more ideas here. There's a circle of ways to get something done, all of them pointing to the result in different ways, like spokes to a hub. It's no longer quite so important which path I choose. Shades of possibilities, where before I thought only only in 'yes' or 'no'."

"'Forget the colors of the threads, but remember the pattern'" I murmured, in translation.

Olaya gave me a look which managed to be puzzled yet also somehow indicated that he understood.

"Something the grand vezier once told me," I explained. "I'm only now beginning to see what he meant by it."

"Ah, you move in high places," del Guercino said, "A very capable man, your grand vezier. If Florence had a few more like him, our northern border would be somewhere up around Denmark by now." He chuckled a little, then went on. "What I used to think was the endpoint often wasn't. Shipping cargoes to Ancona, for example. Six months ago, I would have planned only as far as that. I used to see that as the end. Lately, I realise that, whether I ship the cargo to Ragusa or Ancona or to some other place, it is just one of the paths."

"The real endpoint is making the sale."

"No," he said, "that too is only part of the path. The end-point is having the means to lead an interesting life."

"The Genoese have been trading like that for years," I said. "They often don't even tell their captains where to sail. 'Here's the cargo; go make a profit. Come back in six months. Don't rip the sails.'"

"They learn that from the Ottomans?"

"Don't know. Maybe. From trading in the Levant, most likely. The Ottomans probably learned it there too."

"I was taught," del Guercino said, "and oh how my tutors beat it into me, that something can be false, even if true most of the time. If even the smallest link can be proven false, the whole system is false. This doubt is held up—proudly—as proof of the rigor of the logic."

I thought of the Hungarian cavalry in the woods. "But a thought which might be true most of the time might then be discarded as false, even if it was false just once?"

"And so it often is," del Guercino said. "Not very clean, even within its own intellectual terms, is it?"

"No, it's not at all. I have read a book about this idea. *Dialectics*. It was in Italian," I added. "Proving a thing to be true by failing to find a situation where it is false. A man wouldn't last two days in the forests thinking like that."

"Nor in the Enderun Kolej, I daresay," Sergio added. "Logic that excludes can't possibly be logic. If something is true more often than it is false, regarding it as false can be just as misleading as taking it as completely true. What I really want to know is: 'how true is my thought for this *particular* case? How true is it *now*?'"

"*'If you only knew*
how many false fantasies of the imagination
are nearer to the truth
than the careful conclusions of the cautious'," I quoted.

"That's good," del Guercino said, "Giucciardino will like that. He is a risk-taker. Is that from one of the authors you are thinking of?"

Olaya nodded. "It is."

"Do you know where I can get a copy of the manuscript it's from?"

"I have one," Olaya said quietly. "It's in Persian. But Kachak can translate it for you, and I can print it. He studied it while an oglan at the kolej."

"Good. Then consider it decided. I must certainly buy a copy. But the Medicis are also planners. They use logic like no one else in the world." He half raised his tea glass to me, "You Ottomans are planners too. I've seen the way you leave nothing to chance when preparing a campaign."

"But, as you said, not one plan, not one answer."

del Guercino nodded. "Because circumstances change."

"Planning too far ahead can be wasted; we know that we will often have to make a new plan anyway. So we make many plans, knowing all the time that many of them will not come to pass. But the one which finally does is worth all the others."

del Gurecino opened his hands. "I like that. Complicated, perhaps, and surely it takes time, but flexible. Which is why I know I want that book."

"You shall have it. Kachak, how long do you think it would take you to prepare a translation?"

"A month, perhaps a month and a week. It is not a long book."

"Two weeks after he has finished the translation, I will have a fine copy printed for your Giucciardino. Twenty florins for the copy, and twenty florins for the translation."

del Guercino did not even haggle. We drank more tea together, and del Guercino left to return to his lodgings above his office in the merchants' quarter.

"And now, to your business," Olaya said to me. "Thank you for waiting so patiently to get to it. I am sorry if our talk delayed you."

"Not at all. And I am grateful for the translation work. But we should talk of what I am here for in the back room."

Olaya stood and locked the front door of the shop. "It's evening anyway; I doubt I am losing any customers." He sent the shopboy home, then motioned me to the back room where the press was, and where no windows faced onto the street, but only into a little walled garden with its well.

I slid the Expeditionary Hall notebook I had brought with me out of its taffeta bag. "Bahadir wants to know whether you could print copies of these using a press. He thinks it would save time."

Olaya's eyebrows went up when he saw the S.O., the mark of the Expeditionary Hall on the inside front page. He examined the pages, turning them over slowly, studying the handwritten Arabic characters which the Ottomans used for writing Turkish. "These are very clear, easy for a typesetter to select the slugs. It could be done, certainly," he said quietly. "But these notebooks contain naval secrets. How secure would they be here? My house is not a fortress. You know as well as I do that every firenk nation has spies in this city. What if one broke in to get these?"

"Your shop would be watched by Janissaries. In uniform and out. You live on the floor above, and you have a big dog."

"Still, why not set up a printing press at the palace? That way the notebooks would never leave the Hall of the Expeditionary Forces. Or at the Tersane?"

"There are conservative elements at the palace who would frown on it. They see the printing press as a western innovation. They are suspicious of it. There would discussions, debates. It would be quieter to print them here."

"How long?"

Olaya flipped through the book, getting a rough estimate of the pages. "Do you want them bound like this one?"

"No, that's too fancy for sea. Just stitched. With plain leather covers, tanned to keep the spray off them."

"Two weeks. I'll have a number of different assistants work on a few pages each. That way the work will go quicker—and they won't know very much of what they are working on."

The two weeks had nearly passed when Olaya's shop boy came to my lodgings and asked me to come to the shop.

Olaya was white-faced. "The notebooks for the Island of Kos…" he began.

"Is something wrong with them?"

He motioned to the pile in the cabinet. All twenty seemed to be there. He pulled out one that I took to be a copy, but then saw that it was only a piece of wood wrapped in a leather binding to look like one. "One of them is missing," he answered miserably.

"How long ago?"

"I only discovered it this morning. Sometime in the last two days. We hadn't printed all the copies until then."

"How?" I asked.

He pointed to the window that opened into the enclosed garden. I examined the carved wooden shutter. It had been forced with hardly a mark, and presumably very quietly. The garden walls facing the street were fairly high, but not unclimbable, and the dividing wall separating Olaya's garden from the one next to it was lower. "Somewhere, there is a janissary captain who will soon be wishing he'd never been born," I hissed. Where had the ones who were supposed to be guarding the street been?

"If it was during the day, then how could the thief have gotten into your press room without you or your workers noticing? If it was at night, why didn't your dog bark?" I wondered aloud.

"Perhaps it was someone known to me, or perhaps while I was out with the dog. I take him with me often, for safety."

"Who knew you were printing the notebooks for us?"

"No one. I didn't tell a soul."

I believed him, but it didn't mean very much. Even setting only a few of the pages at a time, any of his staff were bound to have figured out what they were working on. A reassuring mention to their families over a meal that work was steady and their income reliable, a boast in a tavern; there were many ways that the information might have spread.

"I need to think," I said. I pulled one of the copies off the pile and began to thumb through it, trying to evaluate how much an enemy might be able to learn from it. A navigation notebook on Kos and its harbors obviously would indicate our navy's interest in that island, but that was hardly news to anyone in the Mediterranean with a brain. As for the details it contained, they would either be more or less accurate than those contained in similar notebooks, which half the navies in the White Sea already probably kept. I had scanned the first eleven pages, and was just beginning to feel that nothing serious had been compromised when I came across a passage that made my skin go cold.

"*...there are strong inshore currents, which—combined with summer winds which blow up suddenly during the evenings—means that great care must be taken on anchoring to keep well away from the opening of the harbor.* Ikbal, Okbashi, *and* Peyam, *having set only two anchors, were nearly blown ashore...*"

"Oh damn," I said, putting down the book for a moment. "Someone has been careless."

"What is it?"

"They know what time of year our ships were there, and even the names of some of the squadron," I said gloomily.

"Oh." A long silence. "I didn't realize those details were in the notebooks."

"Normally they're not," I said. "The amanuensis also writes up a log and account of the voyage, which is kept separate from the navigation notes. Captains who will later be sailing in the same waters are sometimes given both, sometimes not. Sometimes they are allowed to read the log to prepare them for what they might encounter, but usually they are not given a copy. The amanuensis probably intended to delete those details from the notebooks before handing them in, but..," I spread my hands, knowing how it was. "After months at sea, there is a myriad of things to be done upon returning to port, and the haste of gathering everything up, it all probably got mixed up in the ship's dispatch bag. The oglans in the Expeditionary Hall are taught to copy obediently everything they're given."

I forced myself to read the rest of it through. I found mentions of two of the other ships, and a number of details which an alert and intelligent enemy reader, if he knew his business, would be able to glean plenty of useful hints from.

With a heavy heart, I motioned to the janissaries to box up the remainder and load it on a donkey to take down to the wharf where a caique waited to row us across to the palace point. I was sharper with them than I meant to be. I was not looking forward to reporting this to the Admiral.

Bahadir was in the chart copying room. He got up from his chair without a word when he saw the worried expression on my face. He motioned me to follow him, and we walked out into the palace gardens where there was less chance of being overheard. He did not say a word when I told him of the theft, only an unemotional "Very well."

I stopped on the path, not sure how to take his reaction. "It contains the names of the ships of our squadron who patrolled there."

"What color is the *Okbashi*'s hull?" he asked.

I searched my memory. "I don't know; I can't picture her."

"And the *Ikbal* and *Peyam*? How many masts each?"

"I don't know."

"In all the time you've spent along the harbor, have you ever seen any of those ships?"

I shook my head. "They must dock down at Gelibolu."

"They don't."

"Then where?"

"Nowhere. It is a squadron," he said with the faintest of smiles, "which does not exist."

"I don't understand."

"Or rather, it exists now in the minds of our adversaries. Think how many ships they will have to pin down on Kos patrolling for a squadron which will never come. Nor were the janissaries unvigilant. They saw the intruder go in through the house next door—it happened last night, by the way—and come out again the same way. They followed him to the house of a merchant named Etienne de Marsan, who is now also being watched."

"French? Rhodian?"

"Perhaps. He could be working for any country. It might not even be him, but someone in his household. We never had reason to find out too much about him until now. He arrived in Istanbul three years ago. Has given no trouble. He is what he says he is,—wool and iron to Istanbul, cloth, spices and hazelnuts back to France via Ragusa and Ancona. At least on the surface. So, with your help, and that of your Andalusian bookseller, we may have uncovered a previously unknown enemy agent."

"Three years ago. About the time Aubusson signed those letters of marque we captured?"

"You always were sharp. That connection is...intriguing, isn't it?"

"You intended for the notebooks to fall into enemy hands!"

"Yes, the original was carefully composed for the purpose, together with the fabrications of the ships' names and various other details. They're mostly accurate; we want our adversaries to be impressed by what our captains know. It was intended to lead and mislead. Best of all, it was stolen in a manner that suggests our opponents did not want us to notice the theft, or at least not for a while."

"They're hoping we send more, so they can repeat it?"

"We hope so. We think it might be time for our adversaries to discover our navy's sudden interest in the port of Taranto."

It was not my place to ask, but something in Bahadir's expression indicated that he wanted me to.

"Why Taranto?"

"To distract them from our navy's much more intense interest in Rhodes."

"What shall I do with the others?"

"Keep them separate. We might be able to sell one or two. If the Rhodians have one, the Spanish or the Neapolitans are bound to want one too."

Chapter IV
A thousand hidden ways

The second notebook, one of the Taranto set, was stolen just over a week later. Yigit, Mete, Erhan, and I—dressed as Tersane workmen—were on the roof of Olaya's house when it happened, having arranged for him and his dog to be out on that particular evening. People forget sometimes just how good Mete is with a rigging knife. I don't, and if ever I should do so, Yigit and Demircan and the other janissaries are certain to remind me. It also helps that he is two people. Or at least, most people think he is. From the time that they were young, he and his older brother Evren played the game of 'seldom seen in the same room at the same time' with the grownups. I think many brothers who look alike do this, perhaps without intending to. It happens once by accident; an innately-timed entrance and exit misleads someone into supposing they are two people, thence the possibilities dawn on them: their doubleness opens a secret door, a door that they alone possess the keys to. Those of us confined to one skin seldom realize it is there at all. Being in two places at one time can be played so many ways. Mete is also silent on his feet, which is why the thief never heard us behind him a few doors before he got to Marsan's house.

Bahadir had ordered us to find out where the stolen notebooks were being sent. Rhodes? France? Naples? Spain?

"I want the entire route, before the seas open next spring and our convoys sail. We simply cannot afford to have firenk spies slipping out of Istanbul with details of our sailing schedules and cargoes."

Therein lay our problem. There were a thousand hidden ways the notebooks could leave de Marsan's residence. A thousand ways they could find their way aboard either a ship bound for Europe, or be sent across the Bosphoros to Usküdar on the Asian side to be put into the saddlebags of a donkey caravan taking the road which led south and east to Bozburum. From Bozburum, no more than an eleven-mile strait of water separated Rhodes from the coast of Anatolia. Even in winter, those were sheltered waters, no obstacle for a well-handled ship.

Winter narrowed the choices for us, which was why Bahadir had chosen to carry out the experiment when he did. That, and the fact that, with the crews in port, he had plenty of trained manpower available to carry it out. "And to keep us busy, and out of the fleshpots of the Fener wharfside, no doubt," I commented to Erhan.

"There are fleshpots in Fener?" he rejoined, assuming a look of wounded innocence. "Why doesn't anybody ever *tell* me these things?"

With the sailing lanes closed, we were counting on the courier travelling by road—whether west or east. If the courier left the city by the Yediküle gate, and took the road west to Greece and Italy, we could presume that the notebook would reach the Papal forces (who might subsequently share it with anyone), or else directly to Naples or France. If the courier took the road south to Cannakale and down the coast, then we could cautiously presume that the destination was probably Rhodes.

Unless of course the courier did what we would have done, and doubled back on his tracks to throw off pursuit. If he did, then Ozkan and the others would try to follow.

"It would be helpful to obtain a sample of the spy's hand-writing," Bahadir had said. "There are plenty of calligraphers at the palace who could copy it easily. Then we might be able to send our own misleading sailing schedules."

We took turns waiting and watching with the janissar-ies at both ends of the narrow street, waiting for a courier to leave the house with either the notebook or a copy. We did not even know whether the thief and the courier would be the same person. In fact, we doubted it. The thief, whom we referred to as the Viper, came and went from the house frequently on his normal business, to the customs house, to the taverns of Pera that the merchants used as informal trad-ing houses, but never with anything that resembled the sailing notebook or a copy of one. He was followed all over the city, to the point where we were becoming increasingly worried that our presence—no matter how many times we switched the watchers—would eventually be noticed. It was terribly frustrating. We had originally hoped that the courier would leave Marsan's house with a presumably routine shipment of goods bound for Europe. There would be no way of knowing which of the donkeys carried the notebook, of course, but that wouldn't have mattered at the outset. Ozkan, Berk, and Erhan were keeping watch at the Yedikule gate to follow any of Marsan's caravans that departed by that route. Mounted on Ozkan's superb horses, they would have no trouble following the courier if, for example, the courier broke off from the convoy.

But it had been more than two weeks, and no caravan had left. As urgent as the sailing notebook was, we knew that the courier would not have delayed sending it on its journey. The uncomfortable conclusion was that the notebook was somehow already out of Istanbul and on its way, and that we had missed it. Meanwhile, a third one had been stolen from Olaya's shop. Thira Island this time. In my opinion, the firenks are welcome to that dangerous place and all that comes with it. Prey to sudden, savage storms, and with its harbor exposed to the west winds *and* dangerous rocks lurking just underwater at the mouth of it, no sailor I'd ever met had a single good word to say about the place. It was secret hope that someday all our enemies' fleets would take it into their heads to go there and sink themselves.

"Your coins, my friend," Mete said almost conversationally, his hand clamping over the Viper's mouth from behind and with the point of his rigging knife just touching the nape of the Viper's neck. I ducked around to his left (I had already checked the Viper's knife hand to make sure he was right-handed), getting a good look at his face, as well as his boots. I like boots. They leave prints, prints which I—or for that matter any army scout with experience in the woods—can track. A man tends to wear the same boots every day, no matter how much he might change his outer clothes or his hat. Spot the boots, and you spot the man.

Yigit reached inside the man's jacket for both the decoy purse, where everyone those days kept a few coins in case of robbery, and then deeper for the main one hanging inside his shirt from a lanyard around his neck where he kept the bulk of his money. Yigit found the Taranto notebook as well and took it out, deliberately turning it upside down as if he couldn't read and staring at it puzzled for a moment before tossing it contemptuously on the ground. As we darted off with our loot, we were happy to see the man reach quickly for it and bundle it inside his shirt as he ran for the safety of de Marsan's door.

"So, you got a good look at him?" Bahadir asked.

"Yes, admiral, a very good look," Mete confirmed.

"And he at you?"

"Not really. We kept mostly behind him. Our necks and lower faces were scarved. As any street ruffians' would be."

"Good. That will make them nervous enough to want to get him—and the notebooks—out of Istanbul quickly. Worry them that it has been seen, even by street ruffians who normally don't count in the scheme of things. They can't risk that you might later mention seeing it to someone. Even if you seemed to have no idea what it was."

I paid a visit to del Guercino's office, on the pretext of taking the translation to him. He was very pleased with it. After pretending to inquire into buying shares in a cargo, followed by some very gracious and interesting conversation about eastern authors, I steered our talk slowly around to my main purpose. "Suppose you were trying to smuggle a book out of Constantinople, a book you knew a lot of other people were looking for, how would you go about it?"

"Bury it deep in a cargo that no one is going to bother sifting all the way through by hand. Something with some sting in it. Pepper, say. Then I'd send it to Beruit by galley, and from there back to Europe."

"Or," he continued, "I might simply ship it to Candios. From there, it could be reshipped anywhere. East to Aleppo or Cairo, west to Venice or any port in Europe. Crossroads of trade and gossip, Candios is. Has been for two thousand years."

Wonderful. Candios or Beruit. "Too slow a voyage." I tried another tack. "What if one of your competitors was trying to smuggle it out, and you wanted to find out where it was going? Your competitor is shipping it to someone, and you need to know who. Knowing where it is going is more important than the book itself. And you need to find out without them knowing you've found out."

"Is this one of your 'dangerous manuscripts'?"

"You could say that, yes."

"How urgently is the receiving party expecting it?"

"Fairly urgently."

"Ahh. That helps. It limits the options. It would have to get out of Istanbul quickly then?"

I nodded.

"Well, you can't search every ship and caravan going out of Istanbul, and even if you did, chances are you still wouldn't find it. On the other hand, the ordinary cargo ship or caravan would be too slow for our smuggler's purposes."

So, it would have to be aboard a small, fast ship or in a caravan carrying an urgent—perhaps perishable—cargo. Find out what the cargo is, and you narrow down the destination. You wouldn't ship furs to Russia, for example, or wheat to Egypt. But you would ship alum to Florence, or nutmeg to Genoa."

I nodded. This was a useful approach.

"Kachak," he asked quietly, "just how dangerous is this book of yours?"

At first, I wasn't going to tell him, but then I reconsidered who he was and the risks he had already run in his time among us. "If we do not find out who has it," I answered heavily, "the city could starve next autumn."

He sucked in his breath. "Then I wish you luck."

It was the habit of the Padishah, as it had been his father's and grandfather's, to wander disguised in the streets of Edirne and later of Istanbul, when it became the capital, in order to learn the thoughts of his people. On these outings he was often accompanied only by two janissary guards in ordinary clothes but with yatagans hidden under their jackets for use in case of any threat to his person. No doubt many other janissaries watched over him unseen from a distance. Bayezid especially enjoyed hearing the music of his capital city. He was a formidable composer in his own right. His saz overture, which we had heard played several times at the palace, was haunting and grand, hinting at the broadness of the winds which sweep across the Anatolian plains. Its intertwined melodies reminded me of the rise and fall of the sea, and of its loneliness. He often wrote the words to his music himself. In his poetry, Bayezid was fond of words with double meanings which changed depending on the words surrounding them. A word that you thought meant "earth" in one stanza could change its meaning to "truth" when you read the next line. "Thorn" changed to the "kiss" of lovers, with all the bitter-sweet pain that fitted both words, and back again beneath a cypress tree.

On one of these evening outings, Erhan, Inanc, and I—who of course recognized him from the palace despite his merchant clothes—came across him on a street corner near Eminönü, politely listening to a group of merchants who were discussing wheat prices.

"I know you three, do I not?" Bayezid said conversationally, falling into step beside us after he had disengaged himself from the discussion. "Don't selam," he whispered quickly just as we were about to do so, "Tonight I am plain Merchant Adnih, from Pera."

"Yes, Adnih efendim." I gave him our names formally, though I was willing to lay twelve odds to seven he knew them already.

He smiled. "Ah yes, you're the boy of the threads. And you," he turned to Erhan, "are the one who observed so truly that our treaties are written in our souls. And you," to Inanc, "Bahadir tells me you can shoot the beak off a firenk ship at twelve hundred arshin."

"I hope to do so again in your service."

"Whereas I, on the contrary, hope you will never have to. However, I fear the world will give you all too many opportunities to show me your skill. Daud Pasha tells me that the pope's recent scandals have given us a breathing space, but little more. You know about the new forces stirring in Italy; King Ferrante's death has left the French once more eyeing the empty throne of Naples as an opportunity to make trouble. They say they will finally use Naples as their harbor to launch the crusade that the pope has long been demanding from them. King Ferrante was moderate, sensible; he understood the balance. Last year he sent me two gyrfalcons."

The Padishah stopped in front of a small byzantine building surmounted by an octagonal dome, its small arched windows facing the sloping street. "I think this is my favorite building in Istanbul. It has been here a long time." He was silent for several minutes. "My advisors counsel me that Sultans must not enter the line of world rulers, nor fall prey to the temptation to become the successors of the Byzantine emperors. Prince Korkud agrees with them. He tells me that such a ruler can no longer be himself, and often has to do things he wishes not to."

"Prince Korkud is a formidable scholar," Erhan said. "I have read his commentaries on the Persian poets. His alcove at the Enderun Kolej was the same one that I was later fortunate enough to be assigned to."

The padishah smiled at the compliment to his son. "I think he takes after me in that," Bayezid continued.

"Adnih efendim," I made so bold to ask, "why did you make the law forbidding books to be printed in either Arabic or Persian?"

He considered the question a moment. "Because I think there is something beautiful in the writing, hand-lettered, that I don't think a printing press will ever quite equal. Don't you? Lettering a Koran, or a book of teachings, or an old tale from the east of our forebears, is work of hands dedicated to God. Dedicated to creating something lasting. When one opens a page, the way it feels as one turns it, the way it sounds, the way the letters flow…I want to keep that beauty in my land. The press is fine, very useful indeed, for other languages whose letters are not so liquid. Greek letters, Latin letters, all the European tongues. But the typefaces the Europeans brought from North Africa to use for the Arabic characters are too… unlovely. Everything to its best purpose. And, well, also because the calligraphers guild sent a petition. They asked me to protect their trade."

We continued walking. In one street, his moderate but clearly well-to-do clothing caught the eye of the proprietor of an establishment who—no doubt taking us all for a prosperous merchant accompanied by his assistants—persistently offered him, and us too, the favors of the ladies within.

"New Circassian slave girls, very polite, very clean," the proprietor was saying.

The Padishah expressed polite disinterest in Greek. The proprietor was not the least bit abashed and repeated his offer at a slightly lower price. "Perhaps another night," Bayezid said gently so as not to hurt his feelings. The spectacle of a man whose harem contained the most beautiful and educated women in the world being offered the comforts of the ordinary trade struck us as unutterably funny. Bayezid too. "Yes, it is amusing, is it not? But then, he couldn't know."

I needed to think, and I went in the late afternoons to the place where I could do that best, the shed in the Tersane where *Akdogan* was laid up for the winter. The Tersane workmen who were resteaming her bow frames had left for the day; I had timed it thus to be there alone. I walked around her hull, admiring as I always did, her sharp lines, and enjoying the opportunity to study her out of the water. Avoiding the varnish pots, I sat cross-legged on the dirt floor in front of her prow.

Was there some way around the problem that we weren't seeing? Some way to jump straight to what we needed to know? Perhaps we did not need to know the whole path to know the destination. Perhaps if we untied even only part of the knot, we would get at the one useful fact, or two, that we sought. Almost six hundred years ago, Hoca Al-Kwarizmi had written, "You do not always need to solve an entire equation in order to derive useful information from it." I sent another of the many silent thanks I frequently sent in the direction I imagined his soul to inhabit. If I had read nothing else in my entire time at the Enderun Kolej, that single line alone would have made the study of Persian well worth the effort.

I tried to see with both eastern and a western eyes. To move freely between both, according to the question, borrowing the best from each. "That's the truest of all the al-jabrs," our lala had said, "the real test of a mind." He was right. It was bloody difficult.

Which part? The end or the beginning? Who was the courier riding to? Or, who had sent the courier in the first place? The answers to those questions at least were the same. Two points on the circle which were really one. And every point on the circle had some connection to the point we were looking for. That at least was a comfort. And somewhere out at sea would be the ships who were using the information Marsan's courier sent them. How would it get to them?

"When a thing looks most plausible, lay it bare." A western Roman emperor had written that, a western emperor who had looked to the east for much of his thinking. "Look for solutions in the most likely places; those with the fewest causes." That was straight from the west. Their own best advice, and seldom followed. From the east, I reminded myself not to fall into the western trap of assuming that—just because one method worked—there were not others. The circle analogy was apt. Especially if every suspicion in our bones was right and it was Rhodes. Any information gathered by Rhodes would eventually be reported to their masters the papacy, and anything the papacy gathered would presumably be shared with their wolves on Rhodes.

"And through it all," I reminded myself, "you still might be getting it wrong. A single inspired guess, carefully assessed, may yet give you a better answer than all the calculations in your head."

Thus Mete and Yigit found me two hours later. They brought the cold wind, as well as some plain good sense, in the boatshed door with them.

"Kachak? We thought you would be here. Remember, we're not looking for the book. We're looking for the person who *has* the book." Mete pointed out.

"True. That helps."

"We're looking for the *masters* of the person who has the book," Yigit clarified.

"And perhaps we do not need to find the spy in order to get a sample of his handwriting. After all, the book will likely be translated and copied before it is sent. And probably the copy won't be made by the spy himself, but by one of Marsan's secretaries."

"Who probably also draws up a lot of other routine documents," I said excitedly. Ship manifests, bills of lading, customs declarations, accounts. Who knows, we probably already have samples of that handwriting and we didn't even realize it!"

"The customs office!"

We left the shed and ran along the shore to the solid limestone and brick building which housed the offices of the Limanibashi and his inspectors. It turned out that Marsan had three secretaries, or at least there were documents from his establishment in three different hands, plus a letter in his own. We asked if we could borrow them, and were firmly told no.

Yigit shrugged as we left the office. "That's fine for now. If we need to have them, Bahadir can send an order from the palace. It's an option."

"And a good one," Bahadir said later when we told him our idea. "Let's go down this path a little. We send one of the notebooks and a forged letter, but to whom?" he mused, looking down at the map of the White Sea which he kept always at hand on a corner of the windowsill. "Whom do we chose?" He tapped Rome, Genoa, Lyon, and Rhodes slowly in sequence. "We'd still be guessing at who the recipients are. And even what language he uses when he writes to them."

He let the silence hang, then began again. "Alright. Let's say we send a report to the Knights of Rhodes. Whom would the spy normally address it to? To the *Bisun* himself?" he asked rhetorically, casually slipping into the pronunciation ordinary Turkish sailors used to approximate 'Aubusson.' "Or to one of Aubusson's clerks? If so, how would we find out which one?"

"He'd probably write them in cipher anyway," I felt I had to point it out, even though Mete shot me a discouraging look as soon as I opened my mouth. "Even if we know the hand-writing, we don't know the cipher."

"Hmm. Never underestimate the algebraic abilities of some of our people. There are people in the corridors of this palace who have become pretty good at calculating the frequency and combinations with which letters of the alphabet occur. You'd be surprised what they can read. But that's still not our biggest problem. Even if, by luck, we got everything else right, the odds are that we might still send it to the wrong country."

"And if Marsan's never sent them anything before, they will write back to him asking about the unexpected gift, and the game will be up."

"And we'll lose the slender thread we have gained, which is being able to send misleading reports to watchers unknown," Bahadir cautioned. "We must not lose the whole rabbit for the sake of the paws."

"For all we know, it could be a lone corsair captain paying for the information freelance to make himself richer," Mete said. "Just as dangerous to us, perhaps, but a whole lot more difficult for us to trace than a hostile government."

"Where would you hide a sailing notebook if you were hoping no one would notice it?"

"With other sailing notebooks."

"It's aboard a ship!"

"We'll search every ship in the harbor!"

"We can try, but we can't be sure we'll find it, even if we happen to stumble on the right ship. It's bound to be hidden well, deep in the cargo."

Nevertheless, we tried. Bahadir detached another seventy sailors to assist us. We went through the holds of every ship waiting for spring at the foreigners' wharf like swords through a loaf. We did not find it.

"Finding the book, or the courier, in Istanbul," we concluded, "is like looking for a needle in a heap of straw."

"And the best way to find a needle in a heap of straw is to make the heap smaller. Go to a smaller town where we are more likely to cross paths with him. Somewhere too small to hide."

We took a caique across to palace point and went, rather glumly, to report to Bahadir. We saw him at a distance in the second courtyard, walking deep in conversation with another man in ordinary clothes. Even from a distance, there was no mistaking that it was another naval officer. It shows in a hundred ways, in the way we walk, the way we carry our shoulders, even in the particular way we fold our collars.

As they came to the end of the path and they turned back towards us. Onur, for it was he—bearded, recently married, and returned from commanding a galleot in the Danube squadron—was reporting to Bahadir on the situation in northern Europe. "The Germans have shown no enthusiasm for a crusade. For decades the pope has been collecting tithes and special levies for it, and they are tired of sending hundreds of thousands of ducats to Rome every year with nothing to show for it. They know that most of the money goes to pay for the luxuries of the curia instead. They also are at war with the Hungarians over their disputed border, so they have no wish to help them against us. Holy Roman Emperor or not, Maximilian returns polite replies to the papal envoys, keeps them hanging, but that is as far as it goes."

He broke off when he saw us. "My little cousins!"

We gathered in front of him, in a line to greet him, by habit almost if we were all still oglans at the palace school and he our senior.

After the greetings were done, Onur continued. "You may talk in front of them," Bahadir told him. They've copied enough of your reports by now that you have no secrets from them."

"Yes, well, the Italians are becoming increasingly nervous about the French king's talk of coming to Italy to lead a crusade. They fear his motives run deeper than service to the Church and pressing his claim to the throne of Naples."

"The Italians may have unleashed a dragon on themselves—they use that very word—by inviting Charles to the peninsula to lead the crusade," Bahadir observed.

"Ah. Someone must have already sent you a copy of Ercole's stolen letter too. Yes, Charles' head is filled with chivalric romances. His library at Lyon is said to be full of them. For a while, the duke of Milan and the pope both played on his imagination, exploiting a young man's impetuosity. For a long time no one thought it would amount to much; enough of his advisors were against the idea. Now there are whispers throughout the Savoy that there's real planning going on. He may actually provision an army and cross the Alps this time. The Venetians consider him a more immediate threat to the peace of Italy than they do us, and that's saying something. They are becoming extremely worried."

"Have they pulled the channel buoys out of the lagoon yet?"

Onur stopped for a moment, nonplussed. "Yes, I believe they have. How did you kn—"

"They always do that when they are nervous about a hostile fleet finding its way into their harbor. And what do the trees tell you?"

"Much. As soon as the crops were in, the French crown hired every farmer in Provence to begin cutting in the royal forests."

"The first whisper of an invasion fleet is the crash of falling trees'," Bahadir quoted. "Toulon? Marseille?"

"Toulon most probably."

"Not both?"

Onur shook his head. "I do not think so. Merchant ships of all countries sail in and out of Marseille. Too many spies who could watch the work, count ships, estimate cannon. Toulon is a garrison city. Easier to contol. If he uses Marseille, it will be for the overflow."

"Which brings us to the business of your cousins here, who I think are just itching to tell me something."

We shuffled and stammered it out that, no, we had had no luck in searching the ships in the harbor.

"I think, for caution's sake, we have to conclude that the notebook has left Istanbul and is on its way to whoever is paying Marsan's courier." Bahadir turned to us. "Mete, Yigit, Kachak, if you saw your viper again, say in a port waiting for a ship, would you recognise him again?"

"Undoubtedly. But which port?"

"Bozburum."

"So, it's Rhodes then? How did you know?"

"I don't. But it's the most dangerous of the possibilities. If we are wrong, the consequences are a little less severe than if we guessed somewhere else and missed Rhodes. The next most dangerous possibility is France. Toulon, to be specific. I would like to eliminate one or the other as a choice before going down the list of the others."

"I want all of you to ride to Bozburum and search the road along the way. You can ride together as far as Cannakale, but after that, split up into threes. Six of you together would be noticed. Stay about a day or so apart on the road, that way you can watch more of it at a time. You said that Ozkan, Berk and Erhan are getting bored watching the Yedikule gate?"

"They are."

"Then they will be happy to be on the move. Ask in the towns you stop in, but discretely mind you. When you get to Bozburum, wait there for two weeks or so. It's a small town, on a small bay, no more than twenty streets. If he goes there, he can't avoid you seeing him."

"Make the heap of straw smaller," Yigit nodded.

"What? Yes, exactly. Keep your eyes and ears out for any small ship putting in anywhere along the coast to pick up a passenger or a small cargo. I will keep the notebooks flowing so that they will have something to send frequently. Something should come through in that time. No matter what you find or do not find, I want you back in Istanbul in plenty of time for the sailing season.

He began writing out a series of several short letters. He handed me one of them. "Take this to Tursun Efendi; he will give you money for the expenses of the road. These others will introduce you to the garrison commanders at Cannakale, Izmir, and Bozburum in case you need to ask for official help. I would prefer you to manage things quietly so that you do not have to use them."

"Take Inanc with you. He can draw. It might be useful to have a diagram of any ship they send. Be ready to leave at first light tomorrow morning."

They gave us our pick of the stable of horses maintained across the street from the Gulhane gate for the use of palace couriers. With Bahadir's letters in our pockets and Tursun's coin in our pockets, we were shown to alcoves in a building along the side of the outer courtyard of the palace normally reserved for the servants of visiting foreign envoys.

Before dawn the next morning, excited to be going on our adventure, we rose and bathed and dressed. We were just putting on our jackets when a page stuck his head into our alcove.

"Admiral Bahadir's greetings, and he says you are not to leave. Please report to him in his office."

We looked at each other in puzzlement. Had we done something wrong?

Bahadir looked worn, as if he been awake the entire night. As it turned out, he had been. "Plans have changed. I can't possibly send you out of Istanbul now," he said. "There is bad news. The Padishah has fallen very, very ill. This is a secret; you are not to tell anyone. Go back quietly to the Tersane. We may need to have the fleet fully-crewed and ready sooner than we thought. If the Europeans should find out about the Padishah's illness there's no telling what they might do."

We each nodded silently. Our training was supposed to make us impervious to sudden changes of events, but we knew this was more serious than most. There had been outbreaks of plague in the city and in Anatolia for a month past. If Bayezid had caught it, and should die of it, it would be an irredeemable loss. We could well imagine the panic which would ensue.

"Keep the knowledge off your faces," Bahadir told us. "Do not let your expressions show. No matter what you are feeling inside, you are to behave as if nothing were amiss. The notebooks will wait for another time. It was after all, an experiment. We have made progress. We have a route to send misleading information to the enemy, and we have uncovered one of their agents we didn't know about before. Perhaps in time we will learn more. In the meantime, I have sent a description of the courier to the garrison commanders in Keshan and Bozburun. They might spot him. If so, it would give us the information we need. And if the notebooks were being sent through Candios, that path will be closed to them now. The Venetians won't be letting any ship sail either to France or Rhodes from there."

Those few in Istanbul who were in the know held their collective breath and waited. To explain the Padishah's absence at official functions, the story was put about that the he had gone on one of his frequent trips to the former capital city of Edirne. Supplies were readied at the Tersane, but no overt move to get the fleet ready for sea especially early was made. On shore, the crews began falling ill as well. Fully a third of our crews were sick. Many died. Every afternoon for a month, Erhan went to the palace, and each time he returned, he would shake his head silently. No news.

I myself fell miserably ill, staying in my bed for days and wandering in and out of a fevered sleep whose dreams—although never declining to the state of a full delirium—contained nevertheless the sharpened colors and surreal visual transpositions that come with illness. In one of them, I was swimming in the water next to the overturned and slowly sinking hull of *Akdogan*, the water around me a sea of fire. "From under the sun, a messenger comes with a silver trumpet," a voice called out, but there was no one in sight. My skin burned. I woke horrified to see a thin sheen of blood on my forearms and hands. Either the fever was breaking, or I was dying. I drank some water out of the flask by my bedside and decided I felt a little better than I had.

"You look as thin as an anchovy," Erhan said, poking his head into my room to see how I was doing.

"As pale as one too," I said. The sleep and its dreams, for all their horror, seemed to have purged me. Was I hungry? No, not yet, but at least my body felt as if it might one day want to eat again. This too, I took as an improvement over the feeling of never being able even to imagine food. In another five days, I felt strong enough to get up and walk about, albeit slowly.

Meanwhile, Erhan had brought back cautiously optimistic news from the palace. It was said that the Padishah was gaining strength. The previous Friday, he had appeared publicly at prayers in Hagia Sophia, to our profound relief. Neither the disease nor the recovery was mentioned publicly. We learned, much later, that despite our precautions, the word had slipped out to Europe. A messenger got through to the papal court with the news that "the Grand Turk would die." A Venetian ambassador in Rome reported this to Venice; the worried Venetians reported it—only many months later—to us.

Chapter V
The hunted

Spring finally came, and with it, the time to get the fleet ready for sea in earnest. The sailors who had gone to their homes for the winter began to report back for duty and to gather in the city. It was good to welcome our crewmates back. Our Serbian and Albanian rowers, of which *Akdogan* had a sizeable contingent among her crew, returned earliest, having the farthest distance to travel. They established themselves cheerfully in a group of rooms at the end of the hall of the Tersane barracks, rooms which we took to calling collectively 'Little Serbia.'

"He shaved it off!" Little Eagle exclaimed at dinner one night. Canni had returned to Istanbul with an enviable beard, clearly the work of several months. Generally, only Muslims were supposed to wear beards in Turkey, so he was clean-shaven again.

"Now the rest of us look more manly," someone quipped.

On the morning of the last new moon before the equinox, we gathered in *Akdogan*'s shed and lined up quietly and formally on either side of the hull. I stood next to Captain Hasan in front of her bow. "Time for the falcon to lift her wings again," Hasan said, "time for us to taste the salt, and dance with the waves and wind across the White Sea." He nodded to Berk and Ozkan, who went aboard her and began flaking out the heaving lines so that the ends dangled over the gunwales for the crew to haul on.

"Takozes out!"

In almost one motion, twenty rowers on either side swung their mallets to knock the takozes aside, the rowers at the ropes began to heave, and *Akdogan* slid down the ways into the water even more easily than she had slid up them a few months before. We cheered loudly as she splashed into the Horn; this was our favorite time of year, a time of purpose and coming alive again. We towed her around to the Tersane wharf to reload the oars and restep the masts. The new rope we had made over the winter needed to be threaded through the blocks, tightened, allowed to stretch, then tightened again. We lowered the sails from the rafters and carried them out—rolled like giant carpets—on our shoulders. The procession put me in mind of a serpent angling its way onto the ship, where we bent the sails onto the yards. Hasan did not like the look of some of the reef points, which had frayed over the winter, so we slung the yards in their bridles, hanging them at shoulder level just above the deck so we could untie the old ones and replace them.

"Are they all to come out?" Berk asked me, pulling at a particularly stubborn knot with his teeth.

"Might as well do them all now," I said nodding, and went back inside to get a set of extras.

The equinoctal gales came early that year, and then— just as we thought we had given them plenty of time to blow themselves out—they came all over again, to Admiral Kemalladin's extreme annoyance. They were testing him, he said, and he called upon all the powers of earth and sky to witness that—whatever he had done to deserve this—he hadn't enjoyed it *that* much. Then suddenly, it was warm. The seasons had turned. It was time to be busy again.

The governor of the Tophane had requested Atakan's gunnery expertise at the foundry. After a raucous farewell dinner, at which there were only about two hundred references made to 'the incident,' we left him on shore to his new work. "Treat my bronze beauties well," he told Inanc by way of valediction.

We took the squadron out into the Marmara Sea for short trips to get the feel of the ships again. The first strokes of the season are always a little rough. It takes time to get the timing of the oars together for an entire ship. The sound of the starboard side blades hitting the water at different times sounded like a kind of stuttering thunder. "We're rowing like a bunch of firenk donkeys!" Ozkan shouted at them over his shoulder.

"But I *am* a firenk donkey, sort-of," one of the Serb rowers on the port side hollered back at him, to general laughter. It took us a few trips to sharpen up the blade work and get them in together cleanly and quietly. We were perfectionists about this, and stayed out late one evening, not wanting to return to the city and have anyone see us until we were sure we had it right.

The fleet left the Horn to the sounds of bands playing on the quay. The spring sailings were traditionally a festival. All the ships flew their pennants; there were cannon salutes from the guns on the point. Once past the Dardanelles, the fleet split up into its various squadrons. Our squadron's job was to clear the waters along the western coast and among the Dodecanese islands of as many corsair ships as possible and to smoke them out of their lairs before the Rosetta and Alexandria convoys sailed. Coastal towns, even more than shipping, were the luckless targets of the corsairs' sudden raids. Towns, being stationary, were less chancy to raid than ships, at least the small, undefended ones. While the booty might not have been as rich, the pickings were easier. The coastline was too long for our troops to defend all of it. Even with the best of intelligence, there were no sure ways to predict where the corsairs would strike.

We patrolled belligerently around Kos and Simi, and *Yildirim* wasted the better part of a day standing bows-in towards the rocky shore with her foresail yard aggressively reversed, aft end down and forward end swung up, to get it out of the way of her cannon. We dreamed above all of finding where the corsairs stored their oars and stealing or burning them. Oars were the basis of a fleet. Burn the supply, and it would take two or three years to re-season the wood and make new ones. You cannot make oars out of green wood; they will warp and split.

We ran down to Patmos and watered there. Bayulken checked in with the governor for news of ships sighted and any rumours he could share of corsair activities. Hearing none, we left *Yildirim*, *Hilal*, and *Bayezidiye* in port while *Akdogan* headed east to the cluster of islands which our charts show under the collective name of The Nesae, too small to be inhabited. We dropped anchor off the northernmost one, and Hasan ordered the jali boat swung out. With four rowers, and accompanied by a pair of janissaries armed with bows and yatagans just in case of trouble, we set off for the sandy inlet in silence. One of the rowers cocked an eyebrow at me in question, but I had no more idea than he did what Hasan's purpose was. The bow of the jali boat scraped on the sand, and I jumped out to hold it.

"Wait here," Hasan ordered the boat crew. The two janissaries made as if to come with us, but Hasan frowned them back unwillingly to their thwarts. Beyond the beach was a gently rising hillside, sparsely shaded by olive trees which grew spaced apart from each other like suspicious neighbors. According to the notes in the sailing book, people from Lipsi sailed across the strait every autumn to harvest them, but for now we had the islet to ourselves. At the end of the cove, two fingers of rock stretched into the water, leaving a sheltered space of sand between them, which——judging by the charcoal, fish bones, and charred ends of wood——was where the people who came to the island made their cooking fires. Beyond the rocks, a path led up toward the olive trees. Hasan took it, still without saying a word, and I followed. It wasn't until we had gone a little ways that I realized he was counting steps.

"About here," he said, stopping and looking around. "Ah, there," he stopped and looked down at the pebbly yellowish soil at the foot of one of the trees where the roots spread out. "I want you to see this too, to confirm my navigation," he said. "Also to learn how this is done."

I looked down too. At first I saw nothing, as it was intended that a casual passerby would see nothing. I steeled myself to see and to think, looking for the not-ordinary in the ordinary. What is, what isn't. 'The earth is either the earth or the sky,' as the saying goes. The pattern of the pebbles, so casual-appearing, suddenly snapped into place. I had seen the pattern before, had copied it on charts a hundred times. They were islands, and the one with the tiny twig lying in the dirt above it was Farmokanisi. "A maritime pataran," I murmured half to myself, intrigued.

"Very good. That is the 'where.' Can you tell the 'when'?"

That one took me much longer. The pebbles were mostly the same color as the sandy soil, but as I looked more carefully, I noticed some that were deliberately smaller than the ones which marked the islands, harder to see. There were eleven of them.

"Eleven nights past the new moon?" I hazarded. I could not see the indicator for the moon, as hard as I looked, so I inferred that it must be deliberately absent.

"Eleven before, actually. We do it backwards just in case someone should figure out the rest of it. But you caught on very quickly." Hasan picked up the pebbles and shook them out on the ground like dice, now truly random. "For the next time," he said, and we returned to the cove. He said nothing about who had left the message for us, nor why. I knew that I would learn that in due time, if I needed to know it at all.

The eleventh night before was only five nights away from tonight. I knew that we would not sail directly to Farmokanisi, not after so much caution had been taken to convey the destination so secretly. In this, I was correct. *Akdogan* patrolled, apparently at the whim of each day's wind, off various islands. At each, we sent the jali boat ashore, looking for keel marks in the sand that might be left by a ship recently beached: fireplace remains still warm, recently-cut branches or trees which might have been used for repair materials, or any of the hundred other signs that might reveal that corsair ships were operating in the area. On the fifth afternoon, *Akdogan*'s patrols brought her, as if by chance, close to the uninhabited north shore of Farmokanisi, which possessed several deep bays separated by wooded bluffs.

We beached *Akdogan* in one of these, stern-first with her guns pointing seaward. Hasan sent two of Yigit's janissaries up to the bluffs with a lantern as lookouts. Just as the sun was setting, one of them scampered frantically down the path to the beach. "There's a Venetian galley and a galleot standing in from the west," he told Hasan worriedly. "I almost did not see them against the setting sun."

"There'd better be," Hasan said. "They're late. They were supposed to be here before us, waiting."

Venetian galley *Fortuna*, one hundred and twenty-four oars, made her way into the cove, expertly handled. There is a certain look to a well-handled ship, and the *Fortuna* had it. Her hull was painted a soft buff yellow, another good color for blending with other colors on the horizon, with black gunwales. Not a speck of red paint anywhere. *Fortuna* was a practical ship, crewed by practical sailors who had no need of vain display. *Fortuna* and her escort galleot rounded in, turning their sterns to the shore, guns to the sea, and beached. Their crews swarmed smartly ashore with ropes to make them fast to the trees, while their captains came ashore to consult with Hasan.

"Captain Vincenzo, it is very good to see you."

"And you, Hasan. How have the seas been treating you?"

"They give their bounty, and they hide their dangers. You?"

"Much the same. These are dangerous times."

As if to confirm this, Hasan asked, "No one knows you are here?"

Vincenzo shook his head. "This is officially unofficial. Meaning that my orders are to pick up information any way I can, and no one will ask any questions as to how."

"Captain Andreas, how nice to see you again," I half bowed. He shot a look at me and almost jumped a foot, frowning at the recognition.

"The Council of Ten would not object to my telling you that they have reason to believe there is a spy in Istanbul and they ask for your help in tracking him down."

"Just one?" Hasan quipped.

"True. Well, one that we're interested in, anyway. Fourteen days ago, one of our galleys captured a corsair galleot northeast of Crete. It had aboard it some extremely interesting papers. The first was a list of cargoes and sailing schedules—by name—of Venetian ships expected to sail from Constantinople to Cyprus and onward to the Levant for the coming month. It also," Captain Vincenzo continued, "had a list of yours."

"Do you have it with you?" Hasan asked.

"I regret not. I sailed with the originals directly to Candios. From there, they will be sent onwards to the Council of Ten."

I was disappointed but not surprised. Examining the originals would have told us much about who had sent them, probably more than the Venetians wanted to share. Even a look at the paper they were written on might have told us much.

"But you kept a copy?"

Captain Vincenzo pulled some papers out of his doublet and handed them to Hasan. I read it over his shoulder, trying to deduce as much as I could of the route the information contained in it must have taken. The original report must have been sent in cipher from Istanbul. Once at its destination, the relevant parts had been copied in plain language and distributed to the corsair captains. No sender, no addressee. That information was too sensitive to be risked to anyone who did not need to know.

Fourteen days, I was thinking. How long had it taken the message to get from Istanbul, to be deciphered and copied, and thence disseminated into the hands of the galleot captains? The information in it was less than a month old. I could tell that much by the dates some of the ships had been in port. No time for the information to have been sent all the way to one of the European powers and back. It had to have been disseminated from one of the islands not very far from here.

"And the second document?" Hasan said, sliding it out from behind the shipping list.

"We are not sure what it is."

It was a list of words, more than three pages of them. The words were Turkish names, but written in firenk letters, which was presumably why the Venetians had not recognized them as words and assumed it was a message in cipher. Each of the names had a string of firenk characters—combinations of MMMM, CC, and Xs written next to them.

"It's not in cipher," I said grimly. "It's a ransom list. Names, and the amounts of their ransoms next to them. MMMM is the way the firenks write four thousand."

"Bastards! Where was the galleot sailing from?"

"Kos, we think."

"It begins to fit," Hasan said. "I have some information for you in return," Hasan said. "The Knights of Rhodes are rebuilding their fortress at Halikarnassos Bay."

Vincenzo started violently. "So, it is true then."

Halikarnassos was less than one hundred miles from the Venetian colony on Naxos, and not much farther than that from Crete. Safe under the guns of the fortress, the corsair ships could sally out into the shipping lanes of the Ionian Sea at will and then dart back to its protection where no ship or squadron would dare to pursue them.

And Kos was just offshore from Halikarnassos, I thought. The names on the list swam at me. I knew their sad story without having met a single person on it. Taken prisoner by the corsairs, now sweating under the lash to rebuild the walls of Halikarnassos until death or the payment of their ransoms released them.

"Any activity at Halikarnassos is naturally of grave concern to Venice," Captain Vincenzo resumed.

"And to us," Hasan concurred. "The problem is, what to do about the place?"

"Your army might attack it by land," Vincenzo said, "and our ships by sea."

"That would mean a full-scale war with the Religion, and probably with the Papal States as well."

"Something that Venice has every wish to avoid."

"Short of assaulting it, we'll have to be content with patrolling; keep the corsairs from getting in or out. Related to that, our picket galleys around Crete have been reporting an unusual number of ships sailing from Rhodes to France this early in the season," Captain Vincenzo added.

"Carrying?"

"Naturally, we do not know. We have no brief to stop and search any. But our assumption is that the Knights of Rhodes are trying to stir the King of France to launch the crusade he has long promised. They are itching for trouble. To them, the means justifies the ends."

"How well we know it," Hasan said.

Few things are as fascinating to sailors as the chance to see a foreign ship up close. Our sailors wandered over in twos and threes to examine the Venetian ships, and I could see that the Venetians wanted to do the same with ours, but were tentative and shy about coming over to them. They were wary of us, the terrible Turks they had heard so many tales about. As both crews went about cooking supper on their respective ends of the beach, the Venetians gradually lost their reserve and began to come closer, offering to trade with us for our sash knives and jackets. They offered wine, which a few of our sailors drank (not all of us were Muslim). After supper, almost by common consent, the crews brought out whatever musical instruments they had. Music is as important to the Venetians as it is to the Turks, and no Turkish or Venetian ship would ever have put to sea without at least some musical instruments aboard. After supper, the sailors who had them brought them out, and the singing started.

"That mirror, it doesn't work," Andreas remarked to me sourly.

"Oh? Are you sure you are using it correctly? Do you remember to say the right words?"

"What words?"

I mumbled a few lines out of the *Lay of the Sons of the Night Wind*, which he pretended to understand, and then I left him to his doubts.

A dozen of our sailors were standing in a line, tossing their swords over their heads. The Turks will tell you that they're the ones who taught the Cossacks how to dance, the real stuff with swords and fire, and it's probably true. Being able to dance with a yatagan in your hand without maiming yourself—or anyone else in the room—is considered one of the heights of masculine accomplishment. On sand and barefoot, the stakes were even higher, but our lads were determined to show the Venetians how it was done.

"You?" one of *Akdogan*'s starboard rowers motioned to me to ask whether I wanted to join the line.

"Thanks, but I think I'll leave this to ones who were born to it," I said and stood aside, though I would dearly have loved to try. A small voice inside cautioned me that nothing in my Enderun background would have adequately prepared me. And we were, after all, in front of foreigners.

Blurs of flying elbows and high knees, with swords being spun and tossed between them until—with a final verse of the song and a 'heyah!'—they threw their swords high and caught them by the hilts as they turned and bowed.

"Where did Tur Ali learn to play the Dombra like that?" someone asked.

The Venetians applauded, duly impressed, and began to play some of their own music. It was bright and cheerful, using different modes from those we were used to in our own music.

In the morning, having exchanged information and laid plans for cooperation, the captains held a last consultation. "We will be taking more risks than before," Vincenzo said. "The stakes are higher this year."

Hasan nodded. "We too. I will find a way of informing you about any French ships we find sailing between here and Rhodes."

"Venice will be grateful."

The Venetians sailed west to patrol off their islands, Crete and the Morea. *Akdogan* sailed back to Patmos to rejoin our squadron and our supply carrack. From there, we sailed to meet the Rosetta convoy. Our first view of it was the bows of four Ottoman galleys breaking the morning mist, moving almost silently across a mirror sea towards us. The sight was breathtaking beautiful and arresting in its seriousness. The galley escorts were followed by the merchantmen, their sails mostly slack in the light breeze. We were fifty merchantmen and supply carracks all told, escorted by twelve galleys and galleots, rounded out by a pair of very fast brigantinas for relaying messages back and forth among the warships or to shore.

We turned south with them, towards the Karpathas Straits. On the sixth day at sea, Semih—who was up the foremast on lookout—shouted down "We've got company, sirs." There were sails off to the southeast, shadowing us. I looked over to *Yildirim* and *Hilal* to make sure they had seen them too. Red pennants fluttered to the ends of the main yardarms of all twelve escorting galleys. They had. I counted five or six of the sharp triangular sails belonging to galleys or galleots, accompanied by the large square sails of a support carrack of their own. They stayed well out of range of our guns. Corsairs seldom directly attacked a convoy; the risks were higher than they could stomach. They preferred to wait for a ship or two to stray from the protection of the escorts, and pick off the stragglers. Their tactics were to cripple, not sink, their targets.

Our orders were clear. We had a treaty, and we were on no account to fire on any ship flying the red and white flag of the Knights of Rhodes, unless they fired first. All the corsairs of the Mediterranean knew this, and they flew that flag for protection, even those who were not carrying Rhodian letters of marque and who had no right to. It wore on us, being stalked day after day, always the hunted. Every morning we counted our sails, hoping that none of our ships had strayed during the night. To reduce the risk of this happening, we anchored the convoy at evening whenever there was a bay suitable for this, the escorting galleys keeping watch at the mouth, guns cleared and muzzle tompions out. The sailing ship captains were uncomfortable being crowded so close to shore, and said so. If even one or two ships tangled each other's rigging, the confusion could render a whole floating mass of them unmanageable, such that they would drift into others and could be blown ashore before they gained room to maneuver. This nightmare was in everyone's mind, but the merchant sailors were also professionals; they knew what they were about. It took real seamanship to sail in formation; and this they had in high measure. Even so, precious time was lost each morning setting the sails and getting the convoy under way and in order.

Managing more than a mile of ships on the open sea was far from easy. We sailed in a large wedge, with four escorting galleys at each point of the triangle. That guaranteed that— no matter what direction the wind was blowing—a minimum of one group of escorts was always in the windward position in case of an attack, and could swoop down quickly to reinforce the others. The sailing captains would have preferred to sail in a more open line, or in a shallow arc, but that would have been almost five miles long, much too far for the escorts to move rapidly to a trouble spot if needed, and too easy for the corsairs to isolate stragglers.

In places where our southern coast was sparsely inhabited and undefended, we knew that the corsair galleots often found a bay nearby to overnight in. This too, infuriated us, but there was little we could do about it. We discussed trying a night approach to surprise them in their holes to blockade them and bottle them up in some bay. But we dared not weaken the convoy by diverting some of the escorts, and we also knew that the *corsos* would be posting lookouts on the bluffs who would see us coming, and that we would be sailing into the guns of a beached battery of galleots drawn up stern-first on shore.

On those evenings when we found ourselves off stretches of rugged coastline where it was not safe to anchor, we lit the stern lanterns and rafted the galleys around the supply carracks. This gave us a chance to go aboard them and eat full meals. You can't bake bread on a galley, and biscuit and cheese becomes monotonous after a while, so the more ample ovens of a carrack provided the fresh foods that we hungered for. There was more deck space to sleep on too.

So much depended on the wind. In a calm, the square-sailed cargo ships were helpless against the nimble corsair galleots who could nip in three or four at a time and surround one before the other ships in the convoy could come to its aid. If the wind were strong enough to kick up the waves, the sailing ships could move easily while the galleys and galleots had heavier going and were thrown about by the rollers. In a moderate wind, the odds could shift in an instant depending on the direction. A galley or galleot's triangular lateen sails allowed her to sail much closer to the wind than the cargo ships. Thus a moderate wind with smooth seas was the most dangerous time for us.

The presence of the corsair carrack changed the equation. It meant that they could stay at sea longer and operate independently of the coast. It also meant they had a broadside of floating artillery to retreat behind if they bit off more than they could chew.

The carrack either did not have a name, or else we never got close enough to read it. We took to calling it simply the 'great carrack' or—less affectionately—the 'Square-Sailed Bear.' She was enormous. "Two thousand *tonnilato*, if she's an ounce," Hasan estimated. The sides of her hull rose from the water like walls. She had two full gun decks, with a row of smaller guns on her stern deck and a row on her forecastle, at least fifty in all. The sheer weight of iron which her broadsides could throw was enough to make us gasp. No galley or fleet of galleys could get close to her under such a withering fire. The height of her gun decks meant that she could pour down a rain of destruction on the much lower decks of any ship trying to approach her. Boarding her would have been out of the question; we estimated that she carried a crew of seven hundred at least.

Loose among one of our convoys, there was no limit to the havoc she could wreak. She was the largest warship most of us had ever seen and perhaps the largest warship in the world. Her foremast and mainmast carried two topsails each, while the mizzen carried a lateen sail for maneuvering. In a stiff wind, she would be able to keep up with all but the fastest galleys, and her guns would be high enough above the water to fire even in weather when a galley's risked being doused by the waves. Even becalmed, she would be far from helpless, a bristling floating fortress.

But for all that, she had weaknesses too. She needed deep water for the draft of her keel, I thought to myself. She would not dare operate too close inshore, and there at least we had an advantage. Her high forecastle would make her unhandy in all but a following wind—that much was true of any carrack.

We put in at Eyrinhal, Kemer, and Antalya on our way. Off Antalya, while our ships were safely snugged down in harbor, protected by the guns of that formidable fortress, a storm dispersed the corsairs, who were hove-to offshore, there being no undefended bay they could put into along that well-garrisoned stretch of coast. We knew better than to hope that the storm had sunk them; the corsairs were better seamen that that, but we took no little satisfaction in imagining the hours of drenching, cursing, dangerous wrestling with flapping sails they must have endured. With luck, it might give us a day or two sailing free of them before they intercepted our track again.

They must have been very angry about the storm, because they became more aggressive. More than once they sailed provocatively through our convoy, forcing our ships to alter their courses, in hopes of disrupting our formation and peeling off some stragglers. It was calculated to intimidate. They knew that we would not dare to fire on them, and they were trying to provoke us into violating our orders.

I came awake one morning to a steady southwest wind just strong enough to ruffle the water, but not strong enough to throw even a single whitecap. It was the combination we most dreaded.

"Nightmare time," Berk commented.

Suddenly, the sea was full of corsair galleots, darting close to the edges of our convoy, sometimes daring to sail into our formation between our ships.

On one of these feints, the corsairs got a little above themselves, and the Square-Sailed Bear found herself between some of our ships and the shore. "Let's see them do this," Hasan said. *Hilal* and *Akdogan* suddenly hardened up their sails, and we clawed our way up to windward on either side of her, hemming her in and forcing her even closer towards the shore. In order to change course, she would either have to tack or wear, and that meant risking hitting one of our ships, an action which would give us an excuse to fire. We had hounded her pretty close to shore before she suddenly opened her gun ports to threaten us off.

"Oh, you wouldn't *dare*," Hasan said, narrowing his eyes in calculation as five or six of her cannons ran out. Our galleys dared not risk that wall of iron. "Alright, we've made our point."

We bore off, and had the satisfaction of seeing the carrack almost run down one of her own galleots as she wore hastily across the wind to beat clear of the shoals. She had to haul her buntlines and luff her main and foresails at the last minute to avoid the collision.

Thus we played a dangerous game of cat and mouse all the way to Cyprus. Convoy duty would not rescue any of the hostages at Halikarnassos, but at least we could take comfort that we were saving others from the same captivity. Once in Venetian waters, we could relax our vigilance a little. The Venetians loathed the corsairs and dealt firmly with any that they caught. In return for a two percent customs duty, the Venetians usually permitted Turkish merchant convoys to put into Limassol. I say 'usually' because this concession always depended on the Venetians' mood and the level of tension between their government and other Christian nations. For diplomatic reasons, our warships were not permitted inside the mole under any circumstances. The escorts had to anchor in the roadstead outside. This was dangerous in the event of a sudden storm, and Turkish warships had been lost on previous occasions. We grumbled about it, naturally. It also denied us the opportunity to go ashore.

From Limassol, it was a direct dash south across the open waters of the eastern Mediterranean to Rosetta. Two hundred miles, three days and nights at sea; four at the most. A number of Venetian ships joined the convoy, glad of our protection. The corsairs seldom risked shadowing a convoy in the open waters. Besides the extra uncertainty of a fight in the open sea, where a single well-placed cannon shot by their prey could upset their plans, they ran the risk of encountering naval patrols the Mamluks periodically sent up from the coast of Egypt. None of us had much faith in the efficacy of the Mamluk navy—we knew it to be unskillfully crewed and a cesspool of corruption—but the approaches to Rosetta and Alexandria were thick with the ships of many nations coming and going, and its presence was a deterrent. Although the pickings among so many ships might have been rich, the corsairs knew that no ship was ever more than a mile or so from any other. Help was never far away, and to dare to attack one meant to attack many.

We approached the Nile delta, that vast fan of water and sand which spreads out into the White Sea, with extreme caution. Little Eagle had once commented to me that "'Nile' must be Greek for 'the place where all the sand bars gather'." It took us half a day to get the entire convoy safely into the Rosetta mouth of the river. There were miles of ships berthed there end to end, from every port in Europe—French, Genoese, Neapolitan, Austrian, Venetian, even a pair of nefs from Rhodes. The sailing ships in our convoy 'vailed' their topsails as we passed the fortress at the river mouth, lowering the topmast yards briefly as a customary sign of respect and greeting upon entering a foreign port.

In Egypt, we saw only a few of the wonders of that fabled land. We were too busy loading and unloading to travel far from the port, of course. We did not have leave to travel to the south to see the mountains of stone we had heard about, built upon the desert, much as I dearly wished to. Nor did I get the chance to travel to nearby Alexandria to see the remains of the famous library that first the Romans (accidentally) and then the Mamluks (deliberately) had burned—the Mamluks with the pronouncement that "If a book contains matter which is in the Koran, it is superfluous; if it contains matter which isn't, then it is idolatrous." We did visit the ancient temples in Rosetta, the walls covered with the mysterious pictures that the ancients wrote in.

We spent some of our free time ashore trading in the bazaars for our own accounts. Each sailor, whether on a merchant ship or on a war galley, was by custom allowed some space for his own goods. Particularly in the confined spaces of a war galley, the space allotted wasn't much, but it allowed us the opportunity to supplement our pay. With sailors from so many different nations in the same port, there were some spectacular quayside brawls. The Genoese and Venetians were always at each others' throats; the French and the Austrians frequently had their differences, and the Florentines seemed prepared to take on all comers. Up close, we were constantly struck by how much bigger than us the firenks were. "They eat heavy foods, and their thoughts are heavy thereby," Inanc joked. By tacit agreement, everybody mostly avoided us. The firenks had affairs aplenty of their own, and Egypt—as an Ottoman treaty signatory—was hardly a place conducive to making trouble with Ottoman sailors.

The former ruling Mamluk elite was not—treaty or no treaty—particularly friendly to us as a class. In contrast the ordinary people welcomed us quite warmly. We found that they had never particularly liked their Mamluk overlords anyway.

The port was guarded by a large square fortress of beautiful white stone with its own mosque and minaret that the Sultan of the Mamluks, Kayit Bey, had ordered built some fifteen years before. Inanc obtained permission to visit it, and returned with tales of stacks of granite cannon balls in its magazines, iron being in short supply in Egypt.

"Red granite, I tell you! Imagine the effort of chiseling *granite* cannon balls," he mused. "I'll tell you this, though. They would smash through any ship that tried to enter or leave the harbor unpermitted."

The four firenks blocking our way in the street were drunk, and drunk men should never handle swords. Especially not the long, broad-bladed European swords they were waving over their heads at us. They had apparently run out of money drinking in the tavern at the end of the street, and had decided that robbing a few sober Turkish sailors would be an easy way to continue the evening's festivities, as well as an act of holy merit against infidels. Big gestures, big movements, big sound. Everything about them was big.

The one coming at me swung wide and missed. It required only a small movement of my yatagan to press his sword down to the left before flicking the point up at his now unguarded chest and throat, letting my body weight flow behind the blade, just as Cihan had taught me. I was mostly concentrating on how best to knock his sword away from him without damaging the fine silver work on the hilt. It was a nice sword, and I decided I wanted it because it would be worth some money. The European attacking Inanc tried an over-the-head blow. He was clumsy, and his movements were overly large and therefore vulnerable. Inanc made him look foolish with an agile parry and a long gashing stroke up and across the shoulder of his sword arm, forcing him to drop his weapon with a scream. Cihan's attacker got the pommel of his own sword in his teeth for his pains. My assailant got his balance almost back and tried again, low this time, viciously trying to hamstring me. I jumped back and smashed the flat of my yatagan into the right side of his face as his momentum swung him past me. He tripped as he went, so I did it again and held the point on the back of his neck, stamping on his sword hand to make him let go. Ozkan's attacker, bringing his sword down hard, had missed and bounced its blade into the dirt. With the blade of Ozkan's yatagan now at his neck, he decided that the ground was the best place for his own sword, and he left it there, surrendering meekly. One of them started to yell for help in what I took to be Catalan, then thought better of it. Anyone drawn by his shouts in this district would be on our side, not theirs.

Not at all gently, we slammed them up against the wall. "I think you wish you hadn't tried that," Inanc said, not caring whether they understood. We searched them thoroughly, disappointed that they had already spent all of their money. In addition to their swords, they all carried knives in their boots.

"Hey, what's this?" Cihan said, pulling out a piece of paper. It was of the sturdy type the Egyptians made from the reeds which grow along the Nile, folded in four. He unfolded it slowly, letting out his breath as he did so. Written on it was a list of merchant ships and cargoes.

Another point on the circle.

Perhaps it should have come as no surprise to us that there should also have been spies in Rosetta reporting on our returning convoys. After all, the northbound convoys carried the more valuable cargoes. Still, it was a chilling find. Were we being watched from everywhere?

And this list was different. In addition to the names of the merchant ships, their tonnage, and their cargoes, the paper carried the names of our escorting warships, *and* their captains. Information which—while useful to a corsair captain—would be even more useful to an enemy navy.

"What ship are you from?" Inanc demanded. We tried every language we knew, looking for at least a reaction, but got none.

We marched our four would-be robbers to the fort and handed them over to the military commander to be locked up, then took the paper to Bayulken aboard *Yildirim* to report.

"The guards at the fort will at least find out what ship they're from, and that may tell us something about where the information was being sent," Bayulken said after studying our find. "I will go tomorrow to the captain of the port to ask him to refuse a license to sail to whatever ship that is. In the meantime, you four are to stay on board your ships, or at least not to leave the quayside. Their shipmates may be looking for you. I want each of you surrounded by lots of Turks at all times."

We found this precaution tedious, but had to admit the good sense of it. Rosetta was a small city, and we had already seen most of it anyway. Bayulken had me copy the paper three times, sending each separately by whatever brigantina or cargo ship might be leaving before us in order to ensure that at least one copy got through. The original he kept to take back to Istanbul personally.

"This sword is not the sword of an ordinary seaman," Cihan said, sighting along the blade with a practiced eye. We were sitting on the stern deck, with our backs against the gunwales examining the weapons we had taken from our attackers. He handed it back to me. "Feel the balance."

I did. It was heavier than the swords I was used to, made for someone bigger than me, but I could appreciate how finely weighted it was.

"And the steel of the blade. Fine Moorish work, nothing less. Yes, this steel was quenched in the waters of the Guadaquivir," he said wistfully. "It had its fire from coals of poplar and apple. Strong and beautiful woods for making steel. I'll warrant the firenk you took it from was not its proper owner."

"Stolen, raided, or confiscated?" I wondered. It glinted in the light. There was a small ruby set in the pommel. "I wonder who it belonged to."

"Some Andalusian noble? Killed on the battlefield, or taken prisoner at sea, or forced to flee leaving his goods behind. Perhaps even someone we took to safety two summers ago. It's in better hands now, at least. What will you do with it?"

"I don't know. I had thought to sell it; it must be worth a lot, but now I am not sure I want to. What will you do with yours?" The other three were of plainer make, good for spares perhaps. They were all made for people bigger than we were.

"Take it back to Istanbul. There will always be time on the voyage to think about what to do with it." He held his up against his forearm. "Are *all* the firenks so big?"

One morning, only a few days before we were to sail, when most of the cargoes and provisions were already aboard, Bayulken sent Yildirim's new helmsman, Iskender, to summon me and Little Eagle unexpectedly to the flagship. "I have a special assignment. Go with Canni and Mete." He named the location of a warehouse owned by a Mamluk merchant that lay at the southern end of the city. Canni and Mete had coils of rope slung across their shoulders and gave each of us one to carry in the same way.

One end of the warehouse courtyard was taken up by stone pens for animals—usually sheep—being held for shipment south. Five cursing French sailors were trying to draw out an animal that looked to me like a camel with an enormously long neck, which was visible over the wall, and brown patches on its fur. It did not want to leave Africa, and was making its preferences known. "A present for the king," the merchant's factotum explained. "From far to the south. Few Europeans have seen one."

I heard the sailors say "giraffe" a few times, which sounded like their way of saying an Arabic word for elegant, *zarafa*. "Yes, that's what it is," the factotum replied in answer to Canni's question. "Elegant and graceful, yes. Mean-tempered though. It's not going to be easy getting it aboard their ship."

"Well, I don't envy them," Mete said gratefully. The factotum gave us a strange glance and stopped in front of the wooden door to one of the pens. It had a small wooden shutter in it, which he opened for us.

Which is how Little Eagle found himself eye-to-eye with his first rhinoceros, and one's first rhinoceros is always the special one. He put his face to the opening and was rewarded for his curiosity by a glimpse of a large brown eye and a single enormous tusk belonging to a juvenile African rhinoceros chewing its cud. It apparently had ambled right up against the door out of curiosity at hearing our voices coming through it, so little more than a few inches separated it from Little Eagle in this initial encounter.

"Wahh!" Little Eagle staggered backwards in surprise, so Canni stepped up to look for himself.

"No. Oh no. Oh very much oh no." Canni shot a glance at the coils of rope we were carrying. "No."

"A gift from our sultan to yours," the beaming factotum said, oblivious to our discomfiture. "There is nothing like it in Istanbul, is there not?"

I shook my head. It looked as solid as a small mountain, and several times the weight of a horse.

"No," Mete agreed, "there is nothing like it in Istanbul," and then continued quietly in an aside to Canni, "and I think there is a very good reason why there is not."

Mete asked what it ate.

"Leaves, green shoots, twigs. A special long-bladed grass. We prepared bundles of what it likes for the journey."

"What if it does not want to come?"

"Sirs, do not be so glum. My master had an iron cage made for it to travel in. You will not have to drag it through the streets to the harbor; it can go in a wagon, and you will be able to hoist it aboard ship."

Which was Rosetta's loss. This convenient accessory denied everyone in the port enjoying the sight of Little Eagle attempting to drag a juvenile rhinoceros all by himself up the gangplank of a cargo ship on the end of a rope. And it would have happened too, because we would have stood aside and left him to it for the sheer hilarity of it, and because loyalty to shipmates only goes so far where the wildlife is concerned.

The problem was thus reduced to how to get it to go into its cage. We cautiously opened the door to the pen, closing it promptly behind us. The rhinoceros backed into a corner, stripping the leaves off of some green branches by placing its front foot on one end of them and running them through its mouth. It eyed us nearsightedly, the tacit understanding being that—if we did not disturb its meal—it would agree not to trample us into little pieces, gore us with its horn, and stomp us flat. At least, that is what I took its glance to mean. I was new at such things, and could have been wrong.

Little Eagle held open the door of the cage, and Canni, Mete, and I put our shoulders to the creature's side and pushed.

Nothing happened.

We pushed again. It put down its twigs and turned its head slowly to regard us.

"Put its water pail in the cage," the factotum advised. "They drink often. It will not be long before it goes in."

We followed his advice, and were gratified that, after a little more than an hour, it entered the cage quietly and docilely so that we were able to close the door gently behind it. There was a wagon in the courtyard, hitched to some oxen who had seen it all before.

"And not a word to your masters," the factotum admonished us as we set out for the harbor, "it is intended to be a surprise."

"Oh, I think it will be," Mete affirmed diplomatically.

"And what lucky captain gets to take it aboard?" Canni asked.

"The carrack *Dalaman*," I consulted the note Bayulken had given me, "Captain Kurtoglu's ship."

"Does he know it's coming?"

"I don't think so."

He didn't, but accepted his unexpected passenger with good grace. Four halyards were unslung from the yards and hooked to the corners of the cage. The crew hoisted it aboard and lowered it through the hatches into the space between decks, which had been hurriedly cleared for it. In the end, it was easier than we thought it would be, which gave us time to watch the loading of the giraffe.

This provided a lot more entertainment. The giraffe had no cage, it being too tall for one. The French sailors had to hobble its legs together and sling ropes under its belly to haul it aboard, spitting and roaring.

"We got off easy," Canni said. Today is a good day not to be a French sailor."

After a long, hot summer, we set sail, the holds of the convoy stuffed with cargo. With all the spices on board, the ships smelled wonderful. We sailed our previous route in reverse. Once past Cyprus, we were back in corsair-infested waters again, and they soon began shadowing us. They had become more belligerent over the summer. They shadowed us closer than before, and several times we came very close to opening fire. In the Karpathas Straits, the convoy crowded together under the escorts' guns, muzzle tompions removed and loaded. The beacon on Pighadia was lit as we approached, and this time we were the prey. We had no intention of giving up any of our ships to the corsair galleots who we knew were watching for us from their coves. We had come too far and were too close to home for that. *Akdogan* broke off briefly from the convoy and put in at Nesae, but this time there was no new arrangement of the pebbles.

Once the convoy was safely in Ottoman waters, Bayulken detached *Hilal* from the fleet and sent her east to have a discreet look at Halikarnassos. The information she brought back was not encouraging. "*The fortress sits on its own islet in the middle of the bay,*" Little Eagle wrote in his notebook, "*The bay itself is guarded by a five-mile long island called the Dark Island, which has watchtowers on it. Any ships attempting to enter the bay would be seen long before they entered. Confined to the channel, they would be forced by its narrowness to enter in single file, and would be blown to pieces one by one by the cannon in the fortress as they approached. 30-40 ships can anchor comfortably under the fortress' guns. It cannot be surprised by land. Big dogs—which are tied up during the day—roam free at night to give the alarm.*"

Thus his report continued for three pages, together with a chart of the entire Gulf of Kereme. It ended on one positive note, however. Halikarnassos had no sources of water. Every single surface stream ran bitter (at what risk to himself had he obtained *that* piece of information?), forcing Halikarnassos to rely on fourteen enormous rainwater cisterns for its water supply. "*Certainly it can provide safe harborage, but what use to ships is a harbor with no water to replenish their casks?*

Safe or not, they cannot stay there more than a day or two unless it rains.

Chapter VI
Green over the Bows

Our convoy put back into Istanbul in mid September, when the weather was still relatively fine and the White Sea calm at least three days out of four. As happened aboard any ship making port that time of year, we speculated about whether we would be sent back to sea again, or whether it had now grown too late in the season for a last assignment. We fully expected to be sent out again. There was even a section of the quay reserved for ships like ours who were waiting to hear one way or the other. We busied ourselves doing light repairs, keeping the ships in readiness.

The collision, when it happened, was thus clearly visible to us from our berth along the quay.

Emniyet was returning to the Horn from one of her training cruises. She was well inside the mouth, needing only to make one last tack in the light breeze to take her into her berth. What ought to have been a routine maneuver turned abruptly into chaos when she inexplicably missed stays while coming about. Her mainsail luffed as the wind went out of it. Another gust caught her bow and blew her back across the path of two of the oncoming galleys of the Mykonos squadron, who were also returning to dock astern of her. The galleys dropped their oars and backed water furiously, but it was too late. They were moving too fast to stop completely. The nearest of the two drifted down onto *Emniyet,* and the second galley drifted down onto the two of them. From a distance, the collision did not seem forceful enough to do much damage, but one of the galley's foresail yards came crashing down across first her own deck and then across *Emniyet*'s, binding the ships together in a tangle of sail and rope. I could see people thrown into the water by the impact, swimming, and climbing back up the ropes that were thrown quickly down to them over the gunwales. Helpless to untangle themselves or to maneuver with their oars, the ships were blown slowly into the shallows and onto the mudflats against the shore.

Thus began what would later go down in our navy's lore as "the Afternoon of Loud Curses." Bayulken sent *Akdogan* and *Hilal*'s crews along the shore to help untangle the ships and lever their bows off the flats, while *Yildirim* tried to pull them apart with ropes from the water side, backwatering her oars.

"How much damage?" Bayulken was scowling when we had finally pried them off the mudflat and gotten them apart.

"About ten feet of *Emniyet*'s port side is stove in," Little Eagle reported. He and I had drawn straws to decide who would bear the news, and he had lost. "Above the water line, fortunately. The other two have rigging damage and a broken yardarm."

"Broken oars?"

"At least two dozen."

"Hmph, well," Bayulken muttered. "We'll need space at the dock to repair them. We'll have to move *Akdogan*, *Yildirim*, and *Hilal* somewhere to make room for them."

"Admiral Kemaladdin will have someone's blood in a spoon for this," Iskender whispered to me behind his hand.

"There's room at the docks over at Yenikapi," Hasan suggested.

"Very well. Let's get *Yildirim* and the squadron across then."

In truth, we were all too glad to have a reason to be somewhere else at that moment. We rowed the ships across the Horn and around the palace point to Yenikapi. We were surprised to find a group of eight passengers waiting for us on the docks. They, and their baggage, were guarded by what looked like at least a hundred janissaries. Even more surprising, no less a personage than Huseyin Bey, Bayezid's personal secretary, was also there. He handed Captain Hasan, Bayulken and Gokhan each a letter and a bundle of charts and notebooks that had obviously come straight from the palace by no one's hand but his own.

"You recognize the seal, captains?" Huseyin asked, holding the letters up.

"We do."

"Go with God, then," Huseyin said as he handed them their orders.

Hasan read his slowly. To all of us pretending not to be staring from the deck, and in a fever to know what was going on, it seemed he took an age. "It seems we are putting to sea. Tonight," he said to me very quietly, as he came up the stern ladder on deck. He handed me the bundle of charts and notebooks. "These are the sailing notebooks for the waters where we are going, but you are not to open them until we are at sea. Even then, you are to open only the first one."

I took the bundle, conditioned to obedience, trying not to let my face show the questions that were racing through my head. It was already almost October.

"They need someone who can cross the sea fast. And we are the ones they chose."

"Where to first?"

"Skiros first, then Pireus, and Cape Taynaron. After that, I don't know. Sealed orders. I am to open them only after we leave Taynaron. We'll be sailing close to the coast at least, which at this season is the only sane thing to do."

He turned to Berk, who was grinning from ear to ear at the anticipation of adventure. "I want extra anchors. No telling when we might have to anchor off a dangerous shore. I don't want *Akdogan* blowing onto a shoal."

Bayulken and Gokhan came over to confer with him on the quay. "We need to lighten the ships if they are to rise properly to the winter waves," Gokhan pointed out.

"Yes, I was thinking that too," Hasan said.

"The basilisks, do you think?" Gokhan broached the topic slowly.

"Leave them on shore, you mean?"

All three captains turned the idea over in their minds. "If we run into trouble, we can trust to the culverins and falconetti," Gokhan said slowly. "And without the basilisks, the bows would be lighter by more than two and half tons each."

"Even more, since we won't need the large cannon balls to go with them."

The reluctance was clearly visible in each of their faces. To dispense with the most powerful gun on the ship was not a decision any galley captain would make lightly. In the end, however, they made it. The sea—rather than an unlikely encounter with a hostile ship—was by far the greater danger. One by one, we nosed *Yildirim*, *Akdogan*, and *Hilal* up to the dock under the crane and slung the bridles under the basilisks' trunions. It took four oxen winding the capstan to hoist the weight, but slowly the massive bronze barrels rose out of their carriages and were swung over to the shore.

Evidently the janissaries at Yenikapi had been instructed to give us anything we wanted, and to do it in about half no-time. They saluted Yigit brightly and put themselves at his disposal to help load our passengers' belongings, as well as the supplies for the unexpected voyage. If we were to sail before dawn, there was much to be done. Two of the passengers came aboard *Akdogan* and went below without saying a word, while another four—one of whom seemed to be European—went aboard *Yildirim*. The last pair went aboard *Hilal*. *Bayezidiye* would not be coming with us. Her hull was smaller and lower than the other three ships, too low to risk the heavy autumn rollers we could expect to encounter at sea at this time of year.

Of the passengers, four of them seemed by their clothes to be very important people indeed. The others accompanying them were presumably their servants. Not that we needed the clothing to tell us this. Anyone important enough to be sailing at this time of year was very important indeed. Galleys did not offer the most comfortable accommodations, being built for speed and duty, but *Akdogan* had four small cabins built into the raised space under her stern deck. One of them was Captain Hasan's, who cleared his things out of it and announced that he would sleep with the other officers under the canopy which covered the stern deck.

"So, whatever it is we are doing, it is big," Ozkan said.

Thus we left Istanbul stealthily in the night, no flags flying, no bands playing on the point to see us off. The moon was a waning last quarter, giving us a fairly dark night to hide our leave taking. Everyone aboard had now guessed that the accident that previous afternoon had been elaborately choreographed to divert attention and to provide a plausible reason to move the ships to Yenikapi. It was far less likely that anyone would notice our absence from Yenikapi on the morrow than if there had suddenly been three unexplained empty berths in the naval docks at the Tersane. At the very least, it might buy us several days. Clearly, a staggering amount of planning had gone into this.

"Poor *Emniyet*," Berk said to me. "She's taken another beating for us."

"Someone has gone to a great deal of trouble to get us away unnoticed," I agreed. "Ah, *Emniyet* will mend. She always does. She'll be whole before we get back from—"

"Don't say it; it's bad luck."

"—from wherever it is we're going."

We belted down the Marmara Sea and fetched Cannakale with the wind behind us the following evening. In an hour we had topped off our water casks, and were headed south into the Aegean that same night.

The island chains of southern the Aegean, the Cyclades and the Dodecanese stretch towards each other and funnel the winds which sweep down from the Black Sea. Any ships going with the wind—as we were—can sail as fast as the proverbial arrow that an Ottoman ship is supposed to be able to catch when shot from its own deck. For the rowers, every mile spent under sail was one less mile to row, and they savored the time.

One of our passengers seemed familiar to me. As I stood at the helm, and he paced the stern deck, I tried to place him.

"I think the tall one is Usun Kasim," I whispered to Berk. "We've seen him at the palace."

"Who, the Sultan's Chief Gatekeeper himself?"

"Yes."

"Well, well. That would explain what we are doing sailing west in so much of a hurry. And the European-looking fellow aboard *Yildirim*?"

"No idea."

The identity of *Akdogan*'s passenger was soon confirmed. Before he had become the Sultan's gatekeeper and envoy, Usun Kasim had been the *Sanjakbey* of Gelibolu, in charge of the fleet and arsenal there. During his service there he had been revered by his crews, and it was inevitable that the older veterans in the squadron would eventually recognize him.

After rounding Taynaron's southernmost point, we headed north and then west into a grey and angry sea. As the southernmost point of the Peloponnesus sticking out into the Mediterranean, Cape Taynaron took the winds full on its bluffs. Once beyond it, we were exposed to its full force. Taynaron was a boundary of another kind too, between those waters which we thought of as being mostly 'ours,' and the waters which were home to European fleets.

The October rollers marched steadily towards our port bow, thudding against the hull, before passing under us. The clouds aloft were going one direction; the wind blowing another. A sure sign of trouble. To reduce the sail area, Captain Hasan ordered double reefs tied in both the main and the foresail. Even under reduced sail, the ships of the squadron bounced around like skittish horses. I tried—unsuccessfully—to figure out what was making *Akdogan*'s bow skip awkwardly off the wave crests every time she came down the back of one.

Captain Hasan opened the last of the sealed orders with some ceremony on the stern deck as Taynaron receded behind us and low roiling clouds tumbled across the headlands to our starboard. He read them through silently to himself twice, almost as if he did not believe them, then announced to the crew, "We're to take our passengers to Valona. Once there, the squadron will be given a safe conduct to sail to...," he paused for effect, "Italy."

The West! Beyond the borders of the Ottoman Empire. The world of the firenks. A world almost none of us on board had ever seen. My only experience of the west having been the inside of a prison cell on Crete—which didn't really count—I was as excited and nervous as all the others.

"From Valona, we'll have a dangerous dash across fifty miles of open Adriatic to Brindisi," he said more quietly to me, "and from there, up the coast to Ancona."

The orders having been opened and the squadron now well on its way, Usun Kasim felt able to drop a little of the secrecy. He did not mind it when Hasan addressed him formally on the stern deck by his real name. He was on his way to Rome all right, and the envoy aboard *Yildirim*, Koca Mustafa, was on his way—by express invitation—to Venice. The European accompanying Mustafa aboard *Yildirim* was Giorgio Bocciardi, a papal nuncio. It was Bocciardi's haste to return to his master in Rome which was the true urgency behind our voyage. The third Turkish envoy, whose name no one chose to tell us, was on his way to King Alfonso's court at Naples.

We rowed and we bailed. Every fourth or fifth wave came green over *Akdogan*'s bow, and I thanked heaven for our captains' wise decision to leave the basilisks on shore. When we were under sail, the spare rowers bailed buckets of water out of the hold; when we were under oars, the sail-handlers bailed. Bail as they might—and they bailed like djinns, truly—*Akdogan* never had less than one or two hand spans of water in her hold. It sloshed around unevenly, giving the hull an awkward stagger and a sluggishness when responding to each wave which I found unnerving. She was struggling, and I did my best to handle her gently. The Morea is not a coast you want to make a mistake against. It may have been mostly in Ottoman hands, but rocks are rocks. Apart from the three Venetian colonies of Monemvasia, Modon, and Coron—port cities which clung like isolated apples to their harbors and to a few square miles of shoreline surrounding each of them—the coastline was under our flag. That was some comfort.

I unsealed the notebooks one by one and had Semih read every page of them to me aloud, both for my learning and his. They were not the most reassuring of subject matter, but I was glad of the warnings they contained.

Given the lateness of the season, we stayed inshore of rocky Ithaca and Corfu, which both still belonged to Venice at that time. Contrary to usual practice, we chose to take the sheltered, but slightly longer route, between them and the mainland. It went against the grain, and ordinarily no Otto-man galleys would have confined themselves thus. The risk of being trapped against the land by the surprise appearance of hostile ships normally would have been tactically unaccept-able. We trusted to our treaty with Venice to keep that from happening. We knew that the states of Italy had far bigger enemies than us to worry about at the moment. Off Corfu, a squadron of Venetian galleots came out of harbor to look us over. Bayulken had ordered the culverins pulled well back and secured. The wooden palings in front, which were usually kept opened, were lowered to make it obvious that we were not aggressively inclined. After an hour or so sailing close to us on our windward side, the galleots hauled their wind and turned back to Corfu, their curiosity apparently satisfied.

We made Valona from the southernmost point of Cape Taynaron in just seven days, close-hauled with the wind on our port sides almost the entire distance. You oglans at the palace who will someday be copying these pages may not be-lieve this rate of speed was possible, but I swear on the beard of my captain that what I and Little Eagle have written in our notes is true. You will have stranger things to record before this voyage is over.

Approaching Valona, we passed the southern cape of double-backed Sazari Island, which guards the mouth of the enormous Gulf of Karaburun, in which Valona sits. The gulf's shallow, sandy bottom caused the waves coming in from the sea to pile up high and steep as they got close to the land. The shallowness of the bay caused its waters to change color in vivid bands of green, light blue, and turquoise according to depth. Because of the gently shelving shoreline, the bay was shallow quite far out, and there were no docks long enough to get out to the deep water. All ships putting into Valona were hauled up on the shore stern-first, except for the deep-hulled sailing ships, who rode at anchor in the gulf.

We entered Karaburun Gulf running wing-and-wing before the strong October wind.

"Kachak, have you ever made a downwind stern landing before?" Hasan asked.

I shook my head. "Never in a wind like this. But I've seen it done," I added quickly to show that I was not daunted by the attempt. "I mean, I know the sequence."

"Good. We'll take it very carefully."

In truth, I was daunted. Landing stern-first with this kind of wind behind us was about as complicated a maneuver as a galley can attempt. Risky too. The beach was full of ships being laid up for the winter. The few spaces remaining for us to land in were small, without any room for mistakes. *Akdogan* was fairly breaming through the water, oar blades cleated up and out of the way, the white foam on the crest of her bow wave roaring away from her beak.

When we were still a mile out from the beach, Hasan sent four of the crew up to the main yard. "Buntlines! Mainsail brail up!" he ordered. The sailors at the foot of the mainmast let the sheets go from the pinrail to slacken the sail and allow the sailors on the yard to furl it. The huge sail began to flap and bang in the wind as the sailors fought to gather it in and bunch it up on the yard. As less of its surface was exposed to the wind, it became easier to control. Other sailors on the deck hauled the braces to bring the yard inboard so that it was aligned with the middle of the ship. This was the part which had to be done quickly, fighting the mainsail yard's natural tendency to blow out to one side and to spin the ship as it resisted the wind. We had to make sure it came to rest on deck instead of trailing over the columbarium and into the water. At this speed, if the yard dipped suddenly and caught the waves, it would snap the mast right out of the ship. The feel of the tiller in my hands changed as *Akdogan* lost a little of her speed.

"Loose halyards!" With a squeal, the halyards ran up through the pulleys, the ends uncoiling rapidly and evenly from the deck as the yard was lowered into its forks.

There, the first part was done. Now came the much harder part.

By now we were quite close to the shore, still moving quickly under foresail alone. Because the foremast was too far forward to brail up the foresail in the same way, it would have to wait until we made our upwind turn.

"Helm hard to port!" Hasan called.

"Hard over," I called, and put the tiller over as far as it could go, feeling it bite against the water and fight me like a living thing, trying with all its might to straighten itself and fling me across the stern deck.

The turbulent water seemed to snarl under *Akdogan*'s stern as she rounded hard into the wind, turning sharply one hundred and eighty degrees in less than three of her own hull lengths. From running free before the wind, as she had been a moment ago, Akdogan was now pointing almost directly into it. As intended, she slowly came to a stop as the foresail spilled its wind, her stern now pointing at the beach barely fifty arshin away.

"Let go both anchors and pay the hawsers out. Foresail halyards loose," Hasan commanded, cupping his hands over his mouth. To Berk and Ozkan, almost in the same breath, he shouted, "Blades to water! Hold!" This was the part that had to be done all at once, without a single misstep. The rowers popped the handle ropes off the cleats as the foresail came thundering down. The blades smacked down into the water flat, then were squared to hold water. In places the water burbled white over the tops of the blades as they dragged. We were half a hull length from the beach, almost stopped. The tiller was dead in my hands.

"Ease the hold. Blades half turn. Feather. Slowly. Easy. Very good."

My job now was to keep the rudder absolutely straight as the ship let the wind blow her slowly backwards onto the land. If the flow of water past caught it to one side or the other, it could snap it off the sternpost.

"Oars up!"

There was a gravelly rubbing sound under *Akdogan*'s hull as she brushed the shallows and coasted to a stop. Berk, Ozkan, and I swung down the stern ladders and leapt to the beach, ropes in our hands, to begin making her fast. Sailors from the other ships already on shore ran up to us hauling ropes and tackles which were mounted to rings in stone blocks to haul the ship far enough up on the shore so that she would stay. Up on *Akdogan*'s bow, the foremast crew taughtened the anchor cables to keep her bow into the waves. Doing my best to seem unperturbed, I slowly let out my breath with relief. From the shore, now that my work was done, I was able to watch *Yildirim*, a little slower than *Akdogan*, execute the same maneuver, with *Hilal* close behind her.

We spent two days in Valona, whose huge bay was our navy's frontier bastion, and the edge of the Turkish world. Beyond it lay the West and all the mysteries it contained. The women of Valona did not wear veils, but only hats, and went about with their faces uncovered. This was a new experience for the crew. We were astounded to find that the town—and the hills surrounding it—was full of encamped Turkish cavalry, their tents stretching for miles. There must have been more than ten thousand of them.

Captains Bayulken, Gokhan, and Hasan selected Berk, Ozkan and me to escort them to the house of the Italian merchant who handled the business interests for the westerners in

Ancona and who acted as a sort of consulate for them. Without comment, he handed Hasan the safe conducts our ships would need to enter western waters. They were impressive documents, with big wax seals showing the crossed keys of the papacy.

"I never thought I would ever hold one of *these* in my hands," Gokhan mused, turning it over several times.

"It's almost a 'religious' moment for us, eh?" Bayulken said, slightly awed in spite of himself.

It was then that the merchant told us the astounding news that Charles VIII of France, with an army of thirty thousand men, had made good his long-standing threat and had crossed the Alps and invaded Italy. Charles had declared that his march was not aimed against Italy as a whole. His only intention, he said, was to seize the crown of Naples, which he called no more than his due inheritance. He asked the northern city states for free passage for his army, and promised to make the pope annul Alfonso's coronation and to crown him, Charles the true King of Naples in Alfonso's place. Once that was done, Charles promised, he would carry out his plan to use Naples as a springboard to lead all of Christendom in its long-awaited offensive against the Turks.

"I would guard those safe-conducts well, captains, if I were you. You will be sailing into dangerous waters."

"Why is it everywhere we go there is a problem," Berk commented laconically back on the ship when I relayed what I had heard.

"Problem?" I shrugged. "We don't know the meaning of the word, do we lads? Hey, Inanc," I called him away from sponging out one of the falconetti's barrels, "would you call one of the largest firenk military operations ever mounted in our lifetimes a *problem*, exactly?"

He considered for a moment. "Well, yes, now that you've brought it up, I rather think I would. Exactly, in fact. And the presence of all those cavalry troops here is beginning to make sense."

"Ah well, lads, there you have it. 'Out of the oil; into the hail'."

"That's us alright," Berk said.

Chapter VII

"Out of the oil; into the hail"

At that time of year, the Strait of Otranto could be safely crossed only in daylight. A single day's hard sailing or rowing, perhaps, but a day nonetheless. To be out on the open waters at night would have been unthinkably dangerous. Darkness could hide the signs of an approaching late autumn storm, or make it impossible to read the wavelets that showed the direction and strength of the gusts on the water. In order to give ourselves more time to make the passage, and to take advantage of the calmer waters of the morning, we put to sea in the faint half-light an hour and a half before dawn, and were rewarded by the sight of the sun rising magnificently over the Dalmatian coast astern of us. All sea voyages change you in some way; you return to the land different, more seasoned, than the person who you were when you left. This sea voyage, crossing as it did the boundaries of what we thought of as our world, would change us more than most. Halfway across the Strait, we could see the dark blue line across the horizon that we knew to be Italy. As hour by hour we sailed towards it, it gradually became more sharply defined, eventually forming itself into the rounded hills behind Brindisi.

Because we were under sail, the rowers were free to stare hungrily across at the unknown land we were approaching. Semih and I alternated at the tiller so that we could both have a hand in this crossing and know what it felt like to have steered a ship through western waters.

"Bottom!" somebody lying out on the beak sang out as soon as the dark shapes of rocks and sand below our keel could be discerned. This too was an unwritten tradition upon approaching a new land; calling the shallowing of the waters, the first sign of reconnection with the land.

At Brindisi, we dropped anchor for the night while *Hilal* put the mysterious third envoy and his servant ashore, along with a contingent of twenty sailors and janissaries from her crew to escort them. They were to proceed by road across the peninsula to Naples. At this time of year, it was far safer and quicker—being but two days' ride across the heel of Italy—to go by road rather than to sail around the peninsula and through the turbulent Straits of Messina.

The envoys having been put ashore, the three galleys of our squadron proceeded in company northward up the coast to Ancona. The crescent-shaped, wooded hills which protect Ancona between their two arms came sharply down to the water on either edge of its magnificent bay. One arm of the hilly crescent formed a point of land sticking out into the Adriatic, and sheltered the harbor from the strong winds that blew up the coast. At the hill's crest—its dome visible from far out to sea, was the Cathedral of San Cirio. Next to it squatted the many-windowed limestone block of the episcopal palace where Pope Pius II had died of bubonic plague some thirty years ago while waiting for his warships to arrive, ships which had been requisitioned from all the ports of Europe to carry an enormous army on what was supposed to have been a crushing attack against the Turkish world. Pope Pius' death had dashed those plans. The invasion never sailed. As we sailed past the point and into the bay, we stared solemnly up at the windows that militant pope had died behind.

How little had changed. Again we faced the threat of an enormous European attack. Again the world was poised on the edge of fire and blood.

But some things had. At least for us, Ancona was not a war port. Not yet. As a meeting place and transit point for the trade between east and west, she turned a fairer face to us. By special dispensation from the Vatican, Muslim cargoes could be transshipped there. Even during the inevitable wars, there was always a community of Turkish merchants, keeping low when they had to. In fact, times of war usually rendered cargoes from the east that much more rare, and thus more profitable.

Turgay, their elder statesman and de facto leader, had spent decades in this precarious outpost, and had even rowed aboard firenk ships on more than one occasion. The safe conducts for our journey overland to Rome had been sent to him to await our arrival. He cheerfully made all the on-land arrangements for us, renting a large farm outside the city walls for the crews to live in for the months we would be there. Living aboard a galley for an extended time, especially during the autumn or winter months, was simply not feasible. The cramped conditions would be an invitation to disease.

The squadron was under orders to wait for the embassy's return from Rome and Venice, however long that took. Almost certainly their business in Rome and Venice would last well into the winter months, long after the seas had closed. Our assumption was that we would be wintering over in Ancona and returning to Istanbul the following spring. The captains and their officers would quarter in the farmhouse, while the rest of us bedded down in cramped, but dry, rows on the threshing floors and lofts of the two barns. By the standards we were used to, it was decently comfortable. There was plenty of hay for our sleeping pallets; Inanc and Yigit spent some time jumping on theirs to get the lumps out, to the general hilarity of all of us.

The Venetians had sent a ship of their own to bring Mustafa the final leg of his journey up the coast. It was waiting for him in the harbor when we arrived. In addition to being a much-appreciated diplomatic courtesy, it was a polite way of avoiding the need for a Turkish warship to enter Venetian waters. The last thing the Venetian navy wanted was Turkish warships, crewed by observant sailors, inside their precious lagoon. Defensive considerations aside, the Venetians understandably wished to avoid having to make awkward explanations or denials to their Christian allies.

We did not formally lay the ships up for the winter, although Ancona had the facilities to help us do so, and the artisans along the quay would gladly have taken our money to assist us. With affairs in Italy so uncertain, Captain Bayulken wanted the ships ready to leave at a moment's notice. We 'weathered' them, half-lowering the yardarms and using them as ridgepoles to drape the sails over like tents, to cover the decks. The idea of consigning our precious oars to a firenk warehouse made us uneasy, so we stored them aboard the ships in makeshift cradles in the center walkways between the masts. Storing them in the hold would have been far better for them, but it would have taken too long to slide them all out through the hatches if we needed to leave in a hurry. "If they warp, they warp," Hasan said. "The Tersane can always make us new ones. That's the least of our problems."

Bayulken assigned me the task of keeping track of the days according to our own calendar by keeping count of the phases of the moon, and thus reconciling for everyone the firenk months which were of varying length and did not correspond even remotely with the moon.

Turgay saw to the complicated business of hiring the train of horses and mules we would need for the journeys to Rome and Venice. There was some discussion of the size of the escort that our two envoys and the papal nuncio would need. In addition to defending against the brigands who made the roads dangerous; we also wanted to make something of a strong showing upon our arrival in Rome. It was decided that Usun Kasim and Bocciardi's escort would consist of Captain Hasan, Berk, Ozkan, Inanc, Yigit, twelve of *Akdogan*'s janissaries, and me. Bayulken would stay in Ancona to oversee the squadron, and everyone else not assigned to the escort would wait at Ancona with the ships until we returned. Turgay had procured us good horses and a dozen very patient mules, the kind who look at you mournfully and patiently with big eyes as you tie their bridles to the mule in front of them, and who never once try to bite you.

We left Ancona on the thirteenth day of the month the firenks call November. By one of those coincidences of the two calendars, that day was also the thirteenth of our month of Safar. Inanc chose to take this conjunction as an auspicious omen. The road from Ancona led north along the coast, past long stretches of sand and waves on one side, and flat and prosperous-looking farmland to the other. We stared about us, curious and excited to be riding through a foreign country. About ten miles north of Ancona the road came to the small town of Falconara Marittima. There it crossed the Ensino River over a four-arched stone bridge that had probably been there since Roman times. On the far bank of the river, the road branched, one branch continuing north along the coast, the other turning southwest towards Rome. Crowning a small hill a few hundred yards beyond the bridge on the north side of the river, there was a small castle of warm yellowish-grey stone, built presumably to guard the crossing and to assure the collection of the tolls. I could see one sentry on the top of the square stone entrance tower, and another leaning on one of the machiolations on top of the curved outer wall. As we began to cross the bridge, I noticed dust rising on the horizon in front of us to the north.

Yigit and his janissaries had noticed it too. "Horses! A lot of them."

"An escort?"

"Perhaps," Yigit said dubiously. "It sounds rather large for one."

I reined my horse in. "What is Bocciardi looking so nervous for?"

"Something's not right."

Yigit shot a glance at the castle and lifted his head slightly in that direction.

Hasan followed his glance and nodded back. "If we have to, yes."

As they came closer, we could count between two hundred and two-hundred and fifty cavalry, well-armed.

"Perhaps we should ride back to Ancona."

"I doubt we'd make it. If we have to run, the castle is a better choice. They won't expect us to head for it."

Captain Hasan and I rode forward past the other animals to settle the toll. It was a large one, and it took some time for the toll keeper to tally up all of our animals and decide on the final figure. The horsemen were coming closer. I could not see their banner clearly because the wind blew it towards us, edge on. Then a gust blew it sideways a little, and I thought I glimpsed two golden crossed keys.

It made no sense at all.

They were upon us before we could leave the bridge.

"I am Giovanni della Rovere, Prefect of Rome; halt in the name of the Pope." A big man. I got an impression of a lot of nose, black mustaches, and a bushy beard all pushing out together from under his helmet. His men had light cavalry crossbows, and they were leveled at us. Georgi Bocciardi had turned pale.

"I am a papal nunc—"Bocciardi started to say.

"And I am the Prefect of Rome," della Rovere cut his protest off mildly, but with that casual firmness and control that only someone who has more than two hundred armored cavalry behind him can summon up. He indicated the cross-bows with a significant glance, "as Captain-General of the Holy Catholic Church I trump a nuncio any time. Most importantly, my lieutenant is pointing a crossbow at your head."

The crossbows did not move. della Rovere and ten of his men shouldered their horses roughly past us, towards the pack mules. He motioned to one of his men, who lifted the first of the two of Kasim's boxes off the mule's panniers and set them on the ground. At a nod from della Rovere, he smashed one of the boxes open.

I gasped when the lid flew back, and I was not the only one. They were crammed with golden coins. I had no idea how many; it was more money than any of us had ever seen in one place, not even in the Hall of the Treasury. della Rovere's soldiers crowded around them, excited as schoolboys. It was the moment of distraction we needed, and we knew we would not get another.

"Now!" Yigit yelled, and wheeled his horse around in a tight circle, kicking one of the boxes to the side and scattering a spray of golden coins on the ground. I rode mine into the horse carrying one of della Rovere's troopers, shouldering it off balance and causing it to stumble out of the way. I saw Ozkan do the same with his. The nearest of della Rovere's soldiers were busy scrambling for the coins; others behind them were pushing forward to see what was on the ground. I grabbed the reins of Kasim's horse as I kicked mine into a gallop, and pulled his horse into motion. "My lord ambassador, can you ride?" I asked, mindful of his years.

Kasim tucked himself down close to his horse's mane, "An Anatolian boy like me, and you ask whether I can ride?" and he left me in his dust.

Our horses were fresh; theirs had ridden all the way from Sinagaglia. They were weighed down by armor; we were not. And we were going up a hill, where the horse carrying the lighter burden has the advantage.

Shots rang out behind us. We lowered ourselves as close to our horse's necks as we could and trusted to haste and panic to send the shots wide. An arquebus had to be fired when still in order to be fired with any accuracy. The moment of delay they had wasted to get off their confused shots had bought us another bit of time. I was more worried about the crossbows, which could—in the hands of an extremely skilled rider—be shot from a moving horse. I saw some black burrs go by to my left, and heard the angry hum of the crossbow bolts, but they were high and wide. We thundered up the lane towards the drawbridge. If we could only buy enough time to get across and close it behind us. I don't think any of us had a plan of what we would do after that, or how we would overcome the garrison, if garrison there was.

Behind me, I heard Bocciardi's frightened yell of "*Succur meum!*" abruptly choked off. I wheeled my horse around to take up the rear of our little flying column. Five of the janissaries were doing the same, protecting the escape of everyone else. Kasim's servant was gamely charging along; he was the last of the Turks. The road curved slightly to the right just before the castle, hiding us momentarily from the pursuers.

"Take care of our people first, then worry about Bocciardi only if you have time," one of the janissaries shouted. "He's a papal nuncio. These are *his* people."

From the start of the fracas, della Rovere's soldiers had been closer to Bocciardi than to us, and it occurred to me—much later—that Bocciardi must have been their main quarry as much as the caskets of gold had been. Bocciardi had tried to make a start at getting away when he saw the rest of us break for it, but della Rovere's horsemen were on him too fast for him to get more than a few hundred feet.

We thundered across the drawbridge under the tower and into the courtyard, sliding off our horses in one smooth motion before they had time to come fully to a stop. "The bridge!" Hasan shouted, and we ran for the windlass to raise the drawbridge. The janissaries leapt straight at the counter-weights, using their own weight to swing them down and to raise the bridge the first ten feet.

The first of della Rovere's soldiers on horseback were riding straight at it, less than fifty yards away. The bridge swung up before they could get to it, making a gap they could not leap. In the moment their hesitation bought us, Berk, Ozkan and I had the windlass going, and we slowly raised the bridge the rest of the way. Shots began to ping off the stones, and there was a lot of shouting outside on the topic of infidel dogs, surrendering, and nooses around our necks.

"You lot, up to the parapet," Yigit ordered, "try to hold them off." It was only then that I realized he was still on his horse, swaying, his face grey. A trickle of blood ran out of his right sleeve and down across his hand. He tried to swing himself down from the saddle, and Inanc caught him under the arms as he fell.

"To the captain!" one of the janissaries yelled.

"You'd best not be wearing one of my shirts," Inanc said softly. "You are, aren't you?"

Yigit managed a tight grimace. "You bastard," he forced a laugh. "The blood won't show against the blue."

Inanc laid him carefully on the stones and opened the shirt to the waist. There was blood all over Yigit's chest and shoulder. "It looks worse than it is, OW, stop doing that!" Yigit hissed through clenched teeth.

"Kachak! Water!" I was already running to the well in the center of the castle's courtyard, wishing I had my little box of soldiers' medicines with me, but it was back aboard *Akdogan*.

Yigit was right. It did look worse than it was. Once cleaned, it was not nearly so threatening, though it was still bad enough. The arquebus ball had ripped across the outside of his upper arm, leaving a messy wound, but not a particularly dangerous one as long as it was kept clean. "Someone find a needle," I said, "it needs to be stitched. And some vinegar or wine to kill the infection."

Even in the confusion, Mete and the other janissaries were thinking quickly. They ran nimbly to search the small buildings set along the inside of the wall, and four of them took the stairs up to the guard tower to deal with whatever garrison might be lurking there. Which turned out to be nobody. The only defenders were the two sentries we had seen earlier on the walls. They were presently standing quietly in the courtyard, swords drawn but not pointing them at anyone.

"Who are you lot then?" the senior of them asked.

"We are on our way to Rome. We've been attacked."

"Yes, you certainly have been. You are enemies of the pope?"

"Not at all. In fact we were on our way to him. We're envoys—"

"There's a man out there with a papal banner pointing a gun at you," the sentry cut me off. "I'd say that makes you an enemy of the pope...and probably friends of ours. We have no love for the papal tithes here."

"It's actually the Lord of Sinigaglia—"

"Him neither. Even less. There's a barrel of powder in the guard tower. Not much, but you're welcome to it."

"What is the name of this place?"

"Rocca Priora. It belongs to the Count of Conti. He's in Naples," he said conversationally, as if that was where anyone sensible would have been.

"'First Rock'?" I translated uncertainly.

He nodded. "Close enough."

I stepped backwards and half tripped over something which proved, on subsequent inspection, to be a box of arquebus cartridges which someone had dragged out from against the wall. It had a needle in it for sewing the cartridge bags. I pushed them out of the way, and set about threading it. "Hold still."

"Hey," Yigit said, "are you sure you know what you're doing?"

"Just like stitching a sail." The janissary corps made a point of trusting only its own doctors, but we didn't have one of those, and I was the closest thing to it. Thanks to my Enderun training, which had been handled by janissaries anyway, I did not do such a bad job of it. I tried not to think, "This is *Yigit*'s blood flowing across the ends of my fingers; this is *Yigit*'s arm I'm sticking a needle into," but instead to act as if it were indeed only a piece of sailcloth.

"I hadn't expected to get into a shooting war on Italian soil," Hasan said.

One of the janissaries had made a careful count from the battlements, confirming our hasty count from the bridge. "Two hundred fifty," he reported, "all cavalry. Crossbows and swords, a few arquebuses."

"Spare mounts?" Yigit asked quickly.

"None, efendim. It looks as if they were expecting to come just for the day."

"Well, if we have started a war, at least we've started it by taking a castle."

"What have we got to hold them off with?"

"Nothing heavy, if that's what you mean. No cannon, just our arquebuses and bows. This castle doesn't even have a sally port where we might sneak out and take them by surprise, or try to get away. The drawbridge is the only way out, or in."

We took up positions spaced along the parapet. Nothing much happened for a long time. The horsemen outside drew up at the bottom of the hill, well out of range.

"I am sorry for bringing you and your men to this, Captain," Usun Kasim said.

"It's what we came for, efendim."

"That is extremely gracious of you to say, Captain, but I'm afraid you don't yet have any idea what you came for, or what you are in for."

"Your journey to Rome," Hasan said. "We were told only this much: that it was urgent. I would say that we were not misled in that, at least."

"That it was. But the part you find yourself in now was never intended to happen. That money you saw sprayed out so unceremoniously on the ground," Kasim explained heavily, "was the forty thousand ducats that our Sultan pays the pope annually to keep his brother Cem in safe, and well-fed captivity."

"Our Sultan pays money to the *pope?*"

"Yes. For years. Ever since Cem fled to Rhodes. First it was paid to the Knights, then—after the Knights submitted him to the pope's custody—to the pope directly. In return, the Knights of Rhodes, and later the pope, promised to keep him cooped up and never to let him lead an army against us. Forty thousand ducats a year—less than the cost of equipping eight galleys—was a small price to pay for peace.

"So now you appreciate the urgency of the voyage, and why you and your crew were chosen for it."

Hasan nodded. "We were honored to be the ones."

"And if the money doesn't get to the pope?"

"He may use Cem as the Europeans have always threatened to do, as a figurehead and justification for a crusade. The pope wrote to our Sultan that Charles of France was coming to seize Cem for that very purpose. Having invited Charles into Italy, the pope suddenly realized what a terrible mistake he had made. That is why he sent Bocciardi to ask for next year's subsidy to be paid early. The pope was desperate to use part of the money to pay soldiers to resist the French."

We were paying the pope money to use *against* Charles? My head was spinning.

"della Rovere's brother, the Cardinal, hates the pope and is sympathetic to the French. No doubt that is why he took the money and why he wants to stop us from getting to Rome at all cost. Somehow, despite all of our secrecy, he knew we were coming."

"That would not have been hard. Three Turkish galleys putting into Ancona; horses and mules being hired; impossible for all that activity not to be noticed by someone who was looking out for that sort of thing."

"I'm sure that—as Captain-General of the Church—della Rovere receives a report on every ship that enters or leaves Ancona. The Curia derives a lot of revenue from that trade. That's why he's just up the road, to watch over it."

"And della Rovere will kill us?"

"If he can. Probably. I'm sure he would prefer that there be no one to report these events. He is the Sword of the Church. As non-Catholics, our lives are of no account to him."

"So, this may very well be the start of war."

Usun Kasim grimaced, "a small start of a much bigger war than any of us can imagine. Bocciardi was carrying letters from our Padishah. Bocciardi—not I—because he was the nuncio; I was sent to accompany the gold. I think we must assume that della Rovere has those letters, as well as Cem's subsidy."

They made an attack during the afternoon, galloping suddenly towards the walls from three directions at once, firing rapidly and wildly before wheeling off again. Yigit said that the attack was designed to shake our nerve more than to take the castle by storm. By putting all that lead in the air so profligately, they wanted to show us that they had all the ammunition they needed.

That evening, we lay awake on the parapet on top of the guard tower, lying below the machiolations and out of the line of fire, with our arquebuses propped up in the embrasures. Yigit, with his bandaged arm was lying on his side, cradling an arquebus in the crook of his other elbow, and making the quiet "tattattata" sound that he often makes when he is planning something. The full moon made it easy to spot the soldiers on the flat ground outside and to keep them away from the walls with the occasional ranging shot. We did not have much ammunition, and della Rovere's soldiers knew it. It was only a question of tomorrow. They were content to wait.

"I had not expected to die in some castle in Italy," Ozkan commented, "Or to spend the rest of my days chained to a firenk oar."

Berk shot him an appraising look. "If you think the firenks will have you. You all realize, of course, that they planned the whole attack in order to obtain my incredible strength for their navy."

"I want for you to know," Ozkan retorted, "that I am— at this very moment—looking around for something to throw at your head."

"What do you think went wrong?" Berk turned serious again. "For them to violate the law of nations and attack an envoy and a papal nuncio?"

Inanc straightened out his foot, which had gone to sleep, and began to rub it. "Kasim said that in all the times he has been to the west as the Padishah's envoy, nothing like this has ever happened."

Hasan shrugged. "Who knows? Perhaps a war has started between them and us. Or perhaps it's just run-of-the-mill firenk double dealing."

Berk rolled over on his side and looked at me. "You have your capture story ready, Kachak?"

"No. Not this time. I've run out of stories."

"Don't be foolish," Hasan said. "At least one of us might be able to get out of this. That's an order," he added gently and sadly.

"Sorry captain. These arquebuses, they must have made me a little deaf." I caught Inanc's grin out of the corner of my eye. "I'm afraid I didn't hear you."

Yigit pointed at the castle's two sentries, who had chosen to stand watch with us. "We should remember to tie them up tomorrow when the attack begins," he said, "so that when their compatriots burst in, they can at least say that we held them against their will. It would be the kind thing to do."

Morning came. The castle was surrounded, and slowly della Rovere's men moved up the hill closer to it, shooting occasionally at the battlements to make us keep our heads down. They had the morning light in their favor. It was on their right sides and slightly behind them. We seldom bothered to shoot back, except when they came very close to the drawbridge port itself.

About midmorning, we saw more horsemen coming from the south, almost doubling the numbers.

"Oh, that's just wonderful. Just as I was thinking that the odds were already too much in our favor," Ozkan quipped.

"Their friends don't look at all happy to see them."

Something strange was happening on the field below. della Rovere's men were wheeling around to face the newcomers, weapons drawn.

"I wonder what this is about."

Incredibly, one of the riders wore a turban. "That looks like Turgay," Berk said, puzzled.

"What? With Italian soldiers?"

The two groups formed up. There seemed to be quite an angry discussion going on, from the walls we could see arms raised and gestures, though we could not hear the sounds. Suddenly, della Rovere's men wheeled away and rode back to the road, heading north at some speed in the direction of Sinigaglia. As they passed along the road between the castle and the bridge some of them waved their fists at us. We saw Bocciardi ride by, looking thoroughly miserable, his hands tied together in front of him, allowing him just enough movement to use the reins. His horse's bridle was tied to the two horses on either side of him to keep him from trying any attempt to break away.

The newly-arrived horsemen rode slowly up to the gate-house and shouted up to the battlements, "Everything is all right now. Truly. You can come out." It *was* Turgay.

Up on the battlements, we exchanged the full silent vocabulary of raised eyebrows and questioning shrugs. A trick?

"Have them stand more than a bowshot away from you," Yigit shouted down to Turgay. The other horsemen withdrew to the distance requested.

Thoroughly mystified, we climbed down and released the counterweights to lower the drawbridge. This was the test. If Turgay was under duress, this would give him a chance to run for it, before the others could catch or shoot him.

He didn't. He ambled his horse slowly and unconcernedly across the bridge into the courtyard, dismounted, and told us the story of how he had come to be there.

After the robbery, and our wild flight to the castle, the toll collector had waited quietly until della Rovere's men had surrounded the castle and all their attention was on us, then sent his daughter unnoticed to ride into Ancona with the news. The Anconians had been outraged at the insult offered an envoy on their soil. They had no love for the Lord of Sinigaglia, and they were mindful of the commercial advantages of their trade with the east. They had hastily gathered a detachment of the garrison from the fortress in the harbor, and ridden out with a column of two hundred professional soldiers intent on driving della Rovere back where he came from and escorting us safely back to Ancona. These, our rescuers, we now allowed to clatter into the courtyard.

We rounded up as many of our hired mules as we could find still outside on the hillside. della Rovere had taken three of them to carry the gold; the others had wandered off to graze docilely in the field around the castle.

We thanked the sentries for their impromptu hospitality, and the toll keeper's daughter for her bravery, Kasim giving them ten ducats each from his private purse. We formed up in a column with our rescuers, and dispiritedly rode the ten miles back to Ancona. Even though we were escorted by two hundred Anconian cavalry this time, we Turks formed a tight ring several layers deep around Kasim the whole way, vowing not to let any firenks—friendly or otherwise—get near him again. From their horses, Hasan and Kasim discussed what was likely to happen next, and what the squadron should do.

More than half of us were thoroughly in favor of sailing straight back to Valona and leaving the firenks to their plots. Hasan was of the same mind, and indirectly made his inclination known.

"Our original orders were to wait in Ancona until you had finished your mission in Rome, but that was because everyone had assumed that would be until sometime next March,"

"It is November, too late to risk sailing," Kasim said sensibly. "And I may still need to go to Rome."

With the seas closing for the season, we were on our own in a foreign land. Istanbul could send us no new orders until spring, and we could not report what had happened to us.

An Italian, very well dressed, rode up close to us, trying to get close to Kasim, but Yigit and his janissaries had their yatagans out, and were in no mood to let anyone approach.

"Please," the Italian said gently, keeping his face admirably composed despite the sword points flicking inches from his chest, "I *must* speak to your envoy."

"Oh? And why must you?"

"I am Bernardino Messaglia, the City of Mantua's representative in southern Italy. I am sorry for what has happened, as I know my Lord the Marquis will be. I sent him a letter by courier last night to inform him as soon as I heard the news."

Yigit looked over at Kasim and Hasan for guidance. Kasim nodded. "It's alright, Yigit. Marquis Gonzaga of Mantua is a friend. And even more importantly, he is presently also the commander of the land forces of the Republic of Venice. I met his envoy two years ago when I was there."

Messaglia rode up close to Kasim, and stirrup to stirrup, they conversed for the rest of the journey. Messaglia quickly proved himself to be a good man to have on our side. He was originally Milanese; his family were famous armorers there, and he had opened a branch of the family business in Mantua to serve its increasingly glittering court. His armor—and his discretion—had come to the notice of the Marquis, who employed him in both the armor and diplomatic businesses. Steel of differing kinds was required in both. Hasan still has the helmet he made for him, years later.

And so, waiting idle back in Ancona, wandering the streets and visiting its shops and taverns, tucked amid the stately palaces built by its wealthy merchants, we picked up the news from the townspeople as every day Italy bled. Charles' army seemed unstoppable in its march south. Asti threw open its gates. Rapallo, Fivizzano, and Mordano were taken by storm, the garrisons and the civilian townspeople massacred. Mordano was a senseless bloodbath of wanton butchery where even children were killed for no purpose other than to terrify other towns and cities into surrendering.

I heard people begin to call it 'il diluvio.' The deluge. Even where there was no killing, even in the towns which opened their gates and greeted the French with flowers, hoping to turn away their anger, the invading army brought famine. With thirty thousand soldiers and their mounts to feed, the land could not support them. The army commandeered the harvests and absorbed the produce of the land so that there was little left for the people who had grown it. Even while the French were still in Tuscany, Rome itself had begun to starve; Charles had blockaded the city and no food was reaching it.

As terrifying as the news and rumors were to the Italians, to us they were even more ominous. "If this is what Charles does to his fellow Christians," Hasan said, "it is only a prelude to what he will do to any Turkish city he attacks."

We kept as low a profile in the town as we could. Ancona was accustomed to Turks on its streets, but most of us bought and wore at least a few western clothes so as not to stand out quite so much. Some of the crew bought rather a lot. They bought things for their wives and their sweethearts back home. The lace collar ruffs gave us no end of trouble. Neither Yigit nor I ever quite learned the trick of getting them to stay straight. Kasim, who was used to western clothes from his previous diplomatic expeditions to Venice and Rome, did his best to show us how they were meant to be worn. Some of the crew could carry it off better than others, and some positively reveled in it. It was quite a surprise one day to come across Murat in full western rig, his doublet fitting him as if he had been poured into it, and every point of his lace collar impeccably in place.

A week after della Rovere's assault on us, rumors reached Ancona that Pisa and Florence had surrendered. People refused to believe it at first; Florence could not have surrendered, they said. It was unthinkable. Florentines never surrendered. They never had; they wouldn't know how. Two days later, the confirmation arrived by mud-spattered courier and was read gloomily every few hours for the next three days from the steps of the town hall. Charles was feasting in triumph in Florence, the Medicis had fled, and all of Tuscany and the Romagna lay open to him.

"Well, that's one fucking treaty I guess we can burn," I overheard Kasim—who obviously found the news as difficult to believe as everyone else—observe numbly. "It will be Rome next."

That Rome might surrender, might be conquerable, was even more unthinkable. Except that nothing was unthinkable any longer. Rome was a city that existed in the pages of books. And it made no sense that the firenks were fighting over it. Rome had always proclaimed her enemy to be the east.

We learned by way of one of Messaglia's couriers that Koca Mustafa had indeed gotten to Venice safely. The Venetians, bless their hearts, were protesting della Rovere's attack against us on his behalf. Mustafa had written a formal complaint to Rome. Though what good that would do, or even whether there would be anyone other than the French in Rome to receive it when it got there, was becoming more and more the question of the hour. At our farmhouse, we chewed over every scrap of news, puzzling over what it might mean and what was likely to happen to us. The Venetians sent one of the Serenissima's toughest sea lawyers, Alvise Sagundino, to the Prefect to protest the attack and demand the money back. The Prefect refused, claiming that he had seized it in lieu of payment for a debt owed him by the Holy See.

"Forty thousand golden ducats is a rather enormous debt," Hasan observed. "I wonder what he must have done to put the papacy so much in obligation to him."

Sagundino, who was meantime also the chancellor of the Venetian fleet, refused to take no for an answer and wrote a blistering letter to Rome. The Pope threatened—and later did—excommunicate his own prefect, to no avail. If proof were needed that the pope's power was weakening, there it was. Daily more and more of the most powerful churchmen abandoned the pontiff and swung to Charles' side.

Spring—and the chance to sail away from all this— seemed impossibly far. 'The year is a tree,' our saying goes, 'one part moist and green, one part dry and grey.'" Every day, Bayulken, Gokhan, and Hasan conferred with Kasim. The tension and uncertainty made it seem like a busy time for us, even though in reality we were hunkered down doing next to nothing.

I never held any dislike against Ancona, then or now, for what happened there. Though a place of unfortunate memories for us, it was not the city's fault. Like all of Italy, it was engulfed by events that were too large for anyone to control or withstand.

The hammer blows kept coming. On the last day of the firenk month of November, when the moon was just showing its first faint sickle, a courier galloped into Ancona from Charles' new headquarters in Florence, and stomped arrogantly up the steps of the town hall. The main square in front did double duty as a market and public gathering place, and the drama of his mud-spattered entry assured him a tolerably large audience for the astounding proclamation he read from the top step. Naturally, we Turks were drawn to the square by the same curiosity, so we were hit by the full impact of what unfolded, along with everyone else.

"*Charles, by the grace of God, King of France, Brittany, and Lorraine, and by inheritance King of Naples and the two Sicilies, salutes all Catholics in the name of eternal God. We declare that, as soon as peace and stability are returned to Italy, and we have regained our ancient rights in the city of Naples, we will repel the dirty Turk who incessantly sheds Christian blood, and we shall recover Jerusalem and the Holy Land, and all those dominions where the majority of the population are Christian—*"

"Dirty Turk!" Inanc hissed under his breath next to me. "We're the ones who bathe. The firenks hardly ever wash."

"—*further, we make it known to all Christians that into our hands have come letters written between the Sultan of the Turks and our own Holy Father Pope Alexander VI. Letters proving that Alexander has been in league with the infidel and has defiled his office with an unholy treachery most dangerous to Christendom—*"

There were angry murmurs from the crowd. Those events were definitely news to them.

"*That Alexander has sent his own nuncio, one Giorgio Bocciardi, to treat with the infidel Sultan, requesting infidel Turkish assistance against us, the Most Christian King of France. We make it known that the pope has received moneys from the Turk—*"

"Get everyone back to the farmhouse; stay out of sight," Bayulken ordered under his breath, sensing the direction this was going. "And do it now!"

"—*and further, that the Grand Turk has prevailed upon the Pope by a letter carried by the nuncio, to murder Prince Cem, the Sultan's own brother. In consideration, we Charles—deo gratia rex Francorum, etc.—declare that the Pope can no longer be considered the safe guardian of Prince Cem, and we demand that he release the Prince into our keeping. In proof, we will publish throughout Italy the five letters that the nuncio Giorgio Bocciardi was carrying when apprehended, together with the confession of the aforesaid Bocciardi that he was carrying forty thousand gold ducats to the pope in Rome. The translation of these letters has been notarized in our presence by Filippo de Patriarchi of Florence.*"

The herald paused to draw a large breath before reading out the colophon in ringing and weighty tones, "Given by our hand in the city of Florence on this twenty-fifth day of November in the year of our Lord fourteen hundred and ninety-four, and in the twelfth year of our reign."

"That the Holy Father himself would do such a thing!" exclaimed a woman near me in the crowd.

"He has sold his own flock to the wolves!" shouted another, but we did not stay to listen. We eased our way slowly and as unobtrusively as we could between bystanders to the back edge of the crowd. As soon as we had reached open space and were clear, we darted off to comb the taverns and shops of the city for as many of our shipmates as we could find, ordering them to get back to the farmhouse. Inanc raced to Turgay's house to leave word with him that something dangerous might be afoot, and then deftly found his way along the narrow farm paths between the hedges. I myself ran down to the docks in case anyone were doing some work aboard any of our ships. I found Murat, Cihan, and Little Eagle splicing ropes aboard *Hilal*.

"Something very bad has happened," I told them. "We have to get back, but quietly. No attention. We'll take the path that goes along the point. Keep low between the rocks. I'll explain as we go."

Partway along, Little Eagle slipped, his right foot missing its intended step and plunging into the gap between two rocks, scraping away the skin on the inside of his shin almost down to the bone. We half-carried him, arm-over-shoulder, the rest of the way, blood squelching out of his left shoe and leaving a little trail of red crescents behind us.

Chapter VIII
Juravi et affirmi

At the door of the barn, Bayulken was keeping watch for us and counting everyone in.

"Are we the last?" Little Eagle asked as we came up the path.

Bayulken shook his head, his eyes concerned. "Iskender, Aydin, Musa, and Tur Ali are not here yet."

This worried me; I was sure that everyone would have been back before us. "Where were they last seen?"

"Murat saw them in the street by the Benincasa palace an hour ago."

"Do you want me to go and find them?"

"No. Nobody stray. If people keep going back out, we'll never collect everyone. If they're not back by night, we'll go looking."

By evening though, everyone was back and safe. We kept the candles burning low, and cooked our supper of mushroom and onion soup in restrained light, taking turns to watch at the windows. No one came to bother us, however. The Anconians were buzzing like bees in a hive, but their excitement and interest was directed at the pope and at the French, not at us. The Italian people were not unused to the Venetians and other city states having commercial and diplomatic relations with the Ottomans. What had upset them—as Charles had clearly intended it to—was the news that the pope himself, as leader of Christendom, was having political relations with the Turks. Charles' proclamation had reaped a harvest of anger, and he was using it. Turgay discretely sent one of his assistants up to us once every other day or so with provisions and whatever news he could gather from town.

On the second day of December, Bernardino Messaglia and a servant rode up to the gate. I happened to be on sentry duty there, with some of the crew, and my recognizing him spared him the tedious necessity of convincing the others—who were naturally suspicious of anyone, and who would have taken a lot of convincing—that he meant no harm. I led them personally to the farmhouse and directed two of the crew to attend to their horses.

"I have a letter for Envoy Kasim, from my lord the Marquis of Mantua," Messaglia announced. "I think he will be gladdened by its contents."

"I'll go see if I can find him, your excellency," I said.

Kasim was in the field behind the barn, absently picking the remaining dried heads of wheat off the few stalks that the gleaners had missed, deep in thought. "Efendim," I said respectfully, "Signore Messaglia is here to see you. He has brought a letter."

"Thank you. I will come at once."

We gathered around the fireplace in the kitchen. Hasan motioned to me and Little Eagle to stay for the discussion. Kasim broke the seal and silently read the letter from the Marquis. "Your master is very generous," he said, looking up.

"The Marquis instructed me to offer you hospitality and protection. He wishes you to come to Mantua. This time, you will have a proper escort, and will travel safely."

"I will give the offer much thought."

"I hope your thoughts will be favorable. Meanwhile, I have been able to find out a little more about the letters Charles published in Florence. The Marquis sent me copies, as well as some news."

Messaglia spread them out on the table for us. "Let's see now. Our Prefect has certainly been a busy boy. After attacking you, he rode back to Sinigaglia with Bocciardi in tow. From Sinigaglia, he wrote almost immediately to his brother, Cardinal Giulliano della Rovere—who is with Charles' entourage in Florence—telling him what he had done, and enclosing the letters. Cardinal della Rovere, who we all know hates the pope and is firmly on the French side, received them around the twenty-second of this month. At least, that is what he told the ambassador from Ferrara."

Messaglia looked up to see how we were following him so far. "I have never had any reason to doubt Ambassador Manfredi's word," he said. "According to what Cardinal della Rovere told Manfredi, four of the letters were sent to the Franciscan convent of...," Messaglia consulted some notes, "...San Croce in Florence to be translated from the original Greek into Latin."

He dropped his voice a little. "In case you do not know, San Croce is where the Inquisition in Florence holds its tribunals."

I jumped a little at this detail.

"The translators were a certain Lascarus Ludovico, the Bishop of Famagusta, and Marullus Tarchaniotes, who describes himself as being 'lately of Constantinople.'"

"What, I wonder, is the bishop of a Venetian colony doing in Florence?" Kasim asked, "And working for the French at that. Doesn't that make him suspect in Venice's eyes?"

"Indeed it does," Messaglia said. "The Council of Ten probably would like to have his head on a plate. And that's not the half of it. The fifth letter, the one that Charles claims the sultan asks the pope to murder Prince Cem,—again, this is according to Cardinal della Rovere's story—was supposedly *already* in Latin. On Charles' orders, it has now been translated into Italian."

"To ensure that it can be more easily understood by the common people?"

"No doubt. Charles is making sure that the fifth letter gets in everyone's ears. The other four are just stage dressing. The translations were notarized by, um, a certain Filippo de Patriarchi."

"Charles' proclamation mentioned him" Kasim observed.

Messaglia nodded. "I'll come back to him. In addition to the letters, Bocciardi has given—or was forced to give—a deposition." Messaglia paused, and then continued in an even more serious tone, "I do not know whether the Prefect had him tortured in Sinigaglia, but it is likely he did. As Captain-General, he would have the Inquisition's most effective questioners at his beck and call."

"San Croce was deliberately chosen, then?"

Messaglia gave me a long appraising stare. "You made that connection very quickly, young sir."

"I was the Inquisition's guest. Briefly."

"Were you indeed?" the tone was sympathetic, respectful, understanding. It occurred to me to wonder whether he too, or someone known to him, had also been subject to their attentions.

"In the deposition, Bocciardi says—or was made to say—that the pope instructed him in mid-July to ask your sultan for aid against Charles. To back up Bocciardi's statement, Charles says he will also publish a letter from the pope to your sultan that Charles says Bocciardi was carrying when captured."

"Why would Bocciardi have still been carrying a letter from the pope *to* Bayezid if he was returning *from* Bayezid to the pope, and had presumably already delivered it?" Kasim asked. "That doesn't make sense."

"Our agent in Florence wondered about that," Messaglia nodded. "Nor is that the only thing that doesn't make sense."

"The timing," Kasim said.

"Yes, the timing," Messaglia agreed.

"Bocciardi was in Istanbul by the first of your month of September," Kasim pointed out. "I know that because Mustafa and I were the ones who accepted his credentials at the palace. Even if Bocciardi rode extremely hard on the road from Rome to Ancona, and traveled that leg of the trip in only two or three days, it would take an extremely fast galley indeed to travel from Ancona to Istanbul in twelve or thirteen days. Which is all that would be left to him if the mid-July date of the pope's instructions had actually been true. But it isn't. His credentials from the pope were dated 26 *June*, not July."

"I'd sure like to have a galley who could do *that*," Bayulken muttered.

"Bocciardi was under duress then," Messaglia said slowly, "and he left us a clue by putting in the wrong month. Brave man. He was telling his captors more or less what they wanted to hear, so he was counting on them not noticing the little slip. If they swallowed the bait, he knew that such a detail might unravel their case later."

"Another thing that is odd," Kasim said. "The first announcements of the interception of the letters claimed that four of the five were written in Turkish, and the other in Latin. But everyone—in the diplomatic world at least—knows that Ottoman diplomatic correspondence with Europe is handled in Greek."

"Someone must have pointed that incongruity out to them, because they corrected that detail later."

We stood around the table looking down at the letters.

"Do we know whether Patriarchi reads Greek?" Kasim asked.

Massaglia shook his head. "I don't know anything about him, or—more importantly—who pays him. There's no particular reason to think he does not. Plenty of scholars in Florence do."

"On the other hand," Kasim observed, "the credibility of the translations rests entirely on his say-so. It would be helpful to know whether his Greek is good enough to certify such accuracy." He touched each of the translations with his fingertips in turn, squinting in thought.

The first translation was a conventional letter of greeting from Sultan Bayezid to Pope Alexander, expressing goodwill in the stock diplomatic phrases. It related that Bayezid had received the pope's envoy, Giorgio Bocciardi, and would be sending his own envoy, Usun Kasim with letters to the pope in return.

The second was a letter of commendation from Bayezid affirming that Bocciardi had carried out his commission as nuncio with integrity and accuracy. The third contained Kasim's credentials to act as envoy. The fourth letter struck all of us as odd. The sultan wrote asking the pope to promote Nicolas Cibo—who Messaglia explained to us was currently the archbishop of Arles—to cardinal. The letter praised Cibo's fitness for the task and called the pope's attention to Cibo's years of service, in mind and body. It too bore the superscript of the notary Filippo de Patriarchi attesting to the correctness of the translation, which was ludicrous on its own face because it was mis-dated the twenty-eighth of December—still twenty-six days in the future.

"Why would the Padishah care an Anatolian fig about Nicolas Cibo being made a cardinal? Or need to bring him to Alexander's attention, seeing as Cibo is a nephew of the former pope?"

"I doubt your sultan even knows, or cares, who Cibo is," Messaglia answered brightly. "But della Rovere certainly does. Cibo is a strong French supporter."

"Perhaps the French manufactured that letter to gain some support for their party," Kasim suggested.

Another possibility occurred to Messaglia. "Or to stir up public outrage. If Charles can convince people that the pope is allowing infidel Turks—begging your pardon, Kasim—to interfere in the governance of the Catholic Church, it weakens the pope's hand even more. Subtle. Who would question it? Either way people take the letter, Charles gains by their reaction."

It was the fifth letter that Charles was counting on to cause the most scandal. Messaglia had brought a copy of the Latin 'original' as well as the vernacular Italian translation. In it, the sultan requested the pope—out of concern for his brother Cem's anguish and tribulation at being a prisoner—to find some 'quiet and commodious way' to transfer Cem's soul from this world to a more peaceful one. In return for this service, the sultan promised three hundred thousand ducats upon receipt of Cem's body in Istanbul, and to let nothing trouble the majesty of the pope or the peace of Christian lands. The coda was different from the other letters too, "written in our palace at Constantinople in the second coming of Christ, on the fifteenth day of September 1494" whereas the others said "given in the courtyard under the authority of our Sultan in Constantinople."

"*Juravi et affirmi...et super evangelia nostra*" I read. "Why would our Padishah have sworn by the law of the gospels?"

"Perhaps he was referring to the Koran, and chose to put it in terms that a pope would understand?" Messaglia said, but his tone of voice indicated that he found this odd as well.

I shook my head. "It's *nostra*," I pointed out. "'Our.' The Sultan of the faithful would never have referred to the gospels as 'our' if he meant the law of the prophet.

Kasim nodded across the table at me, agreeing. "I think Kachak's time on Crete learning Latin among the firenks was well spent," he said by way of validation. "If he is correct, it's either a very clumsy mistranslation, or another sign that the letters may have been forged by someone who doesn't know the intricacies of the east. The colophons are curious too. '*Given under the authority*' sounds like the vague writing of someone who doesn't know exactly how the sultan would sign a letter, and did not wish to be caught out by being too specific. The correct formula would be '*Given in our city of Constantinople on such and such day, of such and such month, in the year of Muhammad, 900, and the 13th year of my reign.*' Even if he were writing to a Christian and wanted to use the Christian calendar in order to be polite, the year of the reign would still be included."

Now that Kasim had piqued our skepticism with his diplomatic experience, we read the letters again with fiercer scrutiny. It is easier to find flaws when you have reason to think they are there, and quickly we found more.

"'Second coming of Christ'? Why 'second'? Messaglia asked.

"You're the Christian in the room," Kasim joked in return for the 'infidel' comment, "You tell us."

Messaglia took it in excellent humor. The hunt for the truth through the fog of deception had given us something to do. "Charles comparing himself to a new messiah, perhaps? No, it must be something else. He would not go that far. Not with Cardinal della Rovere standing next to him. People say the cardinal wears armor under his vestments."

"The salutation lines are odd too," Kasim noticed. "'*Sultan Bayezid Khan, by the grace of God, greatest King and Emperor of Asia and Europe...*' That is not how he usually styles himself." Kasim mulled it over in his mind for a moment. "True, he might use the more aggressive title in a letter to a particular foreigner for effect, but certainly not to one on whom he was on good terms. It's usually '*by the grace of God, great Emperor of Asia and Greece.*' He never lays claim to Europe. At least not in any of the correspondence Mustafa and I have handled, and after all, we're his envoys to that continent."

The light suddenly dawned in Kasim's expression. "But his father the Conqueror *did* use those titles in his letters to the European governments."

Messaglia, experienced diplomat himself, was barely a beat behind him. "So the letters must be forged! The forgers needed a model to base theirs on, and they used the correspondence they were familiar with. They must have found a letter of Mehmet II's in an archive, and assumed that all Turkish sultans would follow the same titulary."

Kasim touched his forehead as a friendly salute between two thinkers who enjoy each other's minds at work. "Ah, your western logic. It has its uses. And this could explain the misdating too."

"You think they were copying one of Sultan Mehmet's letters too closely and accidentally copied the date in their haste?"

"On the knuckle," Kasim murmured, using a Turkish expression meaning, 'it stands to reason.' "And I lay you odds that—once I get back to Constantinople and have a look through the copies in the archives—I can probably figure out from the date exactly which letter they copied."

"And, if they had to resort to one of Sultan Mehmet's previous letters, then they must not have captured any of Sultan Bayezid's real letters when they captured Bocciardi. Else they would have had the correct formula ready to hand. So, Bocciardi must have found a way to destroy what he was carrying? I wonder how."

Kasim shook his head, "If he was carrying letters, they would have been in cipher. della Rovere probably has them, but he cannot read them. No one in Europe—except the pope's foreign secretary—can."

"So, all the business about the authenticity of the translations is just so much smoke," Messaglia said. "Whether in Turkish, Greek, or Latin is beside the point. The "translators" would have had nothing they could work with. They had to make the letters up fresh, based on what they expected would be the normal content of diplomatic correspondence. Charles has certainly gone to a lot of trouble."

"He is playing for very high stakes," Kasim replied. "So, yes, we in this room—and a few people outside of it—now know that the letters Charles is publishing throughout France and Italy are forgeries. Other intelligent people will figure it out too. But enough people all over Europe will believe them to be real for the damage to be done. Look, if our Padishah had wanted Cem dead, why did he send Koca Mustafa to Rome three years ago with 120,000 ducats and the lance head which pierced Christ's side, with orders not to give them to the pope until he had seen Cem alive and in good health? I myself spoke to Cem in Rome last year."

"120,000 ducats?" Messaglia breathed, clearly staggered by the amount.

"Bayezid wants Cem safely confined somewhere where he can live in comfort and not do any harm. The last thing he wants is Cem dead and a martyr in the eyes of his former supporters. Our Padishah wants to keep the Europeans from using him against the empire, as they constantly threaten to do."

Kasim broke off with a slightly puzzled look on his face as another thought struck him. "Come to think of it, Cibo was Cem's translator at the conclave. He was also one of the dignitaries the Curia sent to meet Mustafa at Ancona three years ago to accompany him and the lance to Rome. I wonder if that means anything."

Messaglia pursed his lips, considering. "*Everything* means something these days, so I am sure it does. So, what do we do now? We're all of us in this room convinced that the letters are forgeries, but we also know that very few people outside this room will ever believe us."

"It is for that very reason that I have to continue to Rome," Kasim said. "I must tell the pope what the sultan's real message was. He must on no account turn Cem over to the French. I must show him that the letters are forgeries. He is *not* to have the sultan's brother killed."

"It's not safe for you to go to Rome. Not now," Messaglia countered adamantly. "The last thing the pope wants is to see you there. Your presence in Rome would play into Charles' hands. If a Turkish envoy were to turn up at the papal court now, people will be sure Charles is telling the truth. Besides, the pope is smart enough to know Charles forged them to try to get his hands on Cem. You do not need to risk your life to tell him."

"Besides," Bayulken added sensibly, "Charles' army is already drawing a net around Rome. The French may take the city before we can get you there. Or worse, take the city with us inside. I certainly do not want to be a prisoner of the French, and if Charles launches his crusade, we and our squadron will be needed at sea."

Messaglia looked around the room. "Prisoners?" He shook his head. "You won't be that lucky. Has it occurred to you that we nine have figured out something that Charles doesn't want *anyone* to know?" He turned to Bayulken, "Our necks are for sale. If they should capture any of us—and if they get one inkling of what we know—they will not let us live to see the next evening. Do you have any idea how inconvenient we have just made ourselves?"

Messaglia pointed to the letter he had brought Kasim from the Marquis of Mantua. "That letter, at least, is genuine. I urge you again to consider my master's invitation and come to Mantua under his and Venice's protection."

Contrary to Ottoman custom, we did not require three days to come to a decision on this. Bayulken hardly needed to glance around the room to make his decision. We chose with our eyes. Bayulken was firm, however, that this time we would not trust ourselves to the roads, Mantuan escort or no Mantuan escort. The road to Venice ran past Sinigaglia. "We take the ships," he said. "We trust to our own guns and our own swords. I want them, and their crews, out of Ancona and in our control."

Messaglia agreed with Bayulken's logic. "Yes, we can do that. The River Po is navigable as far as Mantua and even beyond. That is how Mantuans usually travel back and forth to Venice." He smiled. "I think the Marquis will enjoy having Turkish warships docked in Mantua. It will give those Milanese puppets of the French something to think about."

"You are Milanese yourself," Kasim pointed out.

"I serve Mantua, and a free Italy."

Bayulken sent a note back to town with Messaglia's servant to let Turgay know what we were doing. If Turgay could obtain licenses to sail on such short notice from the *capitano* of the port, so much the better. If not, we would simply put to sea without them, and dare anyone to protest. We still had papal safe-conducts, and at this time of year it was extremely unlikely that there would be any other ships at sea to enforce the licenses. As long as the heavy guns in the octagonal stone fortress on Ancona's mole did not open fire on us on the way out—and we did not think that would happen—we would be fine.

The farm had a thriving apple orchard. Autumns are mild in Ancona, and the trees were still heavy with fruit crisped by the sea breezes that blew in from the bluffs. "Every man is to take three or four apples with him," Bayulken ordered. "That will be enough to feed us for a day's sailing. There isn't time to buy provisions in Ancona. We'll resupply when we get to Rimini. Let's just get the squadron away."

Quietly, in groups of twos and threes, we left the farm and made our separate ways into town. It was the work of less than an hour to get the sails off the decks, lay the oars in their thole pins, and prepare *Akdogan*, *Yildirim* and *Hilal* for sea. The sight of three Turkish galleys uncovering their decks in early December drew curious onlookers along the wharf. Impossible that it would not have, but they remained merely curious and no one interfered with us. The people of Ancona had remained generally sympathetic to us ever since della Rovere's attack, and we had been careful not to do anything in our time there to jeopardize that store of goodwill.

"Oars run out!" Hasan ordered. The sailing licenses had not come. We would sail without them and risk the consequences.

Little Eagle, Iskender, and I darted down the stern ladders of our respective ships to untie the lines from the bollards, and just as quickly darted back aboard to take up our stations. It occurred to me that ours might thus be the last Turkish feet in the squadron to touch firenk soil. Except of course that neither Little Eagle nor I were really Turkish. No matter. The more time I spent on firenk soil, the more surely I knew that I was not one of them, and never could be.

Barely looking at each other's oar tips, we took *Akdogan*, *Yildirim*, and *Hilal* out of Ancona's harbor almost blade to blade. The garrison of the fort crowded the walls to watch, but no guns opened fire. To save time, we rowed out of the harbor without waiting to bend the sails back on the yards. We could do that on the water. We remained under oars for some miles offshore until the yards were ready to sling into their halyard bridles.

We made Rimini—as intended—in a single long day of rough sailing, our main and foresails single-reefed. One thing about being at sea in December, you have all the wind you can use. I was exhilarated and terrified the entire sail. The windward backstays were taught as lute strings, and when the wind thrummed through them, they sang like them. Little Eagle and I had no charts or navigation notebooks for the northern Adriatic coast; no one had expected us to be sailing into these waters. Even a rhumb line would have been helpful, but we did not have even so much as that. In a hurried discussion on *Yildirim*'s stern deck before we sailed, Iskender, Little Eagle, and I agreed on a course to sail, and that we would stay ten miles off the coast until we passed Sinigaglia, and five miles offshore thereafter to keep well clear of shoals. It made us feel very much on our own, with nothing to rely on but our sea sense.

"And if fog rolls in?" I said, "should we keep to the compass course, or head inshore?" Neither one was a very appealing choice. Inshore, we could blunder onto a shoal. On the compass course out of sight of land, we could miss our destination entirely. The normal thing for a galley squadron in that situation would have been either to anchor or to beach. We all knew we couldn't do either on this trip.

Little Eagle tilted his head and squinted out to sea. "Clouds are moving too fast. No fog today, not with this wind."

"You're right, but it's also December in the Adriatic. 'Adriatic' is a firenk word that means 'the place where there is always fog in December'."

He permitted himself a small laugh. "See you in Rimini."

"Light your stern lanterns," I reminded Iskender. In case *Hilal* and I need to follow them."

"Any ship we see is a potential enemy now," Bayulken had reminded us, "we cannot be sure of anyone anymore," but apart from a few coasting vessels who stayed well inshore of us, we had the water to ourselves. We beached in Rimini for the night, unmolested, refilling our water casks and re-warding our bellies with a large meal cooked on deck. We spent liberally in the markets for fish, biscuit, rice, and enormous round cheeses. It was the Padishah's birthday, and we attempted to celebrate it in the best fashion we could. Back in Istanbul, there would have been fireworks and processions.

From Rimini, we took the next two days' sail at a more cautious pace—there was fog on the morning of the first of these—and found ourselves on the afternoon of the second day at the southernmost of the four largest mouths of the Po. We dropped anchor, and Messaglia went ashore in *Yildirim*'s jali boat to negotiate for three pilots to come aboard tomorrow and guide us upriver for the five or six days it would take us to reach Mantua.

We were in Venetian territory now, and some of the weight and uncertainty we had been feeling for the past weeks seemed to lift from our shoulders. Venice had a treaty with the sultan; and Marquis Gonzaga was the captain-general of the Serenissima's land forces. Flying the white ensign with the red cross and four black eagles of Mantua from *Yildirim*'s fore-mast, we gained a certain amount of authority. We began to feel a little less like fugitives.

The Venetian pilot who came on board the next morning had eyes as big as silver ducats at being aboard a Turkish ship. I introduced myself and Semih to him as the helmsman and underhelmsman, and I could tell he was bursting with all kinds of questions he would have liked to ask us.

As for myself and Little Eagle, every day we were filling page after page of notebook entries on the new coast and rivers we were sailing, knowing that we were probably the first Ottoman helmsmen to see these waters and coasts—from the deck of a Turkish ship anyway—and that ours would almost certainly have the honor of being the first detailed entries on these waters that the Hall of the Expeditionary Forces received.

The Po was a busy river, a highway of barges in constant procession. I was glad to have a pilot aboard who knew the river and the manners of the other shipping. We moved slowly, taking our place in the file, and tying up along the banks at night with the other barges. People gathered along the banks to stare at the spectacle of Turkish warships so far inland. In places we were quite close to the shore, and people sometimes called out to us, mostly curious and friendly, occasionally hostile.

"Who would have imagined this," Inanc said. "It's all upside down. A sea squadron, but not at sea; Turks sailing on land under a firenk flag, and all our orders gone awry."

"And our three galleys perhaps all that stands between Charles' invasion and Constantinople," Semih said. "Do you think fate intended us to be here for that?"

"Fate must have," Ozkan said, "because no one else could have been clever enough to foresee any of this."

"Not even Daud Pasha?"

"Not even he."

"Do you think we can stop Charles' crusade with just three galleys?"

"I suppose that's what we're here for."

"*Inne bilen guyu gazan boluyoruz*," Ozkan said. "We're digging a well with a needle."

"Perhaps we should have brought the basilisks along after all."

"If we had, we wouldn't have made it this far. We'll need something more than a few basilisks to stop Charles' army."

"The brightness of our minds is worth more than cannons," Inanc said. "The Padishah had us all educated for just this moment, and for just this purpose."

Chapter IX
Mantua

Mantua itself gave us a splendid and wholehearted welcome. It was a city that prided itself on being its own master, and concerned itself little with the impressions and reactions of the people in other towns and cities along the banks of the Po. As we rowed into the largest of the three lakes surrounding the island city, a cannon on the roof of the gate tower facing the long San Grigio bridge boomed out a salute, which we—pennons flying—answered. Mantua knew the value of a good harbor and carefully-planned defenses; this was immediately evident in the care her architects had taken to build both. Her perfectly-proportioned half-moon shaped harbor was fully-enclosed within her walls so that her ships would never be left outside at the mercy of an attacker. Except for a narrow entrance—the width of a ship's oars—which could be blocked off in times of trouble with a heavy iron chain, the walls themselves stretched almost entirely across the harbor mouth with battlements on either side of the opening. Moreover, the half-moon shape of the harbor ensured that the guns of any ships berthed inside it would always be concentrated on the entrance—a formidable gauntlet of fire for any attacker attempting to force a way in. It was by far the safest berth our squadron had enjoyed for a long time. The Mantuans billeted us at their army barracks on the city island. Their army being small anyway, and most of the Mantuan troops presently serving with the Venetian army, there was plenty of room for us.

Mantua was a courtly and refined city, filled with beautiful buildings. It was fond of its festivals. Normally, it would have filled the last month of the Christian year with splendid celebrations and fetes. Given the state of war and the horrors pervading Italy that year, the few celebrations that took place were restrained and somber. Nevertheless, the Marquisa, Isabella d'Este, staged a small pageant to show off 'her Turks' to the curious of Mantua. Nor was it mere entertainment; she had diplomatic policy in mind also. She wanted it known, and for agents to report it to foreign courts, that Mantua and Venice had powerful allies and were not to be trampled upon.

Our Mantuan hosts were quick to tell us that the Marquisa was already famous throughout Italy and France as a knowledgeable collector of art and antiquities, a patron of the best and most daring painters, and a sponsor of a literary circle of playwrights and poets. She kept two rooms on the ground floor of the palace, her *grotta*, to be shown to visitors and which were filled with beautiful things. Her library, although not as large as some in Venice or Rome, was nevertheless one of the treasures of Italy. And if we Turks too found ourselves for a time to be curiosities in her collection—exotic imports to be exhibited—then never was—the curiosity of the curiosities more richly rewarded than ours was. She was as eager to show us her fine paintings as she was anyone else. Usun Kasim's courtly manners and travels had impressed her when they had met during one of his previous assignments in Venice. Having heard only snippets of the story of the attack at Roccha Priora, she made him tell her and her husband all over again his latest adventures in full; they said he entertained them as much as any play would have.

Marquis Gonzaga was one of the best-informed people in Italy. We had already seen this at a distance in Ancona. As soon as we found ourselves in Mantua, on his home ground, we were reminded of it even more forcefully. Not a day passed that a courier or two did not come galloping across the long bridge into the city with a letter from a Mantuan ambassador, agent, or merchant in some part of Italy. The couriers were provided with the best of horses too. Three years before, in a remarkable token of friendship, Sultan Bayezid had given Gonzaga special permission to import Turkish Arabian horses from the fabled stud farms outside Istanbul. Those breeds were jealously guarded by the Ottoman government, and to give such permission to a foreigner was previously unheard of. Thanks to these well-mounted couriers, messages arrived in Mantua from Rome after a travel time of only two or three days, and this was accepted as the ordinary way of things, no more and no less than the marquis had a right to expect.

Mantua, despite its small size and even smaller standing army, had become by virtue of her strategic location, one of the hinges of Italy. She was being assiduously courted by many factions. Envoys came and went, gifts were presented, bribes paid, threats uttered and withdrawn. The French, who earlier that same year had unsuccessfully requested safe passage for their army through Mantuan territory on its way south, had not entirely given up trying to keep Mantua friendly to them, or at least neutral. The fact that little Mantua had dared——politely but firmly—to deny mighty France permission to cross its borders had not been lost on anyone. Small or not, Mantua regarded itself as a force to respected.

Coming as we did from a nation that felt itself similarly surrounded by powerful enemies, we instantly felt a kindred spirit with our Mantuan hosts. We were on the same side in a dangerous game, and we did not need to speak each other's languages all that well in order to come to an instinctive understanding.

Charles had not missed the point either. In order to keep Marquis Gonzaga friendly, he had even allowed—indeed he had positively encouraged—Gonzaga to send a Mantuan envoy to accompany the French army as a member of his suite, even though he must have known that the envoy, Signor Ghivizzano, was sending back reports on everything he saw. Charles probably originally had intended for him to do so that his news would intimidate the rest of the peninsula. Meanwhile, the pope, the Milanese renegades, the Neapolitans, all played similar games from the other side, sending their pleas, promises, and gifts.

As the French jaws closed slowly around Rome, Pope Alexander seemed to swing from panic to defiance and back again. Soon after we arrived in Mantua, one of the Marquis' busy couriers arrived from Rome with the news that Cardinals Ascanio and Senseverino—firm advocates of the pro-French policy—had been confined to the Vatican on the pope's orders, and that the pope had ordered his Swiss guards to imprison Prospero Colonna in the Castel San Angelo.

"Perhaps the tide is turning a little," Kasim observed. "The French are no longer the flavor of the moment. The pope is getting a little backbone back."

We got a further taste of the complexities of firenk alliances while we were there. Marquis Gonzaga's older sister Chiara came to stay later in December. Her husband was Gilbert de Montpensier, King Charles' nephew and one of the most senior French commanders, but no one in Mantua turned a hair at her presence or the presence of so many French servants in her retinue. Meanwhile, on the other side of the family, King Alfonso of Naples was Isabella's uncle.

I happened to be ambling along the Via Legnago late one afternoon, watching the swans on the lake in the sun, on the day the archbishop of a place called Kesztheli, and his escort arrived, green and white pennons fluttering from their lances as they cantered over the long San Grigio bridge into the city. Like everyone else, I stopped to watch the pomp, wondering what new event or alliance it portended. The archbishop rode in the middle of his troops, smiling and making gestures of blessing upon the bystanders lining the way. As he drew closer, I gasped in fear, and quickly drew myself back along the wall behind as many people as I could, ducking my head to hide my face and drawing my sea cap lower. Not that I flattered myself that the archbishop would have any reason to recognize me again, but it was a chance I had no wish to take. I had last seen him a decade ago in armor on horseback, wielding a sword over a village in flames.

I never learned exactly what he came to Mantua for, or what he had discussed in his audience with the Gonzagas——if he was even given one. I found excuses to keep myself indoors for several days until I learned with relief that he had departed as suddenly as he had come.

Kasim kept himself very busy observing and recording all the diplomatic activity. Little Eagle and I were pressed into his service running messages and helping to write voluminous reports and notebooks filled with biographical descriptions and character assessments of the westerners Kasim encountered, which Kasim intended to send back to the Vezier's office in Istanbul as soon as an opportunity should present itself. Although Little Eagle and I were far below the standard expected of court calligraphers, we had observed enough of the real thing in our time at the Enderun Kolej to be able to write disciplined and decently fair hands. Our time as chartcopiers had served us both well. Marquisa Isabella especially admired a letter I had prepared at Kasim's instruction for her signature. During one of her husband's frequently required absences on military inspections and recruitments, she ran the government, and we frequently found ourselves waiting in one or another of the anterooms of the palace with correspondence. The strain of the task facing her, and the danger facing Italy, showed in her face and the occasional dark circles under her eyes. It was during one of these spells, to provide a diversion from her burdens, that she asked us to make time in our duties to hand-letter a collection of Angelo Poliziano's poems for her library.

Little Eagle and I were sitting at a table in one of the three quiet rooms that led off of her study, where the afternoon light was best for copying, working our way across some beautifully smoothed linen paper, imported from Anatolia, when she came out of her study and into the room, a swirl of taffeta heavy with pearls, carrying her one-year old daughter Leonora in her arms. She had just gotten Leonora up from her nap. I was partway through the line '*I'ero gia della mia vita in forse*' and steadied myself to finish it so as not to vary the flow of ink before hastily pushing back the chair and rising to my feet. She came over to the table and looked down at our work approvingly. "It is coming along nicely," she said after a moment switching easily between Latin to me and French to Little Eagle. "Beautiful lettering for the almost neglected words of a poet who captured the joys and fears of his age."

"You are very kind, madonna," I replied.

"And you are very kind to be giving me something precious. Polizano didn't have the time to have his poems printed," she said. "Or perhaps he didn't think they were important enough. They were small diversions compared to his scholarly works, songs and ballads for Carnivale. I am fortunate that my friend Elisabetta was struck by them during a reading in Florence, and wrote them into that letter. It is said that he could write an entire play in two hours."

"He must have been very gifted." I could tell that much from the rhythm of the words in the stanzas I had copied so far. I did not need to be able to understand them fully in order to appreciate the harmony of their sounds.

She nodded pensively, "He was indeed. And his talent gave people a temporary haven from their troubles." She paused. "Has Kasim told you two that you have a new Emperor? At least on paper."

Little Eagle and I must have both looked startled. She had specifically used the old Byzantine term for emperor, rather than 'sultan' or 'padishah,' which she was always careful to use when speaking of Bayezid, so we knew her phrase did not mean that Bayezid was dead.

"Andreas Palealogos has signed over his rights in perpetuity to Constantinople and Trabzond to Charles," she clarified, "in return for a pension of 9,300 ducats."

I must have looked up dumbly. Little Eagle glanced sharply at me as if to say 'watch your reactions.'

"Andreas Palealogos is the son of Thomas Palealogos, who was the younger brother of Emperor Constantine XI, who died fighting the Tur—who died fighting on the walls of Constantinople. That makes Andreas, legally, the Emperor of Byzantium."

Little Eagle and I looked at each other. We hadn't any idea that there still *was* an Emperor of Byzantium.

"Andreas has been living in Rome. He's married to a former prostitute, and he makes ends meet on a stingy allowance the pope gives him in case his claim might one day be politically useful. The pope still has hopes of uniting the Eastern Church with the Church of Rome. Palealogos might serve the pope's purpose in that regard. Meanwhile, he augments his allowance by selling what titles of nobility he imagines are in his power to bestow to anybody credulous enough to pay for one. For one hundred and thirty ducats, you could be the governor of Modon."

"Oh. Is Andreas' younger brother Manuel Palealogos?" I asked.

"Yes, now that you mention it. I believe the courier said he did have a younger brother," Isabella said. "I'm not sure if anyone knows what happened to him."

"He accepted a pension from the sultan," I offered. I didn't see that it would hurt anything to reveal the information. The Vezier's office had deliberately made it public information throughout Istanbul. "In return for giving up any claims he might have had to a title, he took a Turkish name and has lived quietly in Constantinople. He has served with distinction in the Ottoman army and navy."

"Indeed? Then I would say he made the more practical bargain of the two, and lives the more honorably. But to speak seriously for a moment, Palealogus has signed over all his titles to Constantinople and Trabzond to Charles. All he asked in return was for Charles to promise to grant him the Despotate of Morea—assuming Charles will ever capture it—and a pension of 9,300 ducats. You're laughing," she broke off.

I wasn't at all, but my face must have revealed how ludicrous I thought the idea was that whole empires could be sold from one person to another like fish in a market. Was there a set of brass scales on the counter, I wondered, to sell capitals by the pound and provinces by the ounce?

"Anyway, Charles knows it's an empty title. I'm sure he figures it's a cheap way to buy a little extra legitimacy. If Charles is Emperor of Byzantium in name, and he has Prince Cem with him on the expedition, then he has it both ways."

"Madonna, you are experienced in the ways of state," I answered cautiously. "Everyone in Italy says so. Perhaps the reasons are even darker than you paint. Charles must also be thinking that—once he has conquered the empire—which he will never succeed in doing, he won't need Cem anymore."

"Poor Cem," Little Eagle said.

"Don't feel too sorry for him. How much do you know about him?"

"Not much. We know that he revolted against his father and later against his brother before fleeing to the firenks."

"Did you know that he has a temper and he drinks? He is often ill for days because of it."

I looked up sharply. "Madonna, that last part at least cannot be true. He is a Muslim prince. He has made the pilgrimage to Mecca."

"Spiced wine, they say. His excuse is that once it is spiced, it isn't really wine. A painter I sometimes commission—Andrea Mantegna—wrote me a description of Cem from Rome. He has grown heavy with overeating—five meals a day—and quarrelsome with captivity. He swings himself from side to side when he walks, like an elephant. One day one of his interpreters displeased him, and he hit the unfortunate man so hard they had to carry him to the Tiber and plunge him in to revive him."

"Bayezid was always the more rational of the two," Little Eagle said cautiously weighing his words. "It was good for all of us that it was he who got back to Istanbul first, after the Conqueror died."

"What is he like, your sultan? Have you seen him? My husband thinks very highly of him."

"We have both seen him many times when we were in training at the palace," I said. We took turns described him to her as best we could, his astuteness, his love of learning. It occurred to me that Isabella and Bayezid had many qualities in common. They would have had much to talk about if they ever met. "You would enjoy his poetry, madonna. And I daresay his music."

"He writes? Do you know any of them? Could you write them out for me?"

"I have not memorized any of them well enough, I fear. My translation would be partial and incorrect, and would spoil the work. Better a silence than a guttering."

She thought a moment, and nodded. "I will ask Kasim to request your Sultan to send me some. A fine, hand-lettered folio."

"Your request will be a compliment to him."

It was my accidental misuse of the word 'guttering' that did it, for it put me in mind of the candle. Without meaning to, I began hesitantly and softly,

> *My affection's madness is a moth to the candle,*
> *the candle two lovers hold close*
> *upright as the cypress tree planted above a tomb,*
> *upright as a thorn, a thorn with the sharpness of a kiss*
> *oh rose, whose face is pleasure and whose thorn is prayer...'*

"That's a horrible translation," Little Eagle scowled. "It doesn't even rhyme."

He was right, of course. Even translating on the fly as I was, I should have done better. The Marquisa was looking at me puzzled. I hastened to explain that 'thorn,' 'upright' and 'planted' were all related words in Turkish and that it was the gradual weaving of the changes in meaning that connected the lines of the stanza, bringing the moth at last from the candle to his rose.

Her secretary Bernedetto Capilupo called to her from within. She sighed, and with Leonora still in her arms, she went back into her study with some papers. Little Eagle put down his pen and got up to stretch his cramped fingers. There was a book on the credenza, finely bound with the Gonzaga arms stamped on the leather cover. He opened it and turned a few of the pages. "Inferno?" he asked.

"Gehenna," it took me a moment to come up with the Turkish word. It seemed a curious word for a title. Curious now myself, I came over to look. "It seems to be a description of the firenks' hell," I said after skimming the first few pages.

It was illustrated with striking and tormented pictures. "They have a hell too?"

"Apparently they do. It seems theirs is in circles. The worse you were, the farther down you are put. Ah, they place Sheytan at the bottom, in the center. Frozen into a vast lake. Hmm, theirs is cold in the worst places. The opposite of a 'gehenna.'"

Little Eagle shivered despite himself. "I don't think I would want to go to firenk hell."

"I don't think they'd let us in," I said. "Well, perhaps they would me. I made—and then broke—certain promises once upon a time that they might consider binding."

"Perhaps you'll get to choose which hell to go to, warm or cold," he said.

"I'm not sure that's the way it works."

It struck us that 'paradise' and 'hell' were almost the same word in Turkish, differing only in the final consonant and in the addition of a middle syllable. "Are they similar words in other firenk languages?" Little Eagle wanted to know.

"Not in any of the ones I know," I said.

On the last day of December, a starving Rome opened its gates to the French, and Charles entered the eternal city at the head of his troops, "to pay his respects as a good son of the Church," he claimed publicly, "and to view the antiquities." No one believed his proclamations this time. We heard that both of the two surviving della Rovere brothers—the Cardinal and the Prefect—rode into the city with him, as did Archbishop Niccolo Cibo. The pope shut himself up in the Vatican, and Charles' troops ranged their cannons in the square in front of the pontifical palace. They tore down some of the houses in front of it to give themselves a clear field of fire. Both sides settled in to negotiate. For the next three weeks, all of Italy seemed to hold its breath and waited eagerly for each courier from Rome. That winter was an unusually mild one, a fact which Charles lost no time in ascribing to the Almighty's showing favor to his expedition and the crusade which he planned would follow it.

Francesco Gonzaga tried to reassure Kasim as much as he could. "The stakes are as high for Italy as for Constantinople." Kasim—uncharacteristically for him—was sunk in gloom most days, not only about the wider political situation, but also about his own inactivity and his inability to influence events. Gonzaga wrote a long and reassuring state letter to Sultan Bayezid, explaining the circumstances of della Rovere's robbery, and taking great pains to point out that Kasim had faithfully carried out his commission in every detail. Gonzaga assured Bayezid that he was doing everything he could to recover the gold Kasim had been transporting. In addition to the sender's copy to be kept in the Marquis' archive, Kasim had me and Little Eagle make multiple copies, two for himself to keep, and four others to be sent next spring to the court in Istanbul via multiple ships for safety.

One late January morning, word was passed for us to gather in the barracks courtyard. The gates were closed behind us, with our janissaries standing at the doors to keep anyone else out.

Kasim strode in, looking more solemn than we had ever seen him. "A courier arrived from Rome this morning," he announced, "with news that is extremely bad for us. Marquis Gonzaga has given me leave to inform you that—three days ago—Pope Alexander consigned Cem to King Charles' custody for a term of six months. As most of you already know, Charles' intention is to march south with Cem, to Naples. Once Naples has fallen—and given the success of Charles' army so far, no one expects that event to be long delayed—Charles will carry out his promise to launch a combined Christian attack against Istanbul, the Morea, and Jerusalem."

Kasim paused for a moment to let us digest the news. There was a disciplined silence.

"Never, I think, has the danger been so great. Certainly never in any of our lifetimes. By late spring or early next summer, the empire will almost certainly be facing an enormous attack, probably the largest attack ever mounted against it."

All of us knew what the news meant. Ever since the attack at Rocca Priora, we were in no doubt as to the stakes being played for, or that the Europeans were deadly serious in their intentions. The wheels were now in motion against us, and the fragile balance that Daud Pasha had so carefully maintained for decades had been destroyed, probably irrevocably.

Just four days later, Charles was already in Velletri. Within days of his taking that city, the Castle of Montefortino was stormed and sacked, resulting in a massacre. It was Monte San Giovanni's turn next; in little more than seven hours of artillery bombardment, more than a thousand men, women and children died in the rubble there. Each courier brought worse news. On the fifteenth of February, Mantua and the rest of Italy were stunned to learn that the Neapolitans had evacuated the fortress of San Germano without a battle. The Pass of Cancello lay open to the invaders.

"If the Neapolitans were going to make a stand, it would have been there," Kasim told us.

"We have to get the ships out of Italy," Bayulken said after a moment. "Winter storms or not. At least as far as the coast so that we can sail at any moment. We can't risk having them impounded if the rest of Italy changes its mind and throws in its lot with Charles."

"I fully agree," Kasim answered. "Happily for us, the opportunity presents itself. The Venetian Signoria wants Marquis Gonzaga in Venice for strategic consultations at the beginning of March. He would prefer to travel incognito. I have offered him and his staff transportation aboard our ships. What could be more incognito than the captain-general of Venice's land forces travelling in Turkish dress aboard a Turkish ship?"

"That will get us as far as the Adriatic," Bayulken nodded. "Once safely there, we can sail for Valona whenever the weather permits. How soon does he want to depart?"

"A week. Maybe two. The Marquis would like to be in Venice for carnivale."

After Kasim finished, I joined the glum and silent group of sailors sitting on the stairs. The same thoughts were clearly visible on all our faces. For a long time no one spoke.

"Naples stands alone," Inanc said finally. "Between us and 'il diluvio.'"

"Under a capricious and despotic king whom his own people hate."

"Propped up by Aragonese soldiers."

"Their fleet has been soundly beaten—twice—off Genoa when they tried to block the French galleys from landing there."

"And their army. It's retreating as fast as it can."

"But no matter how bleak it looks, Charles is not there yet. Even if everybody is right and Naples does fall, it is still a long way to launching the crusade against us."

"That's true. Charles still has gather his ships in Naples—"

"And revictual them; get his troops aboard them..."

"All of which will probably put the timing just about right for him to embark for Asia or the Morea just as the wheat is ripening."

"Maybe, but he has to get them there. Revictualling his ships will not be easy," I reminded them. "His troops have ravaged Italy. There's no food left to load. If he waits until next autumn when the crops are in, it will be too late to sail."

"He'll have an invasion fleet full of ill-fed, seasick soldiers, trying to get across to Asia or the Levant, or Rhodes, or wherever else he has in mind. His thirty thousand troops may have already eaten themselves out of an invasion."

"But nothing has gone wrong for Charles in this expedition so far. Almost all of Italy belongs to him already."

"And that without a single armed encounter worthy of the name, not since Rapallo."

"The terror his troops inspired at that massacre has rolled up the rest of Italy for him like a carpet," I put in.

"The carpet all stand upon, but none can roll up…" Ozkan mused. "Except, it seems him."

One morning towards the end of February, when the days were beginning to lengthen and grow mild, Ozkan, Berk and I were sitting cross-legged on the dock, tightening *Akdogan*'s mooring lines which had a tendency to stretch when wet, when Semih came running down from the barracks. He stopped a few yards short of the quay and gathered himself.

"Semih, what is it?" Ozkan asked, not used to seeing him so solemn.

"I do not know the words to tell you this."

Berk slowly put the rope he was working on down. "It's alright. Tell us how you think it best."

"Prince Cem is dead."

We all stopped. "Semih, where did you learn this?"

"Ghivizzano's equerry brought the news this morning. I heard it from my lord Kasim. Cem died in Capua, a town just outside of Naples. Three nights ago."

"And they are certain of this? This is not a French lie?"

He nodded. "They are sure."

I don't think any of us were sure what to feel. Cem had been a rebel and a usurper, and his selfish ambition had threatened to destroy the peace of the empire. Every one of us in the squadron knew this. But, now that he had died in an infidel land while in infidel hands, all that seemed to matter to us now was that he had been a Turk, and therefore one of us. Perhaps we would have felt differently had we been back in Istanbul, but here we felt our Turkishness all the more keenly for being in this foreign land.

"There is talk of poison. The French are accusing the pope of giving Cem a slow-acting poison before Cem left Rome," Semih added.

"A poison that takes three weeks to act?"

"Kasim says that the last person to want Cem dead was the pope. He loses everything by it. The forty thousand ducats a year, the chance to be the spear point and leader of the other European powers for a crusade, everything."

"Perhaps Charles had him poisoned. Perhaps Charles intended to murder Cem all along and put the blame on the pope. Perhaps that is why he forged the letters."

"Perhaps, but unlikely. Charles worked long and hard to get hold of Cem. He used every means he possessed—including capturing Rome—to force the pope to give him up. He certainly would not have wanted him dead."

"At least not until after his invasion fleet had sailed," I said.

"Thanks to Palealogos, Charles now has the title to Byzantium. He didn't need Cem anymore."

"I'm not sure of that. Title or no title, the eastern provinces will never revolt in support of Charles. They might have risen for Cem."

"Look, Cem was often sick. He drank and ate far too much. The world knows that. His transfer from the Knights of Rhodes to the pope five years ago had to be delayed for a month because he was gravely ill at the time."

"February weather, plus the effects of being outside after years of confinement..." Berk pointed out, "long tiring rides every day on the march south...it is not surprising that a man who was unwell might sicken and die in those circumstances."

"His death changes much."

Above the lake, a fish eagle glided, its wings angled. It suddenly folded them and dove.

"Did Ghivizanno's equerry say what Charles will do now?" Berk asked.

Semih shook his head. "Charles was already inside the city of Naples when it happened."

"So, he's taken Naples then?"

"Some of it. The townspeople welcomed him. Or most of them did. King Alfonso abdicated in favor of his son Ferrandino as the French approached. Alfonso fled the city that night to Sicily with four galleys stuffed with everything from the royal treasury that could be moved, including many of the books in his library."

"You said, 'some of it.'"

"The harbor fortresses are still holding out."

Berk looked up with relief at that small glimmer of hope. "And without Cem, will he still attack us? Does he still plan his crusade?"

"Bayulken says that French ships are waiting in Genoa, ready to sail south to Naples as soon as the season is favorable."

But within weeks, Charles' triumph began to fray. The people of Naples, who had cautiously welcomed him as an improvement on the capriciousness of their Aragonese-directed puppet ruler, quickly became thoroughly disgusted with the conduct of the French troops occupying their city. One foreign oppressor was much like another. They became sullen subjects, then violent rebels. North of Naples, the fortress of Gaeta was still holding out, although the city itself had fallen. As long as the fortress and its guns were still in Italian hands, Charles could not use Gaeta's port for his supply ships.

Charles' coronation as King of Naples and the Two Sicilies, despite its expensive glitter, was a hollow affair that no amount of expensive clothes or lavish banquets could disguise. Part of the city, along with the Fortress Nuovo and the Tower of Saint Vincent, was still holding out against him. Any riches he might have hoped to gain by capturing the city had vanished the night King Alfonso had fled. Charles had now lost Cem and the goodwill of the pope. His claim to be the lance point of Christendom had begun to sound hollow.

One week later, with Marquis Gonzaga and a handful of his staff having come quietly aboard *Yildirim*, we cast off our lines and ran out our oars. Under the watchful guidance of the river pilots, *Akdogan* and the squadron made their way slowly back down the Po. From its mouth, we turned northward, keeping to the outside of the barrier islands that separated the Venetian lagoon from the waters of the Adriatic.

They kept us outside the lagoon as far as possible, until the last mile in fact. Although the force of circumstance and changing alliances had unexpectedly compelled the Venetians to allow Turkish warships into their home waters, they made sure that we came no further inside than required. In our case, this was barely a hundred yards. We entered the lagoon itself through the narrow inlet at the north end of Lido, a narrow barrier of sand and windswept grass, under the guns of Fort Sebastian. No sooner had we passed through the inlet than we turned immediately to beach our galleys and make them fast no more than a few ship lengths inside.

It was two days past the first new moon in the month the firenks called March. A month that would contain the equinox as well as two new moons. And that, we hoped, made it a time of new beginnings.

Chapter X
The Most Serene Republic

It was good to find ourselves at the edge of the sea again, even if that edge was little more than just that. We were confined by our hosts' request to a sandy strip of barrier island. We were not quite free of the land, but we felt freer than we had for weeks. The Venetians did not allow us into the city itself, of course, with or without our ships. Although the Venetians had a long history of trading with all parts of the world, and were used to foreign crews in their harbors, they were not completely comfortable without at least some separation.

We were billeted, like the other crews from non-Christian lands, on Lido Island. "Faces to the sea; backs to the sand," Hasan called it. There was a crew from Aleppo already there, waiting, as we were, for the spring sailing season to open. We were directed to spread out our bedrolls on the floors of the large stone granaries which abutted the walls of the abbey of San Nicolo. Being late spring, these cavernous vaults with their disconcerting echoes were at their emptiest. The last of the winter stores had been gradually consumed. From our station there we waited out the turning of the season. Warm mild days alternated with surprisingly cold days made even chillier by the raw winds sweeping off the Adriatic.

Kasim was allowed from time to time to take a small boat across the lagoon to the main islands of the city on those occasions when he had business there, or when his presence was requested either by the Signoria or—more rarely—by Doge Barbarigo. It went without saying that neither he nor any other Turk was ever allowed anywhere near the enormous Venetian arsenal entirely shielded from prying eyes by its high brick wall. We could see two of its entry ports from our island, and count the galleys going in and out of it. We saw the *Fortuna*, distinctive in her yellow and black gunwales, putting out from her winter berth one morning to anchor at her place in the roadstead, preparatory to putting to sea.

"I wonder what they've been up to."

"Intercepting the Religion's mail and sinking corsair galleots," I hope.

Every morning, we could see the buildings of Venice rising out of the mists of the lagoon, golden in the rays of each dawn's sun. The morning ringing of bells of the city's many churches carried easily across the still waters. Venetian gunboats patrolled the lagoon day and night.

In being kept at a distance like this, we were not treated much differently from other non-Venetians having business in the city. It was only a matter of distance and degree. Even ambassadors from Christian nations usually found themselves posted to lodgings no closer than on Giudecca Island, across the wide canal of the same name from the city. The French ambassador Commynes himself was lodged no closer than the Benedictine abbey of San Giorgio Maggiore. "And he is watched and followed everywhere he goes," Koca Mustafa told us.

Koca Mustafa, who had been at San Giorgio since the end of November, was able to fill Kasim in on the latest happenings. The Venetian Council of Ten had learned of Cem's death just two days after it happened. A relay of couriers had ridden themselves and several horses practically to death day and night without stopping to get the news to Venice so fast. The Council had dispatched one of its senior diplomats, one Andrea Gritti, aboard a fast galley to carry the news to Istanbul. They had forbidden any other ship except the one carrying Gritti himself, to sail from the lagoon.

"You will be pleased to learn that the pope has excommunicated Prefect della Rovere for his attack on you," Mustafa told Kasim. "They tell me that excommunication means that Sheytan will have della Rovere's soul after he dies, and his retainers are dismissed from their oaths of loyalty to him while alive."

"Hmm. His retainers will obey his money, more than their oaths, I think," Kasim commented drily.

"Perhaps, but it's the open break between the pope and the della Roveres that everyone has been expecting for some time."

"Hmm, and the break between the pope and all the cardinals who have chosen to throw in their lot with the French advance."

"Perhaps Alexander is asserting his will again. The two sides are drawing up for the confrontation."

"And both are calling upon the Almighty to hurl divine retribution at the other?"

Koca Mustafa shrugged. "You've been to Rome. You know how it works."

"I will never know how Rome works,"

While the diplomatic maneuvering went on across the lagoon, we kept ourselves busy training, archery for the janissaries, swordsmanship for us sailors. We ran long miles up and down the sandy shore trying not to lose our sea sharpness in the idle days on land. In our free time, we fished for our daily food or sat on the shore and talked about the fascinations of the city we had heard tantalizing stories about, but which we could see only at a distance. One night five of the janissaries purloined one of *Hilal*'s jali boats and attempted to row across the lagoon for an unsanctioned visit to the Pearl of the Adriatic. They were spotted almost at once by one of the Venetian guard boats and brought back ignominiously under guard. Bayulken was furious at this breakdown of our much-vaunted Turkish discipline, pointing out that attention to duty was the main thing that would hold us together in this foreign land, but Yigit and I interceded for them, pointing out that it was under the strain of being so long under foreign influence that had no doubt caused the breakdown. They were let off with a severe scolding and a week of extra hard work scraping the weeds from the parts of the hulls that could be reached above water.

As March wore on, Koca Mustafa's observations began to bear fruit. Although we hardly let ourselves dare hope, it seemed that public opinion—which so lately and completely had been swung to Charles' side by the false publication of the letters—might be swinging back against him.

"Perhaps Charles doesn't speak for the entirety of Christendom after all."

For all of that, there were setbacks to our optimism, reminders that Italy had a long road to travel before her miseries would end. "The fortress of Gaeta has fallen," we were told grimly sometime in the middle of March. "The entire western coast of Italy now belongs to Charles."

On the twenty-sixth, which was the second new moon of the month, Kasim—expecting that we would be putting to sea any day now—wrote a long and deeply grateful letter to Gonzaga, thanking the Marquis for his help and protection during the past months.

"Don't leave Venice just yet," Koca Mustafa advised him. "There are big things brewing. Things that it might be worth your while to stay in order to hear and report them back to Istanbul."

"Staying a few more days would not hurt," Bayulken said. "We've been away so long anyway." In any case, with the guns of the fortress of San Sebastian guarding the narrow inlet which was the only exit to the sea, there was no question of attempting to sail without licenses.

Mustafa was right. The diplomats had been gathering and talking all month, and on the first of that April in the firenk year 1495, it was formally announced that a League of Italian States had been signed in the presence of the Doge and the Signoria. Among themselves, the Venetians referred to it as the League of St. Mark, but tactfully avoided the term in front of their allies.

"The Pope, Spain, the Holy Roman Emperor...even Milan—who were the ones most responsible for inviting Charles in—have signed," Mustafa reported, somewhat in wonder. The preamble of the compact stated that the primary purpose was to defend Christendom against the Turk, but everyone knew that that was only window dressing to spare Charles' pride and not give him any reason to linger.

Charles himself was furious when news of the league reached him at his camp. He had his own envoy stationed in Venice, by the Venetians' own invitation. They wanted the news to reach Charles undiluted through his own channels, and reach him it did. According to Ghivizzano's succinct report to Gonzaga, no sooner had Charles' own envoy reported the news when Charles haled the Venetian ambassadors who were travelling with him, Antonio Loredan and Domenico Trevisan, into his presence and roundly blamed them for contriving everything and sabotaging his efforts to free Christendom from the Turks. In the spectacular royal tantrum which followed that accusation, Charles gave himself up to the temper of a spoiled young man. He threatened—among other things—to form a counter league of his own with England, Scotland, Portugal, and Hungary.

"With *England*?" Kasim queried. "That same England that has been at war with France for more than a hundred years?"

"And with Scotland," Mustafa confirmed.

"I can't imagine that Scotland is very eager to involve itself militarily in the affairs of the Mediterranean. A bit off their patch, isn't it?"

"And what reason has Hungary to go to war with Venice? Venice sends Hungary money to put down pirates in the Adriatic."

"That alliance has about as much chance of working as birds have of giving milk."

"Charles has surrounded himself with so many lies he no longer knows how the world works. The Italians are so eager to have him out of Italy that the Venetians are thinking of loaning him ships to transport his army by sea."

The Venetians later resolutely denied that rumor, and it didn't matter anyway. Less than one week later we woke up to the bells ringing across the calm morning waters of the lagoon. Not just the usual dawn carillon either, but an ebullient ringing that pealed out in one enormous, exuberant clamor that went on for more than an hour, until everyone north of Pavia must have been awake.

"He's leaving!" Inanc came flying into the granary room, leaping agilely over people on the floor still in their bedrolls. "Hey! Charles has marched out of Naples. He's given up!"

I threw off the blankets and pulled a shirt over my head, hopping from one foot to another on the cold stone floor. "Is it true? Is it really true?"

"Listen to the bells; it's true alright. A boat came over from the city with the news this morning."

There were footsteps in the hall outside, running up and down the stairs. I stuck my head out, and it seemed the courtyard outside was filled with laughing, shouting half-dressed Turkish sailors hugging each other and dancing round in circles. Bayulken was there, a huge smile on his face. "This may end well for all of us," he said, "Turks and Firenks both."

"*The dark curtain is drawing back a little*," Little Eagle wrote in one of his notebooks that evening in his careful hand in a larger than normal script. "*The heavy dagger that has been aimed for so long at the throat of the Land of Felicity is blunted.*"

Charles had indeed abandoned Naples. He left behind an unhappy, and nervous, garrison under the command of none other than Gonzaga's brother-in-law—Sir Gilbert de Montpensier—as his viceroy. Charles was now trying to get the remains of his starving and demoralized army out of Italy and back home across the Alps. The campaign was in shambles; the threat of a crusade against the Turkish mainland was over. All the ingredients were gone. The pope had been discredited as rallying point; the military power of France was frittering away daily like chaff in the wind. Charles' invasion had eviscerated Italy. Naples and its navy was shattered. Our treaty with the Knights of Rhodes would have teeth in it, now that the Knights and the papacy no longer had Cem to hold over our heads. In the north, Hungary and Germany seemed ready to go to war against each other again. Spain—the only other state in Europe which possessed either the military resources or the inclination to attack us—was at the other end of the Mediterranean and hardly interested in us. Her ambition now stretched only as far as restoring Naples and Sicily to its empire.

The women of Naples were getting their revenge too through the spread of a terrible new disease that did awful things to a man's nether parts and face. Aragonese sailors arriving in Naples from the ports of Spain carried a pox. Some people said Spanish sailors had brought it back from their voyages to the recently-discovered islands on the other side of the Western Ocean. It had spread through the ladies of the quaysides, and the occupying French soldiers caught it in turn from them. The troops were soon suffering from it so widely that it was beginning to be referred to throughout Italy in polite speech simply as the 'French disease.'

Two days before Charles had marched out of Naples, a Turkish galleot from Valona put into Brindisi. It carried messages to those Neapolitans who were rebelling against the French, formally offering to send them the eighteen thousand Turkish cavalry who were billeted at Valona to assist them. The Neapolitans, after no little discussion, decided that—as tempting as the offer was—the risk of turning so many Turkish troops loose on Italian soil was too high to accept. The offer was politely declined, with gifts.

The galleot carried orders for us to return home. Among the papers they carried was a letter from her captain:

Sevgili Kachak,

Health and good wishes, I kiss your forehead. Back in Valona, we hear that you and Inanc and Yigit have been putting an end to the crusade menace pretty much all by yourselves. The cavalry sipahis are filled with jealousy, and beg you to leave something for them to do. Atakan writes from Konstantiyye that there was panic there for a while this winter as word of the French plans—incomplete and in delayed fragments only—trickled across the mountain roads between snowstorms. He has been busy for months siting new guns along the seawalls of the city, and the Padishah himself comes to inspect their positions and angles of fire. If all turns out as well as we are hearing, Atakan's bronze beauties will not get the opportunity to use their orange tongues.

As for me and my crew, we've had some wild adventures off the Dalmatian coast, which I will tell you about when next I see you. Whoever tells the best story gets dinner paid for—and if half of what we're hearing in Valona is true, it will be quite a competition.

> *I wait for you with four eyes in Brindisi.*
> *Erhan*

While these orders were still on the way to us, the Venetians signed our licenses to sail. Hasan was ecstatic at the news. We began provisioning the galleys for the journey home. By the time we were ready, there was no longer any possibility of sailing down the eastern coast of the peninsula back to Brindisi and Ancona. Charles' troops, having exhausted the opportunities for plunder in the city of Naples itself, were raiding the outlying lands and particularly the wealthy port cities along the coast. Although the larger and better-fortified ports such as Ancona and Bridisi still held out, the French had gradually consolidated their hold on the territory around them. Travel to and between them was now uncertain; even the Council of Ten with its relays of couriers was hard put to know from day to day exactly where the French troops were operating. We dreaded the possibility that Brindisi might fall while we were en route to it, and that we might sail unsuspectingly into a city already in the hands of Charles' myrmidons.

Instead, we would be sailing with a Venetian escort up around the north of the Adriatic and then down the eastern coast. The Venetian ministry of marine was preparing urgent new orders for their Adriatic squadrons presently based at their colony of Corfu. A pair of Venetian brigantinas was moored in front of the Doge's palace, ready to sail at a moment's notice the instant the ink was dry on them. We heard few details, of course, but it was hardly a secret that the Adriatic squadron would be moving from its base at Corfu to rendezvous with other Venetian ships off Savari Island—the same Savari Island we had passed in our journey from Valona. Once they had collected their forces, the Venetians planned to dash west across the Straits of Otranto and carry out seaborne raids on French positions along the Italian coast, and to support the cities such as Taranto, and now Brindisi, which were beseiged by them. Our squadron was instructed to be ready to accompany the Venetian ships as far as Savari. This was a good thing in Bayulken's eyes, because Savari Island, at the mouth of the Gulf of Karabunun, was uncomfortably close to Valona to have such a large Venetian fleet gathered, even if they were our allies for the moment. It was just as well, Bayulken thought, that we would be nearby to watch them. The Venetians—by directing us to sail with their squadron—were just as sure they were watching us.

"What are these?" Bayulken took the red bundles that the boatman who had brought us the instructions handed him. One of them partially unrolled to reveal a golden paw.

"The Lion of St. Mark," the boatman replied with pride. "Your ships will fly it as a courtesy while you are with our squadron."

As if that would fool anyone. Our hull colors and the low profiles of our hulls proclaimed us for what we were. Even so, it was a tactful nod by the Venetians to their Christian allies to avoid being too obvious that they were sailing in company with Turkish warships. In the end, the joke was on them because they forgot to ask for them back after we reached Savari, and we continued on our journey without giving them back.

Which is why, my oglans who will one day be reading this, three Venetian banners hang—to this day—in the entrance hall of the Tersane barracks. No doubt you have noticed them. In case you have ever wondered how they came to be there, that is the explanation. The pleasant folkloric tale that a certain Lieutenant Ozkan stole them from in front of the very walls of the formidable Venetian arsenal by shimmying up a flagpole in the dead of night is but an invention told by the older cousins to each incoming class of new oglans to test their gullibility. But there, now I've told you, so don't you fall for their tales.

Chapter XI
The Lion on the Walls

It was exhilarating to be at sea again. Despite all the wonderful things we had seen, I was not sorry to be leaving Italy behind. Our time among the firenks had left us confused and frightened. I was—as Inanc reminded me—a firenk myself, yet I couldn't begin to understand them. In company with the Venetian brigantinas, we sailed north around the arc of the top of the Adriatic, across to the peninsula of Istria, where the famous marble comes from. In Istria, we took shelter in Rovinj's many-islanded bay. Rovinj itself was a Venetian colony and was a lovely miniature copy of Venice, perhaps one-twentieth the size. Here we were allowed in the town, and got to sample some of the delights that we had missed in the larger version. From there, we carried on down the eastern coast, to Ragusa, and finally to Corfu. Having discharged our responsibilities to our hosts, we were free to sail eastwards and home.

This we did slowly. After two seasons at sea without major repairs, our poor battered ships were much the worse for wear. Weeds the length of Hasan's forearm trailed from our hulls. The caulking between the planking was wearing thin, and there was now almost always water in the hold. *Hilal*'s foresail split its seam with a bang in a not particularly strong wind east of Corfu, and I expected *Akdogan*'s to follow suit any day. Just south of Inebahti, it did. We tried to restitch it, but the cloth itself was so worn and frayed that there was nothing much to stitch the seam to. In the end we had to cut it down to a smaller version of itself. The loss in speed was inconsequential; we knew that other ships would reach Istanbul with the news of signing of the League before we did anyway.

The Venetians gave special permission to *Akdogan*, *Hilal*, and *Yildirim* to put in to their port of Modon on the Peloponnese on our way home. Modon was a beautiful town, and the crews were excited to see it. I saw it first with a helmsman's eye, so I'm afraid my enthusiasm was somewhat blunted. My impression of Modon was of an endless breakwater with a sharp hooking curve at the end of it, stretching out into a bay filled entirely with dangerous rocks. Not only did the hook make it difficult to round the breakwater safely, there was also a low island in the middle of the bay's mouth, especially well-placed to snag any carelessly-handled ship unlucky enough to stray from the channel. To the Venetians, Modon and Coron were 'the eyes of the Republic.' They were welcome to them as far as I was concerned. Still, Modon was a useful watering and revictualling stop, and we enjoyed our time there.

As we made our long, careful return along the coast of the Morea towards Istanbul, the news from the west seemed to leapfrog us. Often there would be ships next to us when we put into shore each evening, and the accounts they shared grew better and better.

On our second to last day at sea—as *Akdogan* and her sister ships sailed easily before a light summer breeze—I left Semih happy at the tiller and went forward to join Inanc, Berk, and Ozkan sitting out on the beak. We had passed the Darda-nelles and were running north through the Marble Sea.

"Can it be that the threat is over, truly over?" Ozkan was saying quietly.

"Kasim thinks it is. He says we shall have peace for many years," I said.

Inanc was staring down at the curl of white water hissing away from *Akdogan*'s bow. "I heard Bayulken say that he doesn't think that the Europeans will be able to pick up the pieces again. For years. Maybe not ever."

"The fear we've lived with for more than forty years..." Berk said. "Now truly past."

We sat in silence for a moment as the slow rise and fall of the ship's beak moved the sunlight and the shadows from the foresail in diagonal lines across our faces.

"We're coming back to a different world," Ozkan said.

"We're bringing back a different world," Inanc appended.

"We've been away a long time."

"It feels strange."

"Do you think anyone will believe our stories?"

Ozkan shook his head. "I wouldn't if I were them. I mean, did all of those things really happen to us?"

"I put them in the notebooks; I hope the oglans in the Expeditionary Hall believe them at least."

"Some ship captain looking at them years from now will think we were crazy."

The city's seven hills rose out of the horizon to meet us as every mile brought us closer until, with surprising suddenness, it was real, not a miniature painting in the distance. It is always thus when approaching the land. One moment, it is still far away and out of reach, belonging to another world entirely separate from the sea. The next, you are close enough to see people moving on shore, smoke rising from chimneys, boats going to and fro in the harbor, and you realize that life onshore has been going on without you, and you are almost home, connected to the land again.

An outbound carrack vailed her topsails to us as she passed, and as we passed the point, the cannons on the wall began one by one to boom out a salute. Our gunners cleared the tompions from the muzzles of our leeward guns, and Inanc put his linstock to the touchholes to fire our guns in reply.

There was no question of *Akdogan* or the rest of the squadron going to sea again this season. As soon as the mast and sails were down and the thole pins out, we towed the hulls straight to the shallows of Kagithane for the ritual sinking. That business taken care of, Little Eagle and I presented ourselves at the Hall of the Expeditionary forces with the piles of notebooks we had so painstakingly filled on the voyage. The oglans at the chart copying room practically gasped when we dumped them out on the table, and we were kept busy for days clarifying notes and helping them make sense of it all as they made the fair copies which would go into the records boxes in the treasury.

The news followed us to Istanbul that Marquis Gonzaga, in command of the armies of the League of Italy, had surprised the retreating French army in a mountain pass near Fornovo. In a confusion of mud and mist, the battle had been less decisive than the Italians would have wished. Nonetheless, it was being hailed throughout the peninsula as a great victory over tyranny. Charles' army had been left in disarray; it was hungry and demoralized and fleeing north as fast as its blistered feet and soleless boots could take it. The Marquis of Mantua, who had had at least one horse shot from under him, was acclaimed the hero of the hour, and suddenly Istanbul had a firm friend in the west's halls of power. He sent Kasim one of the medals that had been struck in thanksgiving for the victory, *ob restitutam Italine libertatem,* enclosed in a letter describing the battle and the droll incident afterwards when the French king had sent his herald under a flag of truce to request the return of some captured account ledgers and a pornographic book "which the King much values," and which had been among the booty taken in the wagon train.

"I naturally returned them," Gonzaga recounted, "for I wished Charles to be able to pay his troops accurately, lest they mutiny and refuse to march out of Italy for lack of salary. As for the book, I have no need of such aids."

By the end of August, Charles' army was back in France and in no position to be a threat to anyone. The token garrison left behind in Naples soon found itself under a relentless and vindictive counterattack.

"Now it is time to turn our attention to the Knights of Rhodes," Bahadir pronounced one evening as Little Eagle and I had finished going over for the oglans our notes on the approaches to the Po estuary.

"They'll have to mend their ways. They're on their own now. No one else in Europe is talking crusades anymore.

Christendom has no ships to send to back them up if they get themselves in trouble."

"So it is all right if we go harder on Marsan?"

"No need to be subtle. We can shake the tree a little. Tracing the path of the notebooks is not so important any more. We're not going to be sending false reports to Europe by that means for the foreseeable future."

"Can we spring Atakan from his duties at the Tersane for a day or so? And some janissaries?"

"Gather whomever you need."

"Come," Atakan said, "there's something I want to show you." He led me to a large building at the end of the Tersane shore, new and obviously built over the winter while we had been away. The janissary guards at the door saluted him and, suddenly recognizing me, threw me a separate salute as they opened it for us. Inside, I came face to face with a wall of wood which rose into the gloom. It was the hull of an enormous ship, braced on its ways and nearing completion. I had never seen a ship so large. She towered above us, three decks high, with a forecastle and stern deck which rose even higher. I counted twenty-two gunports on her maindeck, with an additional six on her forecastle, and four on her stern. She had steps for four masts and a bowsprit. Below her gundeck, there were smaller ports for twenty-five oars.

"She's the *Goke* (Sky Blue)," Atakan explained proudly. "Admiral Kemaladdin's new flagship. We're building a second one just like it down at Gelibolu for Admiral Burak."

"A sailing ship...but with oars?"

"To move her when the wind is weak. It's a class the Venetians call a 'galee grosse.' Our sailors shorten it to 'galleasse.' She's not as fast as a galley, but she can put to sea in weather a galley never could. Flat calm or heavy storm, she can travel no matter what." He motioned me over to the wall of the shed where there was a row of long cylindrical objects under tarpaulins. He drew the tarp off of one of them proudly. It was a bronze cannon, not a culverin but a full-bore cannon, very new with beautiful lettering on its muzzle band. I put my hand across its muzzle to get an idea of its bore. It was wider than my palm and first finger could span.

Atakan smiled. "*Goke* will carry the largest cannon ever mounted aboard a ship. Her sides are thicker than any firenk galley's guns can penetrate. No one will threaten our convoys ever again."

"May it be so," I said, smiling up in the gloom at her sides and seeing with my mind's eye her sails curved and full in the wind. "Speaking of convoys being attacked, we could use your help on a project."

"Certainly. Anything."

"It involves the Knights of Rhodes, and perhaps some large bangs."

❖　❖　❖

"Alright, how many people do we have?" Atakan asked briskly, all business, as he cupped the fuse in his hands and blew on it gently until the end of it was well alight.

"Fifteen of us, and forty-eight janissaries," Yigit said.

"Have everyone stand back, then," Atakan said. "This one will go quickly once it starts."

The explosion blew the door to Marsan's garden wall entirely off its iron hinges and blew the hinges themselves out of the stone sockets, as Atakan had fully intended it to. We were here to make a point, and part of that point lay in making sure the neighbors saw and reported widely on the example we intended to make.

We poured into the garden and the courtyard, and then broke the door to Marsan's house itself down with a few shuddering blows of an axe, kicking the splintered remnants aside and storming into the house, swords ready. The Viper appeared at the head of the stairs, yelling something at us. The janissaries hit him low and hard and bowled him over in their first rush up the steps. Two of them held him down and tied his wrists while the others charged past him. They had orders to seize everyone in the house, and they went to work with a will.

Inanc, Berk, Ozkan and I went through the downstairs. The first door on the right of the entrance hall was a reception room for clients. Beyond it was the dining room. On the other side of the hall was an office, with a large room next to it where the secretaries and money counters worked during the day. We smashed open every cabinet, grabbing armfuls of ledger books, correspondence, customs receipts, and spreading them out in piles on the tables and desks. We were looking for a document none of us had ever seen. It did not matter; we would know the look of it if we found it.

"Aha!" Berk suddenly called out. "I think this is it." He spread out a paper with columns of words on it and rows of MMM, MCXXs, and CCCCs.

There was a box made entirely of silver and full of papers. These were clearly special and, kept separately. Each of them had a name and a number at the top of it, corresponding to the names on the paper which Berk had found. We spread them out on the table and began to piece the structure together. The scope was enormous; Rhodes, Genoa, Rome, Halikarnassos, it was a web that stretched across the whole of the White Sea, and it took our breath away.

Niccolo del Guercino stuck his head around the door. He had come, as previously agreed, as soon the noise of the explosion had rocked the merchants' district.

"Ah Niccolo, thank you for coming. Help us out here if you would. We need your eyes and mind."

"With pleasure."

Four of Yigit's janissaries had found Marsan upstairs and dragged him into the room. By now we had found enough of the papers we were looking for to have a pretty good idea of how it worked.

"This is an outrage. You have no authority——"

Yigit stared calmly down at the short sword in his hand. "We have every authority."

I picked up one of the lists, and began to read, "Barhan, pilgrim from Beyoglu, one thousand five hundred. Is that in ducats, florins, or akce?"

"I don't know what you're referring to."

"I am referring these ransoms, and to the three percent commission you received for handling each of them. I am referring to the ransom lists you have been handling for the corsairs for almost four years now."

"You're how the lists get to Istanbul, aren't you?" Inanc prodded.

He stood there sullenly, but when Niccolo bent forward to examine the papers, his expression changed, became ever so slightly uncertain. del Guercino was the real thing, and Marsan knew it. If anyone could untangle the maze of notes, signatures and bills of exchange, it was he.

"Here," del Guercino indicated quietly to us, after reading for a while and arranging the papers in different piles. "This is where your trail begins." He laid out the papers we had found in the silver box next to some others. "It begins with a cargo, but a cargo different from the others. Something is missing. Not everyone would notice, but it is what's missing that gives it away. It has no insurance *commenda* attached... hmm, why not?" He turned to Marsan. "Because captives are the one cargo there's no purchase price for in advance. The one cargo you do not have to insure. Is that not right, Marsan?"

Marsan refused to give him any reaction. "These," del Guercino flicked the stack, "are promissory notes. Promises to repay money—ransom money."

Yigit did a quick count. There were more than two hundred of them, in varying amounts.

"It is charitable work," Marsan said. "Kindness to those unfortunates. We do not take a penny in interest."

"Naturally not. For to make a profit on the misery of others would be a mortal sin. But you and your partners do not go unrewarded. Your profit is buried in the repayment, which is in a foreign currency you specify—in advance—at an artificial exchange rate favorable to you."

Marsan stared defiantly back. No one would ever be able to prove that, and he knew it.

"Listen," I said. "You'd better answer us, and you'd better answer us well. Every single janissary stomping around in your house tonight was hand-picked for a specific reason. Care to hear what that reason was?"

"Please. I am all ears." Silk couldn't have been smoother.

"Every one of them is related to someone being held on Halikarnassos."

His smile slipped for a moment, but only for a moment. Then was replaced by something that was more like a falsely-confident grin. I wanted very badly to smash something into it. "Halikarnassos? I am sorry; I do not know the place."

"You call it 'St. Petrum'," Little Eagle said. "'Bodrum' to us."

Niccolo was taking us quietly through the next ring of the circle, where the real money was made—the banks who lent money to the corsair captains to buy and outfit their ships, then collected on the other side of the business by lending ransom money to the families of the corsairs' captives. Next came the fees collected by the merchants for negotiating the ransoms.

These were harder to trace. Their remittance was often buried in the sale of supplies—at inflated prices—to the corsair captains in return for the promise to leave the ships of those particular merchants alone. A promise we knew was not always kept.

"The families of the captives, distraught, with nowhere else to turn, sign the notes," del Guercino continued. "Papers that they know in advance will bind them to a lifetime of poverty—of misery, of doing without, of hard scrabbling—to repay it. But they are desperate. Their loved ones are prisoners. It's a race against time. They may sicken and die in those cells.

"Marsan collects the ransom money and sends it—on the families' behalf—to the corsairs. He keeps the promissory notes, or resells them, or uses them as credit according to the market. The corsairs, as agreed, give one tenth to the Knights of Rhodes. Some of this the Knights deposit with their bankers in Rome."

"Who lend it back as ransom money?"

He nodded grimly. "It will not surprise you to learn that the papacy and the Knights of Rhodes use many of the same bankers,"

"And the hub of all this misery, and of all this wealth, is the Fortress of St. Peter at Halikarnassos," Cihan said.

"Where both the former—and present—treasurers of the Order have served as commanders of the garrison. Oh, you did not know that?"

We shook our heads. We had not.

"Quite a circle, isn't it? But I have not yet closed it, not yet," del Guercino continued. "Some years ago, the commander of Halikarnassos had a servant. He must have been an exceptionally daring and athletic young man because he managed to do something very few others have succeeded in doing. He escaped from the fortress on the land side and disappeared into the hills. The Religion demanded his return. The Ottomans refused to send him back. The boy meanwhile had converted to Islam, so they couldn't give him back even if they had wanted to. Which they didn't. So, the Knights began seizing Muslims in the lands around Halikarnassos in reprisal."

Yigit turned to one of his janissaries and asked out of the side of his mouth, "How much money does Marsan have in the house?"

"We have found almost eight thousand ducats so far. There may be more hidden."

"Bring what you've found up here." A good start, but not enough. Inanc supplemented this with the contents of the silverware drawer, which he had been clever enough to find. "We can melt this down."

Yigit motioned to Marsan to sit at one of the desks. "You, and your two will write and sign receipts of repayment for every single ransom loan you have outstanding."

"And del Guercino will watch over your shoulders as you make the entries in your account ledger, to make sure they are in order and that you do not attempt to cheat us."

"When you have finished doing that," del Guercino took up the thread, "you will write a promissory note of your own. The Montefortino bank has an office here in Pera. You will borrow another twenty thousand ducats from them. You have shares in a cargo of nutmeg waiting to be embarked—by fortunate coincidence—aboard a Montefortino ship. You will pledge those shares as collateral."

"They're not worth that much."

"Of course they are not. You'll be in debt for the difference. Since the Montefortini are also the pope's bankers, if you default on the debt, then your soul goes to hell."

Marsan was actually sweating now, not from the fear of hell in the next world, but from the fear of the power of the Montefortino bank in this one. It had branches throughout Europe, and it owned more than a hundred ships used for its own trading. It chartered hundreds more each season. It could crush a small-time merchant like Marsan without even noticing.

"Why would the Montefortini loan money to me?"

"Because you are already a co-signator of four other *commenda* contracts for cargoes carried on their ships," del Guercino said patiently, as if this were the most obvious thing in the world, "and most of all because you will offer to pay them interest of eighteen percent."

"Eighteen per—that's robbery."

"Technically, no. Not if the money's not for us."

"Who then?"

"The prisoners on Halikarnassos. You are going to ransom the rest of them."

Marsan shook his head with malicious triumph. "Promissory notes for prisoners need a countersignature," he said smugly. "Authorized by the Religion itself."

"We have a countersigner," Cihan said.

A snort. "Who?"

"Philippe de Cluys," del Guercino replied and it was as if he had dropped a cannon ball suddenly on the floor.

"The Religion's *treasurer?*" Marsan crinkled up his face, as surprised as Yigit and I were. "Hah! You'll never get away with that. You should have picked someone less prominent. You've overshot your mark."

"I do not think so."

"He will never countersign those ransoms."

"Of course he won't. He's dead," del Guercino said smoothly. "He died last March. In the Morea. They've kept the news quiet until they name a successor."

"Then how do you know about it?"

del Guercino made a gesture with his hands as if he found the question self-explanatory. "I work for the Medici bank. We make it our business to know. Living or dead, it's unimportant for our purposes. There is someone in this room who is familiar with his letters, and can write his hand perfectly."

Marsan looked sharply around at each of us, looking for someone with the social stature necessary to have brought them into contact with a personage who had been not only a Knight of Rhodes but who had also been—two times over—a member of the French nobility. From the way his glance slid over each one of us and passed on, it did not seem that he found any of us likely candidates.

"Cluys' escaped servant," del Guercino said almost soothingly into the pause that followed, and this time it really was as if he had dropped a cannon ball on everybody's foot. "Someone who was with him almost daily, someone who saw his personal papers, who sorted his mail for him. Who knew the back of his hand like the back of his own hand, as the saying goes."

Little Eagle stepped forward, almost shyly. Atakan shot him a stunned glance, and I too was struggling to catch up. del Guercino had traveled much further down a complicated path than he—or any of us—had originally thought he could go. So, that was how Little Eagle had known the streams of Halikarnassos were not safe to drink. And a number of other things too. And no wonder he never let anyone call him by his real firenk name.

Marsan gathered his wits more quickly than the rest of us. "You're the one they've been looking for all this time?

"I will see you dragged back and beaten," he shouted into Little Eagle's face. "I will protest this intrusion of my home, and I will see you clean the streets of Rhodes with your tongue."

Little Eagle said something defiantly back in what must have been Provencale French. Marsan shouted again, but Little Eagle cut him off. "And because I am the sultan's helmsman," he finished in Turkish.

"Protest? To whom? To the Knights of Rhodes? To your pope?" Ozkan laughed. "Haven't you heard? He's a laughingstock. Bought and sold a score of times. He himself does not know who owns him anymore. I saw his gold spread out on the ground with my own eyes as his own prefect took it from him."

Marsan looked around, taking stock. It must have dawned on him that none of us was an officer of flag rank.

"Your commanding officer didn't authorize you to do this, did he?"

I shook my head. "Lantern Captain Bayulken is at a reception," I said, "and is completely unaware of our presence here." Which was, if you took it absolutely literally to refer to this particular evening, quite true. Bayulken had not been told the details of our little raid, only the general purpose. "I think he would prefer to remain unaware, and not to be informed of our conduct at all," I continued. "I feel very confident that he would find your complaint of our behavior interruptive to the festivities."

Little Eagle had sat at the table and was waiting, pen in hand. The janissaries pushed Marsan, the Viper, and the other assistant forward. They began to write "*plenum renumeratur*" and then "paid in full" in Greek on each of the promissory notes, and against the names on the list.

del Guercino gathered them up carefully and counted them against the lines of the ledger to make sure they were all there. When he was sure, he gave them out in batches to the janissaries. They were to fan out through the city to deliver them to the lendees.

One of the janissaries pointed to Marsan. "Him?"

"If the exchange goes properly, we will release him. Until then, they're all hostages."

The following day, we took Marsan to the offices of the Montefortini, guarded by janissaries whose hands were never more than inches from the hilts of their yatagans. I was afraid that Marsan would shout for help or make some sign that he was under duress, or that the Montefortini would sense something wrong because of the presence of the janissaries. We need not have worried; firenk bankers doing business in Istanbul tended not to ask each other questions. The Montefortini naturally had their own guards, as would be expected in any place large amounts of money were handled. It did not surprise them that Marsan would have an armed escort with him to carry so much cash away. They must have ascribed any agitation he might have betrayed to the quite normal tension of making such a large transaction.

With our own ships still underwater at Kagithane, we were disappointed not to be able to escort the ransom down the coast ourselves. Bahadir assigned the task instead to four galleys from the Mytiline squadron who were on their way back to those waters anyway, accompanied by a supply carrack large enough to carry the releasees back to Istanbul. The janissaries, swords drawn, loaded the ransom onto the carrack under Bahadir's eyes.

"Remember what happened the last time we loaded gold onto a ship," Yigit commented drily.

"This will be different, I hope. This time it's stolen from the firenks, *before* it sails."

Marsan and the Viper we put aboard too as guarantees of good behavior, and because we thought it might be better to have them out of Istanbul. Little Eagle asked repeatedly to be allowed to go——I think he would have torn down the castle gates at Halikarnassos with his bare hands——but Bahadir refused categorically to run the risk of putting him in front of the firenks again.

"If you are seen and recognized, they will go to any lengths to steal you back. There's too much knowledge running around in that head of yours for us to let that happen. If I had known about you and your full story, I never would have allowed you to go ashore with us at Crete."

"Someday though, we will have to deal with Rhodes once and for all."

"I know. But not now, not this year."

"Every time we pay their ransoms, we encourage them to take more prisoners."

"Perhaps not for very much longer," Bahadir said, no doubt thinking of the *Goke*. "Things are changing. If we can just get this group back, it may be the last."

I walked down to the sea, the boundless sea. A convoy was headed out of the Bosphoros into the Marble Sea under a cloud of sail. Five squat caravelles flying the red lily of Florence were brailing up their mainsails prepatory to entering the Horn.

Ozkan was skipping flat stones pensively across the water. "In two days we'll raise *Akdogan*."

I smiled. "Yes. It begins again."

"Let's go paint some oars!"

HISTORICAL NOTE AND ACKNOWLEDGEMENTS

The Sultan's Helmsman is a work of fiction. Nonetheless, the historical details—the gunnery, the *devshirme*, the training regimen at the *Enderun Kolej*, the political situations in Europe and the Ottoman Empire, and the handling of the ships—are accurate. *Akdogan* and her sister ships are fictional, but their sailing characteristics are true to Ottoman types, and their names are of the kind which plausibly could have been given to galleys of the time. An Ottoman galley named *Hilal* was in fact captured by the Knights of Malta a century after the events in this story.

Sultan II Bayezid ("the Just") possessed one of the widest-ranging intellects of any Renaissance ruler, west or east. His personal interest in the palace school, and his attendance at examinations of the oglans are well attested. Grand Vezier Daud's admonishment to Kachak to "forget the colors of the threads but remember the pattern" is a synthesis of passages from several Sufi writings. There was much interest in, and study of, Sufism at Bayezid's court and at the Enderun Kolej, so Daud's observation is consistent with ideas in circulation at the time.

The Enderun Kolej blended traditions of the east as well as those inherited from the Platonic academy of the Greeks. The British public school system imitated many of its methods in turn. Its graduates were brilliant and many were famous. Some were infamous; Vladimir Drakula, (yes *that* Dracula), was an alumnus about forty years before Kachak's time, before the school moved from Edirne to Istanbul. According to the Turks, he was a discipline problem during his four years there, though that assessment may have been colored by his subsequent misbehavior as ruler of Wallachia. If I have shown presumption by matriculating my narrator there, it is because—even at the distance of five hundred years—I have benefited much by studying its curriculum.

Some readers may be surprised at the apparent informality of the characters who address the Sultan directly and who are allowed to see his face. It was not until later, under Bayezid's grandson, Suleiman I, and his great-grandson Selim II, that court protocol developed the mystique and rigidity we tend to associate with Ottoman sultans. The earlier sultans tended to remain true to the nomadic tribal roots of the Turkish people, holding audiences seated on cushions on the ground in the open air at which all and sundry could present themselves. Bayezid consciously reversed formalities introduced by his father, the Conqueror Mehmet II.

A ducat was worth approximately $40 in today's money. However, because wages in many professions were generally lower, the purchasing power of a ducat could effectively be much more. Cem's stolen subsidy was thus approximately $1.6 million. A warship could be built, equipped, and the crew paid for a season for between five and eight thousand ducats (approx. $320,000)

Purists may be dismayed by my interchanging the titles Sultan and Padishah throughout the book. Padishah is the Turkish—and more exalted—term; a sultan could be any ruler. As most readers are more familiar with 'sultan,' I have used both titles, especially in the mouths of western characters. Padishahs' names were given in the reverse order from western monarchs' names, with their attributes first, followed by their number and name, thus Padishah Fatih (the Conqueror) II Mehmet Khan, and Padishah Adil (the Just) II Bayezid Khan.

In my use of place names, I have tried to tread the fine line between using the names that people of the time would have known, while still making them recognizable to western readers. In some cases, it seemed appropriate to retain the Turkish and Greek names and spellings for islands and ports, in some cases it seemed more comprehensible to use the Latinized names that Venice bestowed in its long administration of the eastern Mediterranean. Those are the forms most western readers are familiar with. I have retained the spelling "Bosphoros" for no more scholarly reason than because I like the way it looks on the page.

The emergency sealift of the Moors and Jews from persecution in Spain really happened. It is one of the most noble chapters in the Ottoman—or indeed any—navy's history. The hijacking of Prince Cem's subsidy and the publication of the letters also happened very much as described, including the flight to the castle. Scholars have debated the authenticity of the letters published in Florence by Charles VIII, with a gradual concurrence that they were probably forgeries. Speaking through Envoy Kasim, I add some of my own reasoning to theirs.

The Lay of the Sons of the Night Wind, quoted by various characters, is my own invention. It borrows stylistic devices, and some of its images, from the Persian epic poetry which was read and studied at the court and at the palace school. The style of the novel, where a narrator who is also an active agent in the story and who periodically addresses the reader directly, was a familiar instrument in Ottoman adventure tales.

Charles VIII's unprovoked and devastating invasion of Italy was a tragedy from which Italy, and the Italian Renaissance, never fully recovered. The collapse of Charles VIII's military aspirations ended the threat of a combined crusade against the Ottoman Empire for the following eighty years. The events at Rocca Priore and Capua bought the Ottomans a period of relative peace. The subsequent economic prosperity and cultural flowering was the true high points of the Ottoman Empire and world culture, a period from which the west later benefited as well.

The Knights of Rhodes continued their piratical ways and preyed especially on pilgrims, who could be held for ransom. The Knights of Rhodes were specialists in this human trade. In 1522, the Ottomans—provoked beyond endurance—launched a seaborne assault on the island and ending up forcing the surrender and evacuation of the Knights, who later moved to Malta and renamed themselves. The fortress at Halikarnassos, which had never been taken by force, was ceded to the Turks as part of the terms of the surrender.

In 1569, another belligerent pope, Pius V, forged a crusading league which led to the wasteful bloodbath of Lepanto (Savash Inebahti, to give it its Turkish name). The battle, for all its drama and appalling loss of life (at least 25,000 Turkish dead, 15,000 European), had little direct effect on the balance of power, or on the treaties that followed it. The Turks rebuilt their navy within a year and took Cyprus. The Christian league, like all the Christian leagues preceding it, broke up almost immediately after Lepanto in jealousy and discord. Venice and a bankrupt Spain soon signed separate treaties with the Ottomans, treaties which, if anything, were more favorable to Ottomans than to the supposed victors. The Lepanto campaign of 1571 was the final serious crusade threat. Europe's attention turned elsewhere. The desperate sacrifice of the Turkish sailors at Inebahti—a battle they came closer to winning than the numbers show—perhaps spared their land an even worse disaster.

Researching a historical novel is always a great deal of fun, and a fascinating intellectual journey of its own. Events which at first seem obvious turn out upon deeper examination to be complex; explanations initially accepted must be rethought. For historical sources, I am particularly indebted to: Caroline Finkel's history of the Ottoman ruling house and empire, *Osman's Dream*, Baretta Miller's *Palace School of Muhammad the Conqueror*, Kenneth Setton's *The Papacy and the Levant* for its details of dates and correspondence, Godfrey Goodwin's *The Janissaries*, Palmira Brummett's *Ottoman Seapower and Levantine Diplomacy in the Age of Discovery*, Gabor Agoston's *Guns for the Sultan*, Idris Bostan's article "Ottoman Maritime Arsenals and Shipbuilding Technology in the 16th and 17th Centuries," Johann Burchard's diaries of the papal court (which contains the Latin text of the Florence letters and of Bocciardi's deposition), and Guilmartin's magnificently detailed *Gunpowder and Galleys*. Usun Kasim's, Franscesco Gonzaga's, and Bayezid II's diplomatic correspondence is preserved in the archives of Mantua.

I recommend the above sources to anyone wishing to delve more deeply into Turkish history. To the reader interested in exploring the differences between eastern and western philosophy, I recommend any of the various collections of Sufi tales. Their approach to empirical observation of the world—more flexible and adaptive than we are used to in much of formal western philosophy—offers much that is broadening and intellectually stimulating.

The Maritime Museum (Deniz Muzesi) in Istanbul is a wonderland of many informative exhibits and artifacts dealing with all aspects of the Ottoman navy, right down to the stones which were used to print the commissions of naval lieutenants, and a model of the Goke. Displayed on the grounds are probably a hundred or more ancient basilisks, culverins, demiculverins, and falconetti which saw use aboard *Akdogan*'s real-life sister ships. The Deniz Muzesi is notable also for possessing the world's only surviving 16th century galley (the date is approximate, she may have been built as early as 1560 or as late as 1650). She may well have been one of the galleys hurriedly built to replace the losses after Lepanto. Addicts of naval history will find much to feed their habits there.

Barcelona's Maritime Museum possesses a modern reproduction of the galley Real, the flagship of the Christian League forces at Lepanto, also well worth visiting for those who wish to get a sense of what life afloat was like at that time.

CPSIA information can be obtained at www.ICGtesting.com
Printed in the USA
LVOW071947040512

280410LV00001B/84/P